SPEAK IN WINTER CODE

S. M. HARDING

BELLA
BOOKS

2017

Bella Books, Inc.
P.O. Box 10543
Tallahassee, FL 32302

Printed in the United States of America on acid-free paper.

First Bella Books Edition 2017

Editor: Cath Walker
Cover Designer: Linda Callaghan

ISBN: 978-1-59493-535-0

Other Bella Books by S. M. Harding

A Woman of Strong Purpose
I Will Meet You There

Acknowledgments

I'd like to thank all the Bella Book gals who do such a wonderful job for me—and Cath Walker, I hope you didn't pull out all your hair working with me! Thank you for your patience.

I'd also like to thank you readers who make this all possible. I so love sharing the characters of McCrumb County with you and am so grateful you like them too.

Dedication

For all in the LGBT community who have suffered from the rage of "straight" people in so many forms, especially the victims of Pulse in Orlando, Florida—and their friends and families. Perhaps, someday, the hate will end.

The Spirit of Place, IV

The work of winter starts fermenting in my head
how with the hands of a lover or a midwife
to hold back till the time is right

force nothing, be unforced
accept no giant miracles of growth
by counterfeit light

trust roots, allow the days to shrink
give credence to these slender means
wait without sadness and with grave impatience

here in the north where winter has a meaning
where the heaped colors suddenly go ashen
where nothing is promised

learn what an underground journey
has been, might have to be; speak in winter code
let fog, sleet, translate; wind, carry them.

From "The Spirit of Place," IV, *A Wild Patience Has Taken Me This Far: Poems 1978-1981*, Adrienne Rich

PROLOGUE

He stood like a statue of a Civil War hero and remained unmoving as he viewed the fence-lined paddocks before him. The Blue Ridge Mountains rose to the west. He controlled his breathing but he couldn't control his anger. The wide-planked floor creaked as he turned and walked to the head of the table. He examined each of the ten men who sat stiffly around the long, polished table. "Can any of you tell me how this goddamn disaster happened?"

They looked down at their clean writing pads.

All except one, a trim man with a full head of dark hair shot through with gray. "An unfortunate convergence of circumstances—"

"Specify them."

"We had no intel that this sheriff had connections to MCIA, none. Nor did we have any idea that Mohan Shamsi stored his arsenal there. He left us quite blind to his movements."

"No intel is not acceptable, nor is dealing with an arms dealer without knowing his every move." He turned to the man on his right. "Is McCrumb County on our test list?"

"No sir."

"Put it on the top of the list. Do we have any associates there?"

"No sir."

"A militia group?"

"Yes sir." The gray-haired man flipped through his files. "The McCrumb County Rangers. 'An undisciplined group of loudmouths' was the description I was given. They're in our network, but mostly re-post our articles. No incentive of their own."

"Pull Waterstone from the training camp. Tell him to sniff around, hook up with this group. If there are men there worth training, take them back to camp. Train them. Get eyes on the sheriff and anyone else concerned." He put his fists on the walnut dining table and glared at each man in turn. "We spent a year and a half and over four million dollars to obtain those weapons. We have *nothing* to show for that investment. This will not happen again or heads will roll. Your heads, gentlemen."

That statement was rendered more threatening because it was delivered in a soft Virginia accent.

"One more item. We have found a candidate for the office of president. He is an egotistical rabble-rouser and an imbecile. However, he listens to whispers. Get our media concerns in touch with him.

"We cannot stop now, we cannot postpone. The time is here for revolution."

CHAPTER ONE

Sarah

I watched the snow swirl down outside the window, beautiful in its dance for now. The flames in the fireplace moved to a different song, a different rhythm, as the increasing winds gathered the force of the impending storm.

I'd left work early knowing I'd be on duty when the blizzard hit, directing the McCrumb County Sheriff's Department to help the fools out on the roads. I also wanted to be home when Win arrived from her teaching job in Bloomington at CELI, a language institute run for the military and spies. Our weekend together at home would be shortened by the snow emergency and with our first wedding anniversary just past, I wanted to be at her side and feel her by mine.

I put another log on the fire and paced from one front window to the other. "Come on, Win, get your beautiful butt home."

Des, an army-trained Belgian Malinois who in a past life had been named Destroyer, paced beside me. She whined. I went back to the couch and plopped my feet on the finished slab of black walnut that served as a coffee table. She jumped up beside me and I threw my arm around her and let her nuzzle my neck. "Your nose is too cold to be Win, so you better watch yourself." She snorted.

What a tumultuous year it had been. I'd come out to the county in a newspaper interview with the *Greenglen Sentinel* for a series Zoe had been doing on marriage equality. The initial responses had crashed both the paper's website and Facebook page. Twitter had hit national trending. The same old haters were still out there, their vitriol uncontrolled and damn wounding. But I'd been surprised by the support I'd received from unexpected quarters, including some clergy and their congregations.

If those turbulent times hadn't been enough, Win had proposed adopting Bahar and Dorri, two gorgeous little girls from Afghanistan where she had served multiple tours with MCIA. We discussed it and argued about it. I kept asking how we were going to manage and Win kept saying we could and would. She settled the argument when she'd said, "They have no future there. None."

Their parents were dead and their extended family stretched very thin to care for them. Win had been sending money, but conditions for the whole family had continued a downward spiral.

Via Skype I'd fallen in love again. I relied on Win to translate the words, but all I really needed to see was how their eyes lit up when they saw her. And how Win's face softened when she talked with them. What could I say but okay? Win had started the process. We still had issues to iron out like who was going to care for them when Win was in Bloomington. Dad had offered to babysit, excited at the prospect of grandkids when he'd given up hope. We expected them to arrive by early summer. I was scared to death that something awful would happen to them in the interim.

Des barked and I heard Win's truck coming up the hill. Her headlights flashed across the room and I went to the door to welcome my wife home.

"Salt trucks aren't out yet," she said on the porch as she stamped the snow from her boots. She kissed me, then stooped to take off her boots and put them in the boot tray. "You have to go back to work?"

"Yeah. I need to leave before the storm hits. But according to the weather reports, I have about two hours."

"Enough time for dinner and dessert?" she asked with a wicked smile.

As soon as she had her parka off, I moved into her arms. "Shall we have dessert first?"

* * *

I beat the first squalls of the storm to work by ten minutes and shook the snow off my parka as I entered the station by the back door. As I walked to my office, I saw Dory, our dispatcher, scurrying around with five pencils stuck in her white hair. Disaster time for sure.

"What are you still doing here?" I asked her when she stood still momentarily.

"Stayin' for the weekend Sarah, 'cause we're gonna need extra people for dispatch," she said. "We got food in, most of patrol brought sleepin' bags. Did you?"

"I've got one in my truck, part of my emergency kit."

"You better go get it in, Sarah, they're talkin' a foot an' a half. Win get back safe from teachin'?"

"Yeah, and she said she didn't see a salt truck the whole way. I sure hope Roads get their butts in gear or we're going to have people stranded all over the county."

"We've set up a line with Roads so we know where they are. They ain't usin' salt, said it wouldn't do no good. Trucks are gonna go out when we got six inches."

"Hell." After I got my sleeping bag from my truck, I found my dad in my office.

He grinned up at me. "Reckon my electric ain't gonna last the storm an' I'm too old to make do. So I come to town."

"Plus, you thought we might need a few more hands on deck?"

"Couldn't hurt," he said with a shrug. "Win get home okay?"

"Yeah. We had time for dinner," I said as I sank into my chair.

He sat up straighter on the couch and leaned forward. "How's them little girls? You talk with 'em recent?"

"Tuesday. They have such incredibly beautiful spirits, Dad. I mean, they just emit joy. They make me feel better every time we get to talk with them."

He grinned. "Can't wait 'til they get here. Gave up on grandkids a long time ago."

"So did I when Hugh died." I'd spent fifteen years in an arid wasteland, lost, until Win had come back into my life to show me spring's fresh growth.

"You know, I used to worry 'bout Win when she was a kid. Fred was always workin' an' Marjorie had her heart set on a little frilly girl after birthin' them boys," Dad said with a shake of his head. "Always thought Marjorie was a tad on the cold side to Win."

I told him how the family had turned their backs on Win when she came out to them. "Fred Junior wouldn't let Win near her nieces and nephews."

He shook his head again. "What amazes me is that Win can be such a lovin' woman with that kinda growin' up."

"Maybe we were part of it—she spent a lot of time at our house and you and Mom were always good to her."

"Twern't hard, Sarah Anne. We always thought highly of her once she got over her darin' the boundaries." He pushed himself off the couch. "You get any more of them anonymous letters?"

I shook my head and took a deep breath. "Maybe the sender's getting tired of screwing around with me."

"Doubt it," Dad said.

CHAPTER TWO

Win

After Sarah left to manage the county's blizzard, I settled on the couch, put my feet up. Des jumped up, licked my face, then settled and gave a contented grunt. I ran my hand through her thick fur. Wondered how she'd get along with the kids. I thought she'd be a great protector once the bond was made. They were old enough they wouldn't pester her.

Never in my life had I thought I'd marry. Ever. Much less dreamed about having kids. I remembered my years in the military, trading my sexual identity for a career. Hookups without any emotional entrapments. When I'd come home, I was a constant flood of jumpy nerves, adrenaline and paranoia.

Finding Emily, my shrink, turned the tide. Finding Sarah in this new context—not just friend but lover—was a miracle.

The phone rang and I looked at the caller ID. Major Laura Wilkins, an MCIA agent who'd come to Indiana to help catch an international arms dealer. Instead, she'd been captured and brutally tortured by Shamsi's men. She'd be staying in our home except she had an obsessive crush on Sarah.

I answered and I heard her take a deep breath.

"Barry and Linda were supposed to be home three hours ago and they're still not here, and I'm really worried."

"The family you're staying with? I drove in from Bloomington about that time and the roads were messy. Did you try calling them?"

"Of course, but you know how spotty the coverage is around here. They could've had a slide-off or broken down or...I'm worried. They understand I don't like to be alone."

Part of her own PTSD. Emily was treating her, found her a place to stay with the Browne family. "Have you called the sheriff's department?"

"No. They wouldn't understand, Win. They'd think I was some hysterical fool."

She probably was feeling on the hysterical edge right now. Her healing was slow. "You have a gut feeling about this?"

A long silence. "Yeah," she said in a small voice. "They've been getting threatening letters."

"About what?"

Another silence. "Me," Laura said in a whisper.

I wanted to ask why, but I could hear her fraying. "Give me details. Make and model of car, license plate if you know it. Their route."

"They took the truck, but I can't remember the make or model. They were coming home from visiting family, but I can't remember the name of the town. Something Crossing. I should've written it down, but I'm trying not to cling."

When I'd come home, I'd pushed everyone away. Sat in my hell alone so it was hard for me to understand clinging. Yet I got it. "I'll call Sarah—"

"No! She'll think I'm a crazy woman. I can't have her think that, Win. Please!"

"There's nothing I can do but call. At this point, I can't even get down the drive. No problem, it's good to report them overdue. Call me when they get home."

I didn't call Sarah when I hung up, I called Emily. "Laura sounds like she's experiencing a meltdown. There's no way you can drive, but I thought a phone call might help." I explained the situation.

"She called you and not Sarah?"

"Yeah. Afraid she'd think less of her."

I could hear Emily's sigh. "Got it."

Sarah picked up on the second ring. "You all right?"

"Des and I are enjoying the fireplace, watching the snow come down outside." I briefed her about Laura. I didn't mention the possible threatening letters because I hadn't assessed the threat myself. "They may have run into trouble."

"Dory's here and I'll have her run their truck. She probably knows the family they were visiting and can call to see if the Brownes have left." Her chair squeaked. "You guys really okay?"

"Wish you were here." I sighed. I knew better than to ask her when she'd be home. When the storm was over and the damage under control. "Try and get some sleep, Sarah."

"When the snow's stopped, Win. When the storm's over."

* * *

Before the storm I'd put the plow on my truck, backed into the garage. What I hadn't figured on was the fierce winds. The biggest drift was smack-dab in front of the garage doors. I'd waited for a lull to shovel a path to the garage, but it never came. It kept coming the whole weekend. I'd begun digging out Monday morning. It took me until lunchtime to get the doors open and pull the truck out. It took the early afternoon to plow out the clearing and the drive. Then to begin on the county road the drive spilled onto.

Des had done her best gazelle imitation for the first half hour we were out, then started following the cleared path. Then asked to go inside. "Slacker," I'd said. She woofed at me as much to say, "So get me a shovel." When I'd gone in at lunchtime, a walking icicle, she was sound asleep in front of the embers in the fireplace.

Monday night, Micah called. "We been goin' full out, Win. Reckon Sarah be home sometime tomorrow afternoon."

"Everybody okay? You hear anything about the Brownes?"

"They're out there somewhere. We just don't know where."

"Anything I can do?"

"Stay off the roads, Win. We got Roads plowin' the Brownes' route from her sister's house."

Tuesday morning, CELI called and canceled classes for the week. Good. More time with Sarah if she ever got home.

She didn't make it until late that afternoon, exhausted and wired. "Too much coffee, Win. The whole county's a mess, Roads started too late and half the roads haven't been touched. They can't even get through some of the drifts."

"How'd you make it home?"

She'd leaned against me. "Thanks for plowing. I was thinking about getting out and hoofing it when I hit the section you did."

I wrapped my arms around her. "Go take a shower and then I'll give you a massage. You need sleep."

"I've got to go in tomorrow," she said.

"Sarah—"

"I've got to, we're shorthanded because so many of our deputies can't get in. Hell! They can't even get out of their homes or down a road that'll take them somewhere. This is worse than the last time. Those assholes at Roads didn't even start until the storm passed."

I could feel her shudder. Anger and fatigue were a potent combination. I turned her around and gave her a gentle push. "Shower."

I think she fell asleep about five minutes into the massage.

CHAPTER THREE

Sarah

I'd slept so deeply, I don't think I moved a muscle all night. I awoke with the sun already up and the smell of coffee twitching my nose. The sound of the shower quit and in moments Win appeared in her robe, toweling her hair.

"Morning." She leaned over and kissed me. "Your chief deputy called and said to tell you not to rush in. More of your deputies have managed to dig themselves out."

"Alleluia and thank the heavens for Caleb." I glanced at the clock, then grabbed the tie of her robe and pulled her to me. "I don't want to get out of bed yet."

"Is that an invitation to join you?"

"You better believe it."

Coffee and breakfast came later. I was downing the second cup when Win asked about the Brownes. "No word yet. They may not have followed the route we thought. But honestly, it doesn't look good. It's been four days, almost five. How's Laura?"

"Not good. I thought I'd try to get through to her today, plow the driveway so she can get out if she needs to."

"If the Brownes don't come home, what happens to Laura?" I asked. "She's not finished with Emily yet, is she?"

"Don't know. I don't talk to Emily about other clients. Rules." She swirled the coffee left in her mug as if it was a breaking news story. "They've been getting crap letters too."

"Barry and Linda?"

"Yeah and Laura said it was about her. If I make it to her place, you want me to pick up the letters?"

"Take a pair of gloves, an evidence bag and have Laura sign off. She give you any idea what the threats were about? Because they were harboring a lesbian?"

"No idea. Is that what's behind the letters you've been getting?"

"How'd you—oh, Dad. There doesn't appear any specific one reason, the venom touches all areas of my life. 'Die, bitch, die' seems to be a general theme."

Win walked around the island, put her arms around me. "Please be careful. Bahar and Dorri need *two* parents to show them how to love."

I leaned into her. "They'll have two. Until the writer, well, paster of those letters gets careless, we don't have a good way to track him down."

"He? Did you find fingerprints?"

"No. No DNA on the envelope flap either."

Win moved to my side, examined my face. "How do you know it's a male?"

"Sounds like a jerk-off. Emily agrees."

"You talked to my therapist about this and didn't bother to mention any of it?" Win didn't expect an answer. She stalked away. "Don't you ever do this again, Sarah. We're partners. For life. If you ever hold back on something like this again…"

Win smacked the counter. She turned away.

I walked to her, put my arms around her. "You'll do what?"

"Don't mess around, Sarah. I'm serious about this."

"I didn't want you to worry."

"That's my job in life," Win said, turning to me. "To worry about you. Yours is to worry about me. I don't hold back. You can't either or this won't work."

A hundred excuses ran through my mind. But Win was right, we couldn't afford to be less than fully honest with one another, not if we wanted to walk the long path together. "You're right. I promise, no more trying to protect you from bad news."

She scanned my face. "I'll hold you to that, Sarah. I want to see those letters. Bring them home tonight."

* * *

I'd no more reached my desk when Mike Bryer, Fatal Accident Crash Team head, tapped on my door. In my mind, he was a harbinger of death.

"I'm on my way out to the Browne truck. It was spotted in a ditch off SR Fifty-Four."

"Any sign of life?"

"Not from what I heard. Don't know how much crash reconstruction we can do with all the snow."

I got the exact location. "I'll follow you shortly. Give it your best shot because apparently they'd been receiving threats."

His eyebrows rose and he gave a sharp nod.

I called Win and asked if she'd contact Emily. "If Laura was unraveling before…"

"I'll get right on it," Win said. "I guess the first thing we have to do is find another family for Laura. She won't be able to stay there, not alone."

"Ask her to stay with us, at least until Em can find her another place."

"Really not a good idea. I'm not saying a flat no. We'll see, okay? I'm on the way over now."

She disconnected. Damn. I knew Win was worried about Laura's "crush" on me, which I hadn't really seen. But being thrown into a gay life in middle age, I was oblivious to a lot of things. As long as I didn't return the feelings or encourage her in any way, I thought it would pass on its own.

I tried Em's number but it was busy, so I grabbed my parka and followed Mike out to the accident scene.

I pulled into a space behind his cruiser. I could see him working his way down to the car. As he cleared the snow from the driver's side window, he looked up at me and shook his head.

I tried Em again and this time got through. "I'm on the scene of the Browne crash—"

"Did they survive?" Em asked.

I stood on the berm, surveying the scene. With the flat, straight section of road through snow-covered fields, it was hard to see why the crash occurred. Winds had been strong that day, but steady, not gusty. Patch of ice? An animal that had wandered onto the road? Perhaps they just lost sight of the road in the blizzard conditions.

"No, though I don't really know cause of death. Anyway, I was thinking Laura's going to need a place to stay—"

"I'm working on it," Em said. "But I agree with Win—your place is at the very bottom of my list. So is your dad's. Until she's healthier, she doesn't need to be in proximity to you or your old room. Trust me on this, Sarah."

"Uh, okay." Emily's words sounded like a warning. "If it turns out to be something more sinister than just running off the road in a blizzard, I may have to question her as a witness."

"Let Caleb or one of the detectives do it."

"Really?"

"Really." She disconnected.

I sighed. I didn't want to get in Mike's way, but some preliminary word would be good.

He kept moving around the vehicle, wiping off snow with a soft broom until the driver's side was clear. Then he moved to the other side, again brushing off snow. He stopped by the front wheel, bent over for a minute then reappeared. "This could be the reason, a flat tire," he yelled. "If it blew with snow on the road...I'm going to call Bernie, get this out of the ditch and these poor folk to the ME. Okay?"

I nodded. "You have any idea of cause of death for them?"

"That's Doc Webster's job."

"Come on Mike, give me something."

"Looks like they didn't have seat belts on. Either bled out or froze to death."

I nodded, climbed back in my car and called Win.

CHAPTER FOUR

Win

I thought Major Laura Wilkins appeared all angles, sharp and piercing. Fragile too. Bony elbows and knees as she grabbed a piece of the pizza I'd brought. Dark rings under her eyes, her cheekbones sharply modeled. I sat on the floor across a coffee table from her. I'd gotten napkins from the kitchen and handed her one before I took a piece.

"Thanks for the food," she said, wiping her mouth. "I'm not much of a cook. Been slim pickings around here. Linda cooks. Not one frozen dinner I can pop in the microwave."

If Linda Browne had been like most people in the county, she'd cooked stews and soups in the winter and put extra in the freezer. I didn't think Laura had looked or maybe the idea of fixing a meal was too much for her. She was running on pure nervous energy.

I ate a piece and then excused myself. Her concentration was on the pizza, not me. I walked toward my truck and hit the speed-dial for Emily.

"She's not doing good," I said. "I can't leave her here."

"Crap. The people I've contacted aren't plowed out. I've got no solution for you, Win."

It was my turn to cuss and I did. "I don't think she's been eating or sleeping. She looks like shit. Smells just about as bad."

Emily expelled a long breath.

"Besides, she's been threatened along with the Brownes. She shouldn't be here alone. I'd stay, but I don't have a weapon."

"Can this get any more screwed up? I was thinking about having her admitted to Roudebush, but there's no transport."

"The VA hospital in Indy? That would be a damn fine solution, Emily. I could take her—"

"Interstate's closed, Win."

"Back roads?"

"Worse north than here." Emily cleared her throat. "I realize you're concerned with her physical safety, but her mental safety is my responsibility. She can't stay by herself. You're going to have to take her to your home because we're not near to digging out right now."

Last thing I wanted to hear. "Fuck."

"Don't let her alone with Sarah. She'll let the fantasy build, Win. She can't help it right now and she might initiate some…intimacy with Sarah. I'll keep working on finding her another place. Hopefully this will only be today. Okay?"

"I don't have an option, do I?"

"No. But you have one advantage—you've experienced this yourself, so you have a clue what's happening with her."

"I wasn't captured or tortured. Bird of a different stripe, Emily."

I clicked off. Walked back into the house. The rest of the pizza was gone and Laura sat on the couch with her head back. "I'll help you pack your stuff. You're coming with me."

* * *

Laura dozed on the way home. Maybe if we could get her in better physical condition, her emotional life would stabilize. Dream on, Win. Laura hadn't begun to find her demons, much less face them. She'd been a confident woman when she'd accompanied me home from Tucson.

At least appeared that way. Were the cracks in her foundation already there?

I backed into the space in front of the garage. "Laura, we're here."

She opened her eyes wide. I could see the fear. She looked around, saw the house. I got out of the truck with her bag and unlocked my front door. Des swarmed me, then noticed Laura. Sniffed. Sneezed. She went about her business without greeting Laura, though she knew her from a previous visit.

Laura followed me in and to the guest bedroom. I tossed her bag on the bed. "How about you take a shower? Get some clean clothes on? I'll fix dinner in a bit."

She nodded but didn't move. "You don't want me here, do you?"

"Not particularly, Laura. We'd planned to get this room ready for the kids—"

"Kids? Sarah's pregnant? With twins?"

I glanced at Laura. Didn't like what I saw. Avid interest and no judgment.

"Adoption."

"Oh." She walked to the bed, unzipped her bag. "Sarah would be so lovely pregnant."

I sighed and went into the kitchen. I kept an ear out for the shower. Relaxed a bit when I heard it. I called Sarah.

"We've got company."

"Laura? How come?" Sarah asked.

"No other option. Do you think you could come home late?"

"Hell, I was just getting ready to leave. But there's always paperwork. How late is late?"

"I'm going to feed her some carbs, so she should succumb to sleep in an hour. Hour and a half?"

"Yeah, okay. I'm beginning to wonder what we did to call down disasters upon us." She disconnected.

I started the water for pasta, let Des in. She had a big question mark on her face. "Easy, soldier. Laura's just frazzled."

Des snorted and looked at her food bowl, always clear on her priorities.

I heard the shower stop. Took some sauce from the freezer, dumped it into a pan. I kept waiting for her to appear in the kitchen, clean. Revived a bit. When she didn't, I went looking for her. She wasn't in the bathroom, not in her room. I glanced into our bedroom. Laura lay on the bed, arms wrapped around Sarah's pillow. Fuck it all. Time for a dose of reality.

"This isn't your bed, Laura. It's Sarah's and mine. Our bedroom is not where you belong."

"You're just jealous," Laura said as she sat up. "You know Sarah and I have a special bond. You must hate me for that."

What the hell could I say? She was too deep in her fantasy. "No, I don't hate you. Until you face your pain, you're going to stay in this haze. Nothing in your life will have solidity. I know. I've been there."

I motioned her out. Herded her into the kitchen and fed her dinner. By the time Sarah got home, Laura was in her own bed. Asleep.

CHAPTER FIVE

Sarah

"What are we going to do?" I asked. "We can't have her staying here, Win. Getting in our bed is downright creepy."

"She doesn't mean it that way," Win said, rubbing my shoulder. "I don't know if I can explain it to you. When I was recovering in Germany, the one thing I didn't want to think about was the IED. Looking back, I doubt if I could've survived had I kept replaying that explosion. I was in so much physical pain. As I healed, my need for a fantasy relationship with my doctor lessened. But Sarah, that whole time, I knew it was a fantasy. It just gave me someplace else to go to get away. Emily helped me realize my sex life those years was the way I failed to deal with what I was feeling. This fantasy with my surgeon was the same thing—only I never allowed it to become physical."

"You think Laura's crush is the same thing?"

Win nodded. "But she doesn't realize it's not real. For right now, this fantasy of you is what's keeping her alive."

"You think she's suicidal?"

Win shook her head. "No idea. That's a question for Emily. I was hoping to hear from her with another bunk for Laura."

I put my arms around her and drew her to me. "It never gets easier, does it? We survive one crisis and another comes."

"This one's my fault. I shouldn't have brought her here. But I couldn't leave her there alone. She hadn't been eating, probably not sleeping. In a deep state of hypervigilance."

"It's a no-fault situation. You didn't have another option and I know that." I lifted her chin, kissed her and pulled her closer. "Do we have to be celibate tonight?"

Win groaned. "Maybe just quiet. I'll post Des outside the bedroom door." She started to unbutton my shirt, but stopped after two buttons. "I don't want to have to tiptoe around our own home. I want to get that room ready for Bahar and Dorri. I want to teach. Live life like a normal human being. I've had enough drama in my life for ten lives. Am I being selfish, Sarah?"

"No. You deserve a peaceful life, even if your wife's the sheriff." I pulled her into a long kiss, feeling her full response. "We'll call Em the first thing in the morning. I was going to take tomorrow off, but maybe I better wait until she's out of here."

"I've been looking forward to your day off." She unbuttoned another button. "But I can wait until it's safe to play in the whole house all day long. As long as we can play a bit tonight."

"Give Des her last walk for the night and I'll be waiting for you in our bedroom."

* * *

At dawn, I left our warm bed before Win woke up, understanding only a bit what Win had told me about creating fantasies. If I didn't want to think about something, I just didn't. I heard Em's voice in my head saying, "And how's that opening you for new growth?"

I congratulated myself for remembering to leave my anonymous letters on Win's desk and grateful she hadn't asked about them last night. Maybe she'd be able to remove the gray sense of dread I felt when I handled them.

The countryside was tucked underneath a heavy coverlet of snow, nothing breaking the sculptured surface but trees. I watched four ravens swim across the gray sky. They made it look so easy. Did they ever wish for a normal life, one without drama? Was a commonplace life the only norm they knew?

Not wanting to be there I pulled into the lot behind our building. I'd been going full steam for over a week and I desperately needed a break. I went straight up to our forensics lab on the back half of the third floor. Detectives occupied the front, but I saw a glow from only one desk lamp. I took the evidence envelope Win had picked up at the Brownes into the darkened lab, flipped on a light and wrote a brief note to examine the letters for fingerprints and DNA.

I walked back to the detectives' loft and poked my head around the corner to see John Morgan, head of the Investigation Division, bent over a report on his desk.

"Awful early for you to be here, John."

He jumped and looked up. "Morning Sarah. I woke up thinking about those damn letters and it occurred to me maybe we were headed down the wrong path. Some of the language reminded me of this." He punched up a website on his computer.

I scanned the site. "McCrumb County Rangers? Is this new?"

"This MCR site's been online about a year, but there're others. They're one of the militias that've joined forces with the sovereign citizen movement."

"How long have you been following these groups?" I asked.

"Since I was on patrol and had an unfortunate experience with a sovereign citizen." He rubbed the back of his neck. "Seemed to me at the time we were dealing with a bunch of crackpots, but I checked out one of the sites. They'd had over a hundred and fifty thousand hits. Scared me."

"That was the guy who shot at you, wasn't it?"

John nodded. "Claimed I didn't have the authority to arrest him. Then he refused the authority of the court. Judge sent him away for a long sentence and he's been in trouble ever since."

"You think he or one of these people might have sent the letters?"

"Possibly. We can't prove it, but some of the language on these websites is identical. Don't know why I didn't think of it before."

I did. We'd thought the threats were directed at the first openly gay sheriff in southern Indiana. Me. But maybe we'd assumed something we never should've. "Send me what you've got on all of these groups. Notify our internet czar about this particular one."

"I presume you mean Nathan."

I started to leave. "Oh, and there are similar letters from the Browne home. Take a look at them when Leslie finishes dusting them."

John nodded. "Right. Rumor has it the Brownes were harboring a CIA agent and that fits right in with the kind of paranoia MCR exploits."

"CIA?"

"I don't know anyone who trusts the CIA, but these guys are much worse. New world order, also called Obama World Order—imagine *Nineteen Eighty-Four* on steroids—all facilitated by the CIA."

"Hell. If these idiots did anything to cause the Brownes to run off the road, we can go after them hard." I glanced at my watch. "I doubt if we'll hear anything from Mike before noon. Have Leslie let me know when she's finished."

Barely eight in the morning and already I had full day's work ahead of me. Rangers?

* * *

When I got back to my office, I called Em. "We've got a situation."

"Laura?" she asked.

"Yeah. Win thinks she's unraveling quickly." I told her how Win had found Laura in our bed, hugging my pillow.

"Shit. I don't have anybody lined up yet who can take her right away."

"Can you talk to Laura? If you want to take her up to Indianapolis, I can arrange a ride with our deputies. Interstate just opened."

"I hate to push her, but that's a possibility. Let me make a few more phone calls, Sarah."

"Uh, one thing you might take into consideration is that she was the target of threatening letters sent to Barry and Linda Browne. We found their car and they're dead. It could be an accident from the storm, but we're running a death investigation."

Em didn't say anything for a long time. "That changes things. Can Win bring her to my office?"

"Sure, but clear it with Win. She seems to understand what's going on with Laura and tried to explain it to me, but Em, I don't understand. I don't want her in our home. That kind of behavior really spooks me."

"I'll call now." Em disconnected.

Around nine thirty, Mike walked into my office and placed an evidence bag on my desk. "Cause of the Browne crash. Found it in the flat tire."

I examined the slug in the bag. "Rifle?"

"Looks like a thirty-aught-six to me, but Vincente will have to verify."

"So it wasn't an accident. Well, hell's bells."

CHAPTER SIX

Win

I got off the phone with Emily, got Laura packed up. With Des riding behind me and Laura at shotgun, we headed for Emily's office in Greenglen. At this point, I'd tried everything I could. Laura was in her own world. This morning she'd wept and apologized for sleeping with Sarah.

"We were just swept away. I never meant to hurt you, Win," she said, looking so mournful. She glanced at me without turning her head.

What the hell could I say to that? She'd lost touch with reality. I shivered. Maybe because I could've slipped into that same mist so easily.

I deposited Laura and Des in Emily's waiting room, then tapped on the door. I went in, closed the door behind me. "She's flipped out."

"Tell me what happened," Emily said. After I did, Emily's response was short. "Crap."

I started pacing. "Are you going to have the deputy drive you there?"

"I didn't think it'd be necessary."

"Is that a no?"

"I didn't make arrangements."

"Let me go with you. She's not only fragile but…"

Emily stared at me. "You think she's dangerous?"

I nodded. "Explosive. Maybe. I don't know, but I'm getting a feeling."

"Then let's get going, and I'll be glad to have you ride with me." Emily grabbed her coat.

"Give me a minute," I said. "I need to let Sarah know where I'm going."

She nodded and went out her door and into the waiting room.

I called Sarah, told her what was going on. "I don't know how long it's going to take to get her admitted, but I should be back by dinnertime."

"You think Laura's dangerous?" Sarah asked. "I mean, able to hurt someone?"

"I don't have a good answer. She's on the edge, but I don't know which edge."

"Is Laura armed?"

"Oh, crap. I hope not. I didn't even think of it and I should have." She'd come with her service weapon, but I'd lost track of it.

"Check before you leave, Win. Please stay safe."

"You too." We disconnected and I opened the door.

The waiting room was empty. Except for Des, her lead tied to a closet door.

* * *

Des whined, clearly uneasy with what had occurred. I untied her and ran out the door. I slid to a stop at the empty space that had held Emily's Jeep when we pulled in. I let Des jump in my truck first, followed her with my key turning the ignition before my feet were all the way in.

I followed the Jeep's tracks to the street entrance, turned right to follow them. Fairly easy since the street hadn't been heavily used. But when I came to an intersection with Market Street, the slush was too churned up to yield any information.

I called Sarah as I began a sweep of the area for a battered old blue Jeep.

"She did what?" Sarah asked. "Are you sure Emily didn't just take off?"

"I'm not sure of anything, Sarah. Is this my paranoia kicking in? Possibly. But Emily asked me to come along. Why would she leave without me? My gut's telling me Emily's in danger."

"I'll put a BOLO out and notify Greenglen PD. Where are you?"

"Doing a grid search. I lost the trail at Market, been working my way north. I don't have Marty's number with me. Could you call her? Find out if she's home?"

"You think Laura might head to her home? What happens if she meets Em's partner? Will that blow her up?"

"Don't know. Where else around here does she have?"

"The Brownes' empty house. I'll be with you soon."

"Thanks, Sarah. For not doubting me."

As I headed back south minutes later, I saw headlights flashing in my rearview mirror. Pulled over. Got out with Des and walked to Sarah's SUV. I opened the back door, Des jumped in. I followed into the front seat at shotgun. "Hear anything from the BOLO?"

She shook her head. "I called the woman who lives across the road from the Brownes. Nobody's been there since you left with Laura, but she'll keep an eye out and call if they show up."

"Then it's Emily's. You want to do a drive-by?"

"Slow down, Win. We don't know they're at Em's. Laura knows this car, so a drive-by might heighten whatever she's feeling. Do you know what she's feeling?"

I leaned back, closed my eyes. Tried to get back into the old frame of mind. "I think she's had a break with reality. I did, but mine lasted a couple of minutes at most. This seems longer, maybe a deeper break." I opened my eyes. Didn't want to dwell in that black space anymore. "Those days alone must have terrorized her. Maybe this is her way of regaining control."

"Do you think she's capable of violence?"

"Yeah. There's nothing worse for a marine than feeling afraid and not being able to take control of the situation. Even though she spent most of her career behind a desk, Laura's a marine." Had been trained to stop the enemy. To kill. "I didn't even think about her service weapon, just assumed someone had taken it away."

Sarah rubbed her eyes with the heels of her hands. "I called Marty. She's not at home and Em doesn't expect her until dinnertime. She also said they don't lock their doors, front or back."

"We need to get close to the house, Sarah. There's a woods behind it. You know the quickest way in?"

"How fast is the clock ticking?"

"Fast." I hit the dashboard. "My whole perspective could be skewed because I owe Emily my life. If she hadn't been there for me, I wouldn't be here. I wouldn't be with you. Let me get to the back of the house, get eyes on what's happening."

"Are you armed?"

"No."

"We're not even sure Laura's there. Win, we're not sure of anything." She shifted into drive and began to head for Emily's house.

CHAPTER SEVEN

Sarah

My phone rang just as I pulled up to the path through the woods. I checked the caller ID. I put my hand on Win's arm. "Wait, it's Em."

"This should be interesting. Prove whether I'm nuts or not." Win turned to me. "Play along with whatever she says. If I'm right, the call's coerced."

I put it on speaker. "What's up, Em?"

"Hey, Sarah. You have any idea where Win is? This is the second appointment she's missed without calling."

"No idea." I watched Win pantomime driving. "I'm out on patrol and haven't heard from her since I left this morning."

There was a long silence. "Uh, do you think she's been acting strange lately?"

Win nodded emphatically. Wrote on a pad.

"Yeah. Sometimes I get the feeling she's not living in the real world. Uh, says things I know aren't true. How do I handle that, Em?"

"Play along." She paused and I heard whispers. "Sarah, I'd like you to come over and we can talk about this. For Win. Come to my house. Let me give you directions. Have something to write on?"

"Hold on."

Win pointed to her watch, then made a stretch it out sign.

"Okay." Em gave detailed directions which I didn't need since I'd been there numerous times. "As long as I don't get called out, I should be there in about forty-five minutes."

"You can't make it sooner?" Emily asked.

"Not unless you want me to slide into your driveway with siren and lights flashing."

I disconnected. "You're right. She made the call under duress. I'm calling SWAT."

"No," Win said. "I don't want to make this into a standoff. Before you do anything, let me get eyes on the house. See if the back door is unlocked. We need intel first."

"Don't take any action on your own. Promise me."

"Promise. Come along if you want. But not you, Des. Stay."

I parked at the back of the woods and we jogged down the trail to the place where it opened to backyards. Win turned into the woods, and even though they didn't provide a lot of cover in their winter nakedness, Laura would have to be looking out a back window to see us. We stopped behind Em's and sank behind a big oak still feathered with a few dried leaves.

"How do we do this?" I asked. "If we rush the back, she'd have time to hurt Em."

"You're going to have to go in, at least walk up the front walk. I can rush her while her attention's fixed on you." Win searched my face, for what? Fear? Uncertainty? "I can slip in the back. If the door's unlocked."

"Marty said—"

"Laura may have locked it."

"But there's no way to know and you can't check now because she could see you."

Win shook her head. "I'll work my way farther down, come from next door. Cover me?"

"Don't take unnecessary chances. Please."

She began working her way through the trees and brush parallel to the houses. When she got two doors down, she walked casually from the woods to the back door of the house, the hood of her parka up and with the shorter gait of an older person. As soon as she was out of sight from Em's, she moved rapidly to the back of the house. She ducked under windows and moved to the kitchen door. Slowly she reached up to the doorknob and turned it. I could see it turn all the way.

Win signaled success and got her phone out. "Go on," she whispered. "When you get back to your truck, call Emily, tell her your callout was canceled. Ask her if you should wait or come on. When you get to the front door, I'll begin entry. Keep this line open so I know what's going on."

"Affirmative." I disconnected, kept as low as I could and ran as soon as I hit the trail. When I got back, I opened the car and started the engine. Des whined and kept looking through the woods. "It's okay, girl. Win's okay." I reached back ruffled her fur and took her lead off. She'd managed to get it tangled on the console between front seats. I imagined she'd done a lot of pacing while I'd been gone. The heat felt good on my feet.

I made the call. Em didn't pick up until the fourth ring. "Call was canceled and I'm making better time than I thought. Should I stop at the station or are you ready for me?"

A pause. "I'm not doing anything but waiting for you, Sarah. Front door's open, just come on in."

"See you soon." I disconnected and called Win. "She's left the front door open and I'm supposed to just walk in. I'll knock on the door before I go in."

"Roger that."

I unzipped the slash pocket on the front of my parka and tucked the phone in. "Can you still hear?"

I heard a muffled "Affirmative."

"Here we go."

I drove slowly, around the block twice and back to Em's street. As Em's modified A-frame came into view, I said, "Target in sight. Pulling into drive."

"Enough play-by-play. Remember what Emily said: go along with the fantasy."

I cut the engine and turned to Des. "Stay."

I got out, walked up to the front door and tried to slow my pulse. I knocked, opened the door and left it slightly ajar. When I stepped into the living room I saw Emily in a side chair. Laura stood behind her, a service pistol in her hand.

"What's going on?" I saw quick movement in the kitchen. "Why are you here?"

"We were just having a little fun," Laura said, moving toward me. She seemed to have forgotten the gun in her hand. "I've missed you so much, sweetheart."

She put her arms around me and kissed me, began unzipping my parka with her free hand. I pulled back and could feel her stiffen. "You know I'm not comfortable with public displays of affection, don't you, Laura."

"Public?"

"In front of other people." I motioned to Em. She began to turn when a blur flew past my shoulder. It knocked Laura down and fastened a jaw around her wrist. Her weapon went slithering across the floorboards. I couldn't understand. Des was in the car.

Win shoved past me. "Des! Release!"

Des let go of Laura's wrist when Win recovered the gun. She sat beside Win, licking her chops.

Laura was crying and holding her wrist. "All I want is you, Sarah. I want us to be together all the time. Not sneak around anymore."

I helped her up. I didn't read her her rights, but I cuffed her. If she was as loony as Win thought, then she didn't need jail, she needed treatment. Win helped Em to her feet.

"You people have got to stop hanging around me because I'm tired of being used as bait," Em said, her voice shaky. "I don't want any more of this crap. Ever."

* * *

When Laura grew more hysterical, Em gave her a sedative and we took her to the hospital in town. While we waited for the paperwork to be completed, Win hovered. She kept asking Em if she was okay. She'd brought Des in, afraid to leave her in the car again and I thought needing Des close. For a woman who'd been so cool and in command, she was a tad puddly now.

"We're all safe, even Des." At Em's, when we'd gone out to the car, we found the back window down. We looked at Des and she'd just smiled. "I swear the window was up when I left the truck. I think this hero is an escape artist." I motioned to the row of chairs. "Now sit down and collect yourself."

"Sorry," Win said as she sat down. "Just wound up."

Des sat by her and stuck her muzzle into her lap. The two stared into one another's eyes. I wondered who Des had charged in to save, me or Win? She'd never taken to Laura and avoided her when she could. Perhaps this was just her own form of taking advantage of the situation. No, she'd do anything to keep both of us safe.

Paperwork done, Em signed it. "Ladies, I'm going home. Laura will be transported to the VA in the morning. I'm turning her case over to the psychiatrist there." She ran her hands through her hair. "She'll be okay eventually. She's got a hell of a lot of work to do to get there. I'm sorry, Win. I should've paid more attention to what you told me. If you need to talk about this, call me."

"Same to you," Win said with a big grin.

As we walked to my car, I felt a complex stew of feelings, but the predominate one was sadness.

"I'll need to swing by and pick up my truck," Win said as we headed home.

"No way, not tonight. We're going straight home. I'll take you in tomorrow."

"What's the rush?"

"What do you think? We've been walking on eggshells and I need some good release. That is, if you're willing."

"My, oh my," Win said. She leaned her head back and stared out the windshield. "So you kissed another woman today. How'd you like it?"

"I didn't. Too damn sloppy and way too fast."

"Hmm."

"What does that mean, Win?"

"It means it was a new experience. One you'll think about."

"I'm only thinking about kissing you right now and we're almost home. So get ready, Wife."

CHAPTER EIGHT

Win

Sarah made love that night with complete concentration. My lightest touch elicited a response. Her gaze never left my body, as if she was memorizing it. By sight. By touch.

I was right. Laura's kiss had taken her by surprise. Had shaken her, even if it was too much tongue. She was the only other woman Sarah had ever kissed. My second woman was so long ago, I couldn't even remember who she was. Sarah had a hell of a lot more women to kiss to catch up. Would she want to?

Remembering the numbers made me sad. Sex? A hundred? More? One good thing, my emotional count was two. Azar and Sarah.

As dawn lit Sarah's breasts in a rosy hue, I watched her dream. I knew Sarah wouldn't talk about what she'd felt at Laura's kiss. Not until she'd processed her response to it. Her reaction bothered her, that much I knew. She didn't like to talk about "stuff." Had she shared with Hugh? As her husband, surely she'd talked with him. When had she started stuffing down her feelings? Micah said what was on his mind, flat out. Elizabeth, Sarah's mother, was a bit more circumspect. Maybe out of diplomacy, I thought, not lack of awareness. Maybe it was the years Sarah had spent as a deputy, then sheriff. The need to appear professional. Stuff the feelings down and get on with the job.

I wished we could talk about it.

Sarah opened her eyes, yawned. Stretched. Reached out her hand to me. "Last night was lovely. Made me forget it wasn't the first time."

What did that mean? "You want to start over?"

"No. That's not what I meant." She propped herself on one elbow. "I never expected my love for you could grow every day. So, every time we make love, it's new because the love is new. Am I making any sense?"

"Yeah." I took her hand, entwined our fingers. "Yesterday crystalized something for me. You walked into that house and I understood how Azar felt every time I went on patrol. She never said anything, but once I turned around for another look. Saw the worry on her face. I realized my face wears the same expression when you go to work."

"I…"

"I probably shouldn't have said anything. I don't want you to stop being sheriff because I know how much it's a part of you. Down deep. But each time you come home, it's a miracle to me." I kissed her. "Just my klutzy way of saying I understand what you said. About each time being new."

She examined my face. "Be real, Win. I'm behind my desk more than I'm out on patrol."

"Doesn't matter and I don't want you to change to fit into our marriage. I knew what I was in store for. Well, mostly."

Sarah pulled me down to her, kissed me with surprising energy for so early in the morning. "What you said, about kissing Laura, I was honest with you. I didn't like it. Am I curious about kissing other women? Not that I'm aware of."

"So it's possible?"

"But not probable."

* * *

I was just finishing my first cup of coffee when Sarah's phone rang. This was her day off. I'd been looking forward to some snowshoeing. Maybe hot cocoa in front of the fire. And then…

"Not on or off the record, Zoe. It's a private matter," Sarah said. "You tell Mary Ellen Simmons she'd better keep her big mouth shut or she'll find herself faced with disciplinary action from the Medical Board." She tossed me the phone. "Zoe."

"Morning," I said.

"I'm working on a couple of articles about PTSD in our returning soldiers—"

"No."

"Come on, Win. I want to do a good job with this and I've already interviewed several soldiers."

"First mistake. It's not just military who suffer from the disorder. Any first responder is susceptible. Firefighters, EMTs, cops. I don't want people thinking every soldier who comes home from deployment is a ticking time bomb. It's not true. Strictly off the record, the woman who was brought in last night never served in a combat zone. The trauma that happened to her, happened here in good old McCrumb County."

Des woofed to go out. I opened the door and followed. "I have a question for you. What do you know about the Sovereign Citizen movement?"

"In the county? Nothing. Should I?"

"Maybe. You want a story? That might be a good one. Try the McCrumb County Rangers." I disconnected.

I tucked the phone in my pocket. John Morgan had given Sarah copies of all the letters—Sarah's and those to the Brownes. She'd brought them home, left them on my desk. They scared the shit out of me, the way any paramilitary does to the military. I hadn't said anything to Sarah. What had I been preaching? Openness. No secrets. Shit. I hoped sending Zoe McClanahan off on the trail would keep me relatively uninvolved. Her job was to report the news. Mine was to protect Sarah.

Not right, Win. Silence would keep me from active pursuit so Sarah wouldn't find out.

I threw snowballs for Des. High underhand pitches that gave her time to field them. Snow all over her face, we went back inside.

"I really like Zoe," Sarah said. She turned from a skillet of frying sausage. "But why is it, reporters always want to know stuff that should be private?"

"It's their job, Sarah." I refilled my mug. "Zoe did a nice job on our story."

Sarah concentrated on the sausage patties.

"Are you sorry you came out to the whole county?"

"No, never. Sometimes I wish there wasn't a need to."

"Yeah, maybe someday," I said. "Not today."

CHAPTER NINE

He stood in the same position, but the changing seasons had changed his view. The paddock grass had turned from a luscious green to a faded, darker shade and the trees on the mountains stood naked under a light dusting of snow, waiting for winter to finish. He felt utterly impatient with the rate of change.

A soft knock at the double doors stopped his thoughts. "Come." He turned to face his visitor. "Waterstone. Good to see you again and I hope your mission has been successful."

Seth Waterstone stood at attention until the man motioned him to a chair at the long table. "I'm not sure that you'll think it was successful, except in a negative way. The McCrumb County Rangers are pathetic role-players. The only talent we found has been sent to camp for further training. We'll send them back when they're finished, but that may be a while, sir. They lack discipline and sense."

"Shamsi's status? I want him dead before he gives the feds a clear trail to us."

"Hard to reach right now because he's in a well-operated jail. If he was in a general population of a larger prison, it wouldn't be a problem. However, we could take him out with a sniper during his next court appearance. I've placed a sniper for other purposes and he could handle this. But that means we have to wait and we don't know how much he's already said to MCIA. We can put a court appearance into play at any time." Waterstone frowned. "We've found a way to introduce an assassin into the jail before the trial begins. It all depends on what kind of message you want to send."

"I trust your judgment, use whatever method you want but get it done *now*." He stared at Waterstone. "What's the status on the sheriff?"

"She's married to a MCIA operative, retired but still in contact with General William Keller, her old CO. They are a formidable team."

"The sheriff and her husband or…"

"Excuse me, sir. I should've been clear. Sarah Pitt's married to a woman, Win Kirkland, a retired MCIA Colonel. Both are on cooperative terms with Keller. The three form a team, sir."

"I have sincere hopes you've formulated a plan to convince the sheriff to keep her nose out of our business. Now and forever."

"Yes sir. But it's going to take some time and I know you've lost valuable time with the lost missiles and UAVs. I'll push as hard as I can."

"Push harder, Waterstone. If we wait too long, we'll lose our support all over this country. Right now, there's plenty of dissent and anger boiling. We've got to keep it going strong."

CHAPTER TEN

Sarah

I wished every day could be like this one. We'd snowshoed up Foley's Knob, the gnarled siltstone remnant which loomed in front of our house. Des broke the trail for us until she got tired, then Win took the lead and Des followed behind. Back home, we built a fire and cuddled on the couch. I couldn't remember when I'd felt so content and full and at peace. Until Win started talking.

"Why don't you have John send me his files on all those renegade groups he's been following," she began. "I've got a couple of days with nothing to do and while I'm profiling those letters, I can match words and phrases."

I groaned. "You sure know how to break a wonderful moment."

Win moved her arm from around my shoulders and sat forward. "Because you don't want to think about this doesn't mean there's no real threat. If I'm working on the analysis, I don't have as much time to worry."

"Hell, Win. That's blackmail."

She grinned. "Yes, it is."

"Damnation. You've gotten cheeky."

"What do you want for dinner?" she asked as she handed me the phone from the kitchen counter.

"Pizza and beer. I don't want to cook and I don't want you to cook. I want to sit here and watch the fire and be with you."

"I'll call for pizza if you'll call John now."

"More damn blackmail." I made the call, and though John sounded a bit surprised, he said he'd send them right away. When I disconnected, Win was doing the same.

"Forty minutes to enjoy the fire and just be together. I won't even think about this again until you're back at work in the morning. Promise." She sank back onto the couch and pulled me to her. "This is bliss for me too."

I snuggled into her. "Bliss isn't a word I've used too many times in my life. But I can use it now without qualification. Thank you for today."

"Thank you for doing it."

I rested my head on Win's shoulder. "We're supposed to get more snow tonight. Maybe we'll get snowed in and have two or three whole days together."

"We need a vacation," Win said as she rubbed my shoulder. "I know. My fault with my class schedule, but I enjoy teaching way more than I thought possible. When you're ready to retire, you should think about teaching at the academy."

I snorted. "Is this your sneaky way of saying you hope this is my last term as sheriff?"

"No." She tweaked my shoulder. "You want to go four terms, so be it. I think I'm just surprised at how much I like it. My life is good."

"And even better when the kids get here?"

"Yes." She pulled me to her. "Thank you, for everything."

* * *

One of the hardest things I'd done lately was get out of our warm bed and come to work. If it'd been up to me, I would've voted for another day home with Win, but what kind of example would that have given to my deputies?

I needed to start on paperwork, but Win's request propelled me upstairs to the detective's loft. I wanted to know where we stood with the Brownes' murder investigation and if we'd found any link with the letters. Three flights of stairs made me feel yesterday's hike with cranky knees and achy thighs. I definitely needed to get more exercise, and more consistently.

John was at his desk and looked up when I tapped on the doorframe. "Morning Sarah. I was glad you talked Win into going over those militia sites."

"She volunteered. Maybe she can spot something we've missed. Anything new?"

"Yeah, but not necessarily good news. I had Nathan look at the Rangers' website and he's not the provider. It's a national network I fondly call 'the nutwork.' All kinds of radical right groups."

"How'd you get onto this network, John?"

"Southern Poverty Law Center. I subscribe. It occurred to me that the radical right's ideology was rearing its ugly head in McCrumb County. Just talk, but I kept wondering how long they'd keep to talk without action."

I'd heard the rumblings too, but dismissed them as venting frustration with the economy. "How many other groups in the county?"

He laughed and hit a folder icon. Out spilled a list of twenty or more groups. "Now some of these only have three or four members, close as I can tell. But others are part of a statewide or national network."

"Is that what the number column means?"

"Yeah, membership. The column after that indicates the nature of the hate group. Neo-Nazi, White Nationalist, Skinhead, Klan, militia, sovereign citizen, radical Tea Party and a couple of fundamentalist religious like the Dominionists, groups who are loosely linked to the others."

"A toxic mix."

"I have more. Membership rolls for some of them, leadership structure, connections with larger groups." He glanced at me. "All legally obtained from their sites and I've done the work on my own time. When it looked like we might be dealing with McCrumb County Rangers, I downloaded all this onto my workstation."

"I guess I shouldn't be surprised with some of these, though I thought the KKK had died a lasting death a long time ago. They were active in the twenties and thirties—I remember Granddad telling awful stories about them."

"They've never gone away, just been quiet." John tapped another key. "They're recruiting people who think the 'brown tide' is going to overwhelm America."

I could hear the disgust in his voice. "So how do the Rangers fit into this general scheme?"

"Good question that I don't have a good answer for. Most of these sites share videos, stories, that kind of stuff. But the Rangers use only their own nutwork's investigations and reports."

"What the hell kind of investigations are they doing?"

"I printed them out." He handed me a folder. "It's pretty much the same conspiracy theories—the Feds will take away all the guns, put a plan in action for economic dislocation, open FEMA relocation centers and detention camps so that the new global order can take over."

"That's garbage."

"The thing is, they actually believe this stuff." He rolled his shoulders. "I'll dig some more, see how the Rangers have been working locally."

I took the folder and it felt heavy. "Is there a national network of Rangers?"

"I've only been able to find two other chapters, one in Idaho and the other in northern Virginia. They may be affiliated with a group called 1776 Corps, but I can't find a direct connection."

"American Revolution stuff. Strange that they've popped up recently and with that kind of affiliation. What am I not getting?"

He shook his head. "I don't have a glimmer. I'll keep working on it."

"What about ballistics?"

"One hit on NIBIN from an unsolved murder in Idaho. A Coeur d'Alene Tribal Police Officer, though I have no idea how it's connected. I've asked them to send details, but haven't gotten anything back yet."

"Damn."

"I know. Honestly Sarah, I can't even begin to see the pattern in this, but I'm sure there is one."

CHAPTER ELEVEN

Win

Several messages came in from John Morgan and I looked at the links. Why is it when we see a name like McCrumb County Rangers we're dismissive? Bunch of crackpots, we think. That may be true, but it doesn't lessen the danger. I thought of Ruby Ridge, Waco and how that path led inevitably to Oklahoma City. Aryan Nation? Just racists. Branch Davidians? Religious fanatics. Timothy McVeigh and Terry Nichols? We shake our heads and refuse to take them seriously.

I'd been dealing with foreign threats so long, I'd ignored internal ones until General Scott Lester went rogue. That should've rung my bell loud and clear. But I marked it down to a man infected with a deadly case of greed. As I followed John's links, I couldn't mark this down to greed or some other vice. These people believed they were patriots.

Who was I to say they weren't? I'd been on the other side of "through the glass darkly." I'd seen the intel. I knew why we did what we did. Except for Iraq. Humanitarian reasons were different, they were solid. But that wasn't the reason given and when proven false, shook the faith in our government. Was it simply a mistake? Bad intel? MCIA had good intel. I knew that because I'd help gather it. Maybe just too many voices for one administration to listen to. Any other conclusion was disastrous for democracy.

I called Nathan and asked him to track down what he could about the Rangers and 1776 Corps, a group much more in the shadows. "I'm going to call Bill and ask him to get you clearance."

"You think they're that dangerous?" he asked.

"Every time I worked intel, I paid attention when I got a little tingle up my spine. I've no evidence of anything, Nathan. Just the tingle."

I called my old CO, Bill, explained the situation and he said he'd get the paperwork started.

I started going back over the material. If these threats were in Tajik or Urdu, I could tell all sorts of things about the writer. But in my first language? It appeared that the writer either had a poor grasp of grammar and spelling or had run out of some of the letters he needed to paste down.

The first few that Sarah had received echoed Pastor Brown's rhetoric, whore of Babylon type with all caps and lots of exclamation points. But the latest contributions threatened Sarah with rape and eventual decapitation. They broadened the target too. To all members of the sheriff's department, local cops and marshals in the county. The whole damn law enforcement community.

I quit around noon, hungry and thinking I should run into Greenglen to pick up groceries. My phone rang. The ID said Bradway. Marty? Emily's partner?

"Kirkland."

"Hi Win. It's Marty and I'd like to invite you and Sarah over for dinner tonight. A thank-you for you both."

"Um…Emily's still my shrink. Is that okay?"

There was a long silence. "Em's spiraled into a deep depression. I called her therapist—"

"Emily's got a therapist?"

"Of course. Anyway, she said a kind kick in the ass might bring Em back. I thought you guys might be able to provide…"

"A kick in the pants?"

"A gentle one. She knows all the book stuff and is really good at guiding people through the rough times. But she refuses to acknowledge symptoms in herself. I'm the one she wakes with her nightmares. Swears the next morning she doesn't remember anything. She's got me scared, Win. I can only help her so much."

I expelled a long breath. "I owe Emily my life. I'd do anything for her. But I'm not sure this would help any. Besides, Sarah has a say in this."

"I already talked to her and she said if you okayed it, she'd be glad to come. Please, Win."

Sarah. I'd envisioned an "unwind" kind of evening in front of the fire with some good music. "What time?"

"Six?"

"See you then. I sure hope you know what you're doing, Marty."

* * *

I took Des for a long walk before Sarah got home. Des picked up on my anxiety and took it out on small animals who happened out. I was worried about the letters. Those sent to the Brownes and to Sarah had been written by the same hand. Or in this case, pasted by the same hand, a classic example of the poison pen who didn't use a pen. Though I detected a strong tone of anti-gay sentiment, I thought this was more. Was I just projecting my fears? That my relationship with Sarah threatened her just because we existed as a couple? I knew I had to wait for more data from Nathan. Waiting wasn't my favorite game.

I worried about Emily too. What the hell could we accomplish over dinner? If she was suffering from PTSD, she had to recognize it. Acknowledge it. My case had been severe enough I couldn't ignore it. At the rate I'd been going, I would've been dead in a couple of months. If she wasn't suffering debilitating pain, she probably thought she could get through it on her own. "Physician heal thyself." I could hear her saying it. Shit.

Sarah walked in the door looking tired. After she deposited her outerwear and cop gear, she walked into my arms. Tucked her head into my shoulder. I wrapped my arms around her and pulled her closer. "Long day?"

"Yeah."

She pushed away from me. "Let me shower. Maybe that'll perk me up."

Sarah walked back into the living room fifteen minutes later. In a flannel robe and hair slicked back. She looked delicious. She plopped down next to me and put her feet on the coffee table. I loved looking at her feet. Narrow, with a high arch and long toes. Graceful like the rest of her body. I put my arm around her.

"This is the way I wanted to spend the evening. You and me in front of the fire, listening to the new Cris Williamson double album and…"

Sarah reached up and kissed me. Then settled into my arm.

"Then why did you say yes to Marty?"

"Because we owe so much to Em," she said. "We wouldn't be sitting here now, together and happy, if it weren't for her. I don't think we'd be as strong together if she hadn't counseled us from the start. Surely we can give up one lovely evening to help."

"We still have an hour before we have to get ready. How about I put on some slow music and we dance? We haven't danced in a while. I love it feeling you so close. Both of us moving to the same rhythm."

"That happens in this house almost every night, even without music." She grinned up at me. "Will this feeling of desire disappear by the time we have our next anniversary?"

"Not if I can help it. I've never been with one woman this long. I'm still as fascinated with you as the first kiss. More so. I love touching you. Being touched by you. With Azar—"

"You don't have to—"

"Let me finish, Sarah, it's not baggage. With Azar, we lived day-to-day. Planned for the future but with no guarantees the future would include either of us. You and I have promised our lives together, entwined. That's enough to keep me interested as long as I have breath."

CHAPTER TWELVE

Sarah

We pulled into their driveway about ten minutes late, not too bad considering. Win had picked up a nice zinfandel and I clutched it as we slipped and slid up the front walk. "I thought they'd have this shoveled by now."

"Emily's still not back at work," Win said. "The exercise would do her good. I mean if she's...Ah, hell." Win started windmilling and landed on snow to the side with a thump. She started giggling. "Shit, I'm out of shape. Used to be able to climb mountains. Now look at me."

The front door opened and Em leaned out. "Are you okay?"

I held out a hand and pulled Win to her feet. "You've had a week to get this under control. Get with the program, Emily."

"Come on in before all the heat is outside." She opened the door wider and we made it up the stairs like two ancient crones.

Inside, Win bent over to take off her boots and when she straightened up, her eyebrows shot up. "Shit. You look awful."

"Thanks, Win. Wish I could say the same of you," Emily said without a trace of a smile.

"Aren't you sleeping?"

Emily turned away and pointed to the coatrack.

"Good job, Win," I whispered.

"Sorry," Win whispered back. "But she surprised me. I wonder when she last had a good night's sleep?"

We padded into the kitchen and I gave the wine to Marty.

"Where's Emily?" Win asked.

Marty turned from the stove and shoved her hair back with her arm. "Her study. If we're really fortunate, she'll come out and grace us with her company."

"My fault—" Win began.

Marty teared up. "It doesn't make any difference what you say, her reaction's going to be the same. Distant and frigid and angry."

"Well, this is going to be a fun night." Win leaned against the counter. "Shall I open the wine?"

"Chill. We know we're here to help," I said. "What can we do to help get dinner on the table?"

I could see Marty pull herself together and she gave us our marching orders. In another ten minutes, the food was on the table and we were seated.

"We might as well go ahead and eat," Marty said. "I haven't been cooking all day to let this go to waste." She passed the bread.

"How long has she been like this?" Win asked.

"It started right after Laura's meltdown, but it seems to be getting worse and I don't know what to do for her anymore."

"You're a therapist too, aren't you?"

Marty passed the salad. "I'm feeling pretty much like a failure right now. She just won't talk about it at all. I'm too close to her to do any good therapeutically."

Win pushed her chair back. "I'll get her. She may never talk to me again, but this is silly."

I sat open-mouthed. Marty slumped in her chair and I thought she was close to tears again.

"Was Win this bad?" she asked.

"She shut me out after we kissed the first time, but that was about the relationship. What I'm trying to say is I didn't see her much when she was going through the worst of it." I broke off a piece of bread. "What I can tell you is that with Em's guidance, she's much more open than I am. We talk about what she went through and when anything happens now, we talk. She talks and I'm still working on it."

Marty gave me a tired smile. We heard angry voices from down the hall. Then silence. A door opened and Em came in and sat down, looking properly subdued.

Win followed and looked slightly smug.

"My apologies," Em said.

Marty sighed and began dishing up the lasagna, while Emily caught up with the other dishes being passed around. Conversation lagged while we ate, though Win and I gave it a valiant effort. We settled in front of the fire with coffee and I wondered how soon we could gracefully leave.

"I am sorry, Win," Em said. "I've been at loose ends lately."

"End of your rope is more like it," Win said. "But you owe Marty the apology. She's had to put up with your denial and all the other shit."

Em stared at Win open-eyed.

"Isn't that what you'd tell me?"

Em nodded mutely.

Marty's glance had been going back and forth, then settled on Em. Her face softened at Em's nod.

"Meet me at the dojang tomorrow and we'll work on feeling paralyzed in a stress situation," Win said.

"How do you know?" Em asked.

"Because I had to have it trained out of me."

* * *

"How the hell did you get Em to come to the table?" I asked on the way home. "What did you say to her?"

"Between her and me. Let's just say I guilted her into moving again."

"You think she'll meet you tomorrow?"

"Oh yeah."

I knew I wasn't going to get anymore information from Win, so I stopped asking. I just hoped Win had shaken her up enough that she'd get help.

"When's your next day off?" Win asked.

"Tomorrow. You have special plans? Something other than snowshoeing or cross-country skiing?"

"You mean something fun instead of something good for us?"

"I enjoy it once I get started. It's just the starting that's hard."

"That's because you don't get enough exercise during your shifts," Win said, placing her hand on my thigh. "What happens if you have to run a footrace to catch some suspect? You'll be huffing and puffing after the first block."

"You just wait until we get home and I'll show you my endurance. But don't start something now because it's gotten colder and driving isn't easy. I want to make it home, not end up in a ditch."

She removed her hand and stared out the side window. "You get any more intel on the letters?"

"Where did that come from? Or are you distracting me from thinking about what happens when we get home?" I turned to look at her.

"Look at the road, Sarah. It's in lousy condition. Keeping this bucket on the road is hard right now. One bullet to a front tire and we're going somewhere we don't want to go."

I felt my hands tighten on the wheel. We were back to Win's worries. "We're investigating."

"Don't shut me out of this, Sarah. My gut's telling me this is serious. Stay vigilant."

"Hypervigilant?"

"Don't use my weakness against me." Win switched her gaze from the window to me.

I nodded. "I'm sorry. I didn't mean to…"

"You meant to shut me up. It ain't gonna work, sweetheart. I want you to take the threats seriously. I'll stay on your ass until you do."

I grinned. "Promise?"

CHAPTER THIRTEEN

Win

The next morning, we lay in bed. Talking, touching occasionally. Clearing the air.

"I need you to demonstrate you're taking this seriously, Sarah."

"I'll keep you in the loop," she said, moving her hand through my hair. "To be honest, I really don't want you involved. Not after Laura."

"I am involved. With you and with Laura. She was having a rough enough time before this."

"Is this somebody else trying to get back at you?" Sarah's hand was tight on my arm.

"Is that what you've been thinking?"

"Answer me, Win."

"No. I have no enemies left standing."

"Then why Laura? How did they know she was MCIA?"

I traced her jaw with my finger. "It was in the paper. Except for our coming-out interview, I haven't been in the paper. I told Zoe to just say I was a marine who'd served in Afghanistan."

"A marine colonel who's served all over the world." Sarah pulled me to her. "You've been through so much."

"You haven't?"

"We both have. Okay, we'll work the case together."

"But?"

"Just don't put yourself in danger." Sarah stroked my face. "When you stepped out in front of General Lester's truck, my heart stopped. I don't ever want to be scared like that again."

"Ditto to you. You shouldn't have even been on that mission." I felt desire welling. Looked in Sarah's eyes and saw a mirror. "I know I can't protect you twenty-four-seven. That doesn't stop me from wanting to. I know you feel the same way. But if we work together, maybe we won't have to be so scared all the time."

Sarah pulled me down to her. "I love you. It terrifies me to think I could lose you, that I'd have to live the rest of my life without you. You take such risks—"

"The biggest risk in my life is loving you. Now shut up and let me give you pleasure."

We lay still entwined when Sarah's phone rang.

"Ignore it. You've got a whole department to respond. This is your day off."

She tried. But when it rang a second time, she fumbled it off the nightstand. "Yes." She nodded a couple of times. "Okay, okay. Give me half an hour."

I sighed. I gave up on our day together. It better be a fucking emergency of gigantic proportion.

Sarah put the phone back and scowled. "I'll tell you what's going on while I'm getting dressed." She pushed off the covers and rolled out of bed.

* * *

"Officer down" has a different meaning to cops than the military. We don't mourn our fallen troops any less, but we know combat is deadly. Not that cops don't. They do. Going to work means strapping on a weapon. But the expectation is that they'll come home at the end of shift to their families and community. To coaching baseball or basketball. Being a Big Brother or Sister. To cookouts or church-sponsored spaghetti dinners. To bingo at the Grange Hall. Go home to kids, wives, husbands, lovers.

Sarah wasn't sure of the condition of her deputy, but the folks in uniform would surround the wounded man and his family. She'd taken off after a quick shower, gravel spitting from her tires.

After breakfast, I called Nathan. "You hear from Bill?"

"Yeah. It's so cool to hack with government permission. You have time to come over and peek over my shoulder?"

"Yeah." I told him about Sarah's "Officer down" call.

"Anyone you know?"

"No. But she was upset. I am too."

"You think it could be connected to the threatening letters?"

I shrugged then realized Nathan couldn't see. "Could be. Right now, I don't think the department knows what went down."

I drove to Nathan's cabin wondering how I was going to get up to the clearing on the narrow and steep track. As I slowed to make the turn, I saw it had been plowed. Spread with something dark. Whatever it was, I made it to the top with no sweat. I turned off the engine and waited until his lean frame appeared at the door. Today, his long hair was loose.

"What'd you use on the driveway?" I asked as I climbed the stairs to the porch.

"Wood ashes. I've got plenty, it's free and does no environmental harm. Plus, when the sun is out, it helps the snow melt faster."

"Wise man." I stamped the snow off my boots on the porch. Slipped them off as soon as I stepped inside. "So, what've you got?"

"Lots of scary stuff," he said with a smile. "Tea?"

I nodded. Wondered what kind of Miami tonic I'd get today. I remembered the stuff his mother made at change of seasons and Nathan and his sister Mary still made. Tasted awful but seemed to work. At least did no harm.

I padded over to the stacks of electronic equipment that took up one wall. Herbal tea and twenty-first century technology. He'd grown from an inquisitive boy to an amazing man. One who could track as well in the woods as online.

"Where do I find the scary stuff?"

"You're an impatient woman, Win. You should try meditation."

I laughed. "Exactly what Mr. Kim said. That's why he put me in a tai chi class. It's a moving meditation. Speaking of which, I need to be there at two for a special class."

Nathan grinned as he put a mug within my reach. "Mr. Kim is a wise man. Does the tai chi work?"

"Surprisingly well. At least, close as I can tell since I've never been able to do any meditation. You know, the kind that says 'Think about a lotus flower blooming.' I get the image and then I'm off, chasing some other thought because the flower reminded me of another image."

He hit a few keys and four monitors lit up. "These are the main groups in southern Indiana, all with members in McCrumb County. Many of them belong to all four groups. So we've got racists, religious fanatics, militias and sovereigns in one angry stew."

"Shit." I examined each of the four websites. "This is ugly garbage. Who don't they hate?"

"Each other. But they're all connected to national networks and a lot of them are set up through Idaho. I asked Susan to ask around, see if they've heard anything."

"Susan?"

"My ex-wife. She's Coeur d'Alene, lives in Plummer, Idaho. I should hear back tomorrow, but I doubt if it'll be anything specific. Rumors mostly, but maybe it'll give us a lead."

"Nathan, I understand that we need to know about these networks, but is this getting us any closer to finding a shooter here?"

"I thought you liked patterns, Win."

"I do. What I'm seeing is the large picture. What I need to see is how our portion fits into the larger—which I can't do when our part is so sketchy."

"God you're picky." Nathan fastened his long hair and stretched. "I can't show you what I don't have."

"There's got to be a reason why it's so blank."

He turned to me. "Whoever's doing this, they're off the grid."

"Or it's a lone wolf?"

"God, I hope not."

CHAPTER FOURTEEN

Sarah

"As I was leaning over to get my sunglasses, the windshield shattered and I heard the shot," Deputy Ted Perlman said. "Tried to keep it on the road, but I didn't make it. Sorry about the squad car."

"I'm just glad you're here," I said, meaning still alive. He knew what I meant. "So the sun was in your eyes?"

"Yeah. Cloud passed, sun shone through. Bam."

"Then the sun must've been on the windshield. Your shooter couldn't see you lean over and that probably saved your life."

"I will thank the sun every morning, whether I see it or not."

"You didn't have your vest on?"

"No. I don't wear it in the car, well, didn't. I will forever more."

We learn from our mistakes, but cops' mistakes can be deadly. "Do you usually patrol that section of road at that time in the morning?"

He grimaced. "Yeah. Never thought there was reason not to."

"We're going to have to shake up the patrol routes." I made a note. "Anybody gunning for you that I need to know about, Ted?"

He shook his head. "This came out of the blue. My wife loves me, her relatives love me, my neighbors like me. I haven't put anybody away for a major crime and I haven't made any big drug busts."

I put my notebook away. "Ted, take my advice—do what the doctors tell you to do. It's really tempting to push beyond what they allow. Don't."

He nodded. "Guess you learned that lesson the hard way."

I smiled. Since Win and I were supposed to go on our first date the night I was shot in a drug bust gone bad, most of the pushing I'd done was to be healed enough to make love with Win. "Just remember, I've warned you that you'll be impatient with the restrictions. Don't allow the impatience to take over."

I left his hospital room, repeated my advice to his wife. "Don't nag, but stay on his butt when he gets home. He'll push the limits. If you notice a change in his demeanor, please call me."

"PTSD?"

"Just a possibility. We've got a shrink we use for departmental issues. I've seen her several times—there's no stigma in this department about it."

I drove back to the station thinking about Em. I thought a lot of her turmoil came from not identifying Laura's condition soon enough. I also thought about the wives who kept their fear at bay every day their husbands went to work. Like Win.

I walked into the station and was met by Caleb. "We dug a slug out of Ted's front seat, but it hit the frame."

"Mangled?" I asked.

"Yeah. But it looks like a thirty-aught-six."

"Well hell. The same as the Brownes'." I walked into my office. "Have you talked with John? He's been working on hate groups because the threats we've gotten seem to echo their craziness."

"Bunch of nut cases. Guess I've been aware of them, but not what they're up to. Is there any chance the shooter could've thought you were driving?"

My heart did a triple-gainer. "I don't see how. That's Ted's usual patrol route and he makes the round in the same order every day. We need to alter the patrol routes, keep changing them up. I need to speak with Head of Patrol. Is Mark Goodrich here?"

"Yeah. Conference room?"

I nodded and picked up my phone to call Win.

* * *

It was three o'clock before we got all the patrol routes shuffled. As Caleb and I walked to my office, he paused. "Isn't this your day off?"

"Supposedly."

"You want to try again tomorrow? Then you could take two days in a row."

"With all this up in the air—"

"Take some advice from an old married man?" He lifted an eyebrow and brushed his mustache. "When we work all the time, our spouses get restless. They can take a gander around, see someone who could better fulfill their need for companionship."

"You're speaking from experience? Not that it's any business of mine."

"From experience. I almost lost Mary Beth a couple of years ago." He walked me to the door. "I've been thinking. I think we should both reduce our schedule to five days. Mark and John can take up the slack. Good training if anything happens."

"To us?"

He nodded. "You've got kids coming. I've already got them. Life has got to be more than a job, Sarah."

"I'll think about it, Caleb. Really give it serious thought. I think you should go ahead—"

"I won't if you won't. So do it for Mary Beth."

He walked across the bullpen to his office. I sat at my desk and rubbed my temples. Why was it, when the job came up against everything else, the job won? In my heart, I knew Caleb was right. It was bad enough Win worried about me every time I went to work, but to spend more time here… Would she get tired of waiting for me to come home?

"She's so damn beautiful." I shook my head. Talking to myself—a sign of early senility? Or job-related stress?

I didn't know what else I could do today. Information on the slug from Ted's shooting wouldn't be in and that was our one solid clue. We'd found where the shooter had made his nest, but no tracks, nothing we could use to identify him. Our ghost had shot twice, hit both targets and then disappeared.

CHAPTER FIFTEEN

Win

I got to my tae kwon do class early and prepped my students what to do. "You can begin to move, then abort—but I will intervene if I see any two of you active at the same time. Understood?"

They groaned, but all said yes.

"Take it easy on her. No hard kicks. This is more like flag football."

When Emily appeared, I explained the exercise. "The person in the center is 'it.' The rest of these people will form a circle around the person. They'll be able to attempt a move anytime, but only one at a time."

"This is the way you're going to help me?"

"Damn straight. Join the circle for now. I'll be 'it'."

I stood in the middle of the circle. Relaxed. "Begin."

One by one, they tried to attack. Found themselves on the mat. I didn't need to watch their movements, just their eyes. First lesson. After fifteen minutes, I signaled an end. Stepped into the circle with the others. Nodded to Emily. I thought she was going to run, but after a long pause, she stepped to the center.

I watched her eyes. Unfocused. She failed to defend herself time after time. Then I saw the spark of anger in her. People went flying. Emily was good when she was in the groove. After all of the students had a turn, I stepped forward. Emily's eyes widened. She stepped toward me, her jaw clenched, wrath in her eyes. I didn't move. I saw her move coming. Deflected. Took her down.

I asked everyone to sit down. Looked around the circle. "What lessons have you learned from this exercise?"

"Never attack a teacher!" said one young guy. The group laughed.

A couple of them pointed to form and where they'd gone wrong.

"You're missing the central point. At the very end, did I attack Emily?"

I saw lights going on around the circle.

"We use the force of someone's attack to disarm, to deflect," I said, looking at each in turn. "Watch their eyes, not their movements. You will see the moment of attack before they move. Your opponent can also see the moment in your eyes. I did not attack anytime during this exercise. I only watched eyes. Never be the aggressor. Wait for your opponent's eyes to signal.

"Questions?"

There were a rash of them, all beginning with "but." I answered, then bowed deeply to the class. Dismissed them to the showers. Helped Emily up.

"Once you felt the fire, you did good, Emily. How did it feel?"

"Isn't that my question?"

"Only when you're operating on all cylinders. Can I take you to dinner?"

She stared at me. "Fuck it, I've created a monster."

* * *

I called Sarah after I'd showered and dressed. "Are you still in town?"

"Just getting ready to leave," she said.

I told her I was taking Emily to dinner. "You want to join us?"

There was a long pause. "You think that's a good idea?"

"Probably not, but I thought I'd offer. See you at home?"

"Eat fast, Win."

I appreciated her tact. Her understanding that Emily and I shared a different relationship than she had with Emily. Personal versus departmental. And her willingness to bow out even though I knew she was worried about Emily too.

Emily was dressed when I stepped back into the locker room. "Ready?" I asked.

"No, but does that matter?" she responded.

"You want to eat sprouts?"

She smiled. "Your choice since you've shanghaied me."

We walked to Mama Mia's, an Italian place that had great salads and marvelous pasta dishes. We found a back booth, ordered.

"I'm not going to grill you," I said. "I saw the moment you got angry. I saw the anger directed at me when you faced me—"

"I wasn't mad at you—"

"Of course you were. Are. For dragging you into two situations where your life was threatened. First with Shamsi, now with Laura. You have every right to be pissed at me. I just hope you can work through the anger so we can return to a therapeutic relationship. Who the hell can I talk to if I can't talk to you?"

"You're a fucking manipulator."

"I learned from the best." I opened the cloth napkin, put it on my lap. Took a deep breath. "I think what you're really mad at is yourself. For not seeing how close to the edge Laura was. That's why you shipped her off to Indianapolis. *Your* failure. One you can't deal with."

Emily pushed back tears. "You're full of shit."

I shrugged. "What you don't realize is that Laura's a trained agent, used to hiding what she feels. I think when I broke down in Tucson, it scared her. So much so, she felt she couldn't give in to the terror she'd experienced. The way she avoided was to fantasize about Sarah."

"Why didn't I see it?" Emily asked. "I really misdiagnosed. I wish to God I'd believed in your instincts." She shook her head. "I should've."

"First, you didn't get an opportunity to see the way she looked at Sarah. I did. Second, I might've been in some paranoid funk about her." I examined her face. She was fighting an internal struggle. "When the explosion in Tucson happened, I had a blinding headache and couldn't open my eyes without stabbing pain. Couldn't stand up straight. Laura saw the famed Colonel Kirkland immobilized."

"Famed?" She shook her head. "You've become quite a diagnostician."

"Thanks to you. That's not meant to be snarky." I took another deep breath. "What Laura saw has informed her actions ever since. I was in combat, she was a paper-pusher. If a combat veteran could fall apart like that, how the hell would she react if she was in a dangerous situation? That worst-case scenario happened. She retreated totally to fantasy because she couldn't handle the reality. Am I making sense?"

She nodded. "Question is, why didn't I see that in her?"

"Because her hold on the fantasy depended on you not seeing it. I'm sure you saw some strange stuff in her aura or whatever the hell you see when you get all squinty. Can you see erotic emotions?"

"Yeah. I did see it. I tried to get her to talk about it, but she deflected every time. I thought it might be a response to the damage done to her breasts."

"Did you see them?"

Emily shook her head.

"Her breasts are not only disfigured, but she has no feeling in what's left of her nipples or surrounding tissues. What I'm trying to tell you is, one, she's very good at hiding feelings. Two, she couldn't allow herself to fall into the abyss. Like I did."

"But you climbed out."

"She didn't know how, not in her skill set. Nor was she able to allow herself to be guided out. I think I trusted you from the first time I came to see you. But we had the time to let the trust grow."

The dinner came then. I let go of serious talk and told her about the kids, their progress. Anything I could think of. Except the threats against Sarah and how scared I was.

As we walked back to the dojang, she turned to me. "Thanks, Win. You've given me a lot to think about."

"*Think?*"

She gave me a weak smile. "Incorrigible."

CHAPTER SIXTEEN

Sarah

Des, curled up at my side, lifted her head and woofed as I heard Win's truck coming up the drive. Des bounded off the couch and stood at attention at the door. Win opened it wide enough to let Des out, saying, "Be right back."

I put the manuscript on the table and stretched. Shortly, Win and Des came in. I felt two cold hands on my neck, then cold lips on the back of my neck. I shivered. "Getting colder out?"

"Yeah. Can you warm me up?"

Win moved around the couch and sat beside me.

"Sit on your hands for a bit, okay?"

Win laughed and put an arm around me. "Metaphorically? You're not in the mood? Have a headache?"

I pulled her to me in a scorching kiss. "Take that, you little shit."

"Little 'shit.' My, my." She waggled her eyebrows.

"You're a bad influence."

"Now that my lips are warm, I'll work on my hands." She tucked one between my side and the couch and grinned.

"She's still talking to you?"

Win nodded, then glanced at the table and saw the stack of pages. "What's that?"

"I was going to ask you that. Did you write a novel?"

She leaned forward and looked at the cover page. "I'd forgotten all about it." She leaned back. "Before we were together, I found out General Lester had my lines tapped. So I started writing that to keep the analysts in wet dreams."

"You wrote it for men?"

"I couldn't just stop using the computer or they would've know I was on to them. This was all I came up with."

"It's pretty raw, Win." She pulled back, examined my face. "I mean...did you ever do any of that stuff?"

"No. Did I witness things like that? Yes. I was looking for sex." I touched her lips. "Baggage. It's in the past. I didn't mean to snoop, I was just rearranging stuff and found it. I didn't mean to trespass."

She kissed my fingers. "Read the whole thing, Sarah. I don't care. I'm not that person and I never was."

"I didn't read you as the protagonist because that woman had no heart and was just after thrills. Did you know women like that?"

"Sure. Lot of women out there like that." She touched my temple. "I couldn't see any alternative while I was on active duty. But when I met Azar, everything changed. I couldn't go back to that life for anything. I think it was about having roots with someone."

I burrowed into her chest, my arms around her. My roots were Hoosier, one hundred percent. I hadn't been anywhere much except McCrumb County, while Win had been all over the world and met all kinds of people in all kinds of cultures. All kinds of women in all kinds of sexually explicit situations. How could I compete?

"What?" she asked.

I looked up at her. "I'm afraid you'll get bored with me."

"You've got to be kidding. Every day with you is new. Please don't tell me you want to build a dungeon in our basement."

I blushed. "I wouldn't know what to do in one, Win."

* * *

Win had gotten me up at dawn because I neglected to tell her I was taking the day off in lieu of yesterday. Once awake, how could I roll over and go back to sleep?

At breakfast, I told her about Caleb's suggestion to work five days a week instead of six.

"Yes!" she said, then accompanied it with her version of a happy dance. "You don't know how much I'd love to have you home one more day. When the kids get here, well, you know."

I poured another cup. "It's going to be hard, Win. I worry when I'm not there that something will happen to my deputies."

"I'll distract you."

"You already do." I took a sip. "I'll give it a try, but no promises."

"With that attitude, you'll last the week." She took the dishes to the sink. "How's the investigation coming?"

"The bullet that got Ted is so mangled, we can't even tell what caliber it is for sure, but it's in the range of a thirty-aught-six."

"I called Bill and asked him to get clearance for Nathan," she said quickly. "It's come through and now he's officially on our team."

"You couldn't tell me before you did it?"

"You said we could work this together so I wouldn't be scared shitless every time you walk out the door. I was working my end."

"Damn Win." I looked out the window where angel snow floated, waiting for an air current to lift it upward again. That's what Mom used to call it, angel snow, and said it was a blessing. I sure as hell needed a special blessing to catch our shooter. I looked at Win. "Sorry, you're right. It's just going to take me a while to work with a co-sheriff."

"I'm not a co-sheriff, Sarah. I'm your backup with access to data you don't have." She began washing the dishes.

I took my mug to the sink, let it float down into the suds. I wrapped my arms around Win and leaned my head on her shoulder. "I'm not used to sharing the responsibility."

She turned around, wiped her hands and then held my face in them. "I know. You've created this wonderful unit of officers. Then you can't trust them to do their jobs without looking over their shoulders. Take a leap of faith, Sarah. Trust the people you've trained to do their jobs."

"I didn't train you."

"That's not the point," Win said. "I'm not a cowboy and I don't go off half-cocked. You've got to trust my judgment, because I'm not going to ask your permission every time I take a step."

"Whew." I leaned against her.

"These are the things we have to talk about if we want to share the burden. Either you trust me to move or you want me to get permission first."

"It's not that black and white."

She rubbed my back. "In my world, it is. Besides, I told you at the first opportunity."

I pulled back. "If you didn't want to talk about it over the phone, you could've told me when you got home."

"First we got Emily's dinner invitation. Your deputy was shot. I had good intentions."

"Start making a 'to do' list, okay? Things like 'Tell Sarah I've called in the Feds.'"

"Ah," Win said. "That's the burr under your blanket. Going out of the county for help. Something your dad never did."

"No, that's not true."

"Think about it, please. I don't want to argue with you. I don't want to feel like I'm on a tightrope." She kissed me lightly. "Besides, Bill isn't the Feds. He's a friend to both of us."

CHAPTER SEVENTEEN

Win

What I didn't say to Sarah was that I thought the danger to her was real. I felt it in my bones. But, with two days together ahead of us, I'd had enough of cop shop talk.

"So, you want to do anything special with this time? There's a gay bed-and-breakfast down in West Baden. Get away for a while?"

"You've been there before?"

I looked her in the eyes. "Yes."

"With a woman?"

I raised an eyebrow.

"I don't think I want to go."

"It was before we got together."

"I still don't think so."

I threw up my hands. "I give up, Sarah. You're being pissy." I went to my desk. Folded up a list I'd made to furnish the girls' room. Got my truck keys.

"Where are you going?" Sarah asked, her voice tinged with anger.

"Shopping."

"For what? I mean—"

"Furniture for the kids' room."

"Isn't that something we should do together?" She stood at the island in the kitchen, uncertainty in her eyes. "Or are you going to cut me out of that too?"

"Fuck you." I walked to the peg that held my parka.

"Win please—"

"You have real control issues about being sheriff. I understand. But sometimes I get fed up. I need to walk away because I'm getting really ticked off." I put my parka on. "If you want to do something to help, you can begin to take apart the guest room."

Des came up to me, whined and leaned against my legs. Stuck her muzzle in my hand. "Can't take you with me. You'd be stuck in the truck. Maybe Sarah will take care of you."

I gave Des a kiss on the top of her head and left the house without a backward look.

* * *

I picked up the tail as soon as I turned from Clayton Corners Road onto SR 36. I watched for a while, made a slight detour. Yep. Someone was tailing me. I dialed Sarah. "May I have your permission to call Caleb? I've got a tail."

"Someone's following you? Dammit, Win. I'll call him and—"

"No. I want you to stay inside and set the alarm system. Do you remember how?"

"Yeah, but—"

"Sarah, please just do it. I'm calling Caleb now." I ended the call, punched in his number. "Habstadt. What's up, Win?"

"I've picked up a tail. I'm heading to the kids' store in the Old Greenglen section. Can you pick us up? Then tail the tail? It's an older Dodge SUV. Dark green."

"Where are you now?"

"On SR Thirty-six, heading into town."

"Got you covered. I'll be in a black Bronco. You going to make more stops?"

"I was, but I'll pick up my order, head home. Okay? I'm worried they'll target Sarah now. She's home alone."

"Roger that. You get in any trouble, call. I'll have patrol on watch around your house."

"Don't make it obvious, Caleb. We don't want to spook them."

I saw him pick us up about a mile out of town. I'd ordered twin beds, so I parked in front where I could load them and be clearly visible. I'd planned to look at desks. But I want to do it with Sarah, something we do together.

I hadn't realized how much Sarah's dedication to work bothered me. Okay, not just her control over every detail, but how much overtime that took. Time when we weren't together. We had a lot of talking to do.

CHAPTER EIGHTEEN

Sarah

After Win's call I sat down on the couch and cried. This wasn't how I'd planned to spend my time off—Win alienated and telling me to butt out of sheriff's business. I noticed Des curled up in front of the fire and watching me with her head on her paws. Evidently, she was siding with Win.

I took a deep breath, wiped off my tears and set the security system. The cameras showed nothing but skeletal black trees against the snow. I knew why Win was jumpy, but honest to God, she didn't have to take my head off. I walked into the spare room and stripped the bed. I wondered what Win wanted to do with it and everything else in the room. Was she planning to paint? Get curtains? We hadn't talked about it, but I realized what an extraordinary responsibility we were taking on. Could I rise to the occasion and be a mom? A good one?

I lugged the mattress into the hall, then went back in to take the bed apart, piling those pieces next to the mattress. I looked at the bureau, side chair and floor lamp. Leave them? I opened the closet door and saw Win's uniforms, a couple of office-type and one full dress. The shelf above held a variety of caps and one very battered helmet. Something was in a long garment bag. I unzipped it and saw red silk, the dress she'd described to me as being low cut. It looked as if the v ended at her belly button. I zipped it up again, smelled Win's scent on the uniforms and sat in the chair.

Tears came unbidden. Why the hell couldn't Win just let me be sheriff? It was my job! She'd guilt-tripped me over doing my job which I realized I had been putting in a lot of overtime. How often did a storm like that hit? Topped with a double homicide and attempted murder of an officer?

I heard the alarm system beep, indicating someone was coming up the drive. I sprinted into the living room and grabbed my Glock. I looked at the monitor, then heard the old bucket of bolts my dad drove. I held my breath until he made it to the top of the hill. I turned off the system and opened the front door. "Did Win call you to babysit?"

He looked up at me—no, glared. "Caleb called me. Asked me to provide backup for the sheriff. You gonna let me in, Sarah Anne?"

I stood back and let him get gently swarmed by Des. It was a mutual love affair, one that brought back the images of Dad with a series of hounds he'd had over the years. How he'd always been there for me.

"I'm sorry, Dad. Win and I had a fight and…"

"Prob'ly not the first, sure won't be the last," he said, standing. "Win loves you, Sarah Anne. That's clear to see every time she looks at you. When Lizbeth got on me for workin' too much, I guess we had a fight or two betwixt us. First thing you gotta do is listen."

"She said I had 'control issues' at work."

"Ain't that the truth."

"What? Not you too."

"Caleb's got your back. If you don't know that by now, I reckon you don't have the brains I always credited you with. Let him do his job." He gave me a bear hug and didn't let go. "You got a life now. Family. Ride your way through the county with loose reins. You'll find your way just fine."

I felt tears forming again.

"Now," he said, holding me at arms' length. "Why's half the spare room out in the hallway?"

* * *

When Win got home, Dad asked her what she wanted to do with the double bed.

"Give it to Goodwill, I guess," she said. "Or if you know a family that could use it…"

He loaded it into his truck and took off with a warning look at me over his shoulder.

I pointed to the cartons that rested in the hall. "So, how do you want to set these up?"

"I don't know," Win said, her eyes searching mine. "I've been waiting for you to help me plan."

I walked to her, wrapped my arms around her and let my head rest on her shoulder. She didn't pull me toward her and I felt her shoulders tighten. "I'm sorry, Win."

She stepped away. "Sorry isn't going to cut it. We need to talk because I'm beginning to feel resentment. I don't like the feeling."

"Resentment about how much time I spend on the job?"

"Yeah," she said. "How much time you're thinking about the job even when you're home. Silently. You just drift off."

"Can we set the beds up? Eat lunch? Then sit down and talk?"

I felt her stiffen. "I don't care. Whatever." She walked down the hall.

I followed. "I didn't know if you wanted to keep the dresser in here or move it."

"They can't reach the top two drawers. It's empty except for a couple of blankets. You want to use it for your stuff?"

My stuff? "Yeah, sure. Let's move it."

We picked it up and Win duck-walked backwards until we were through the doorway to our bedroom. "Where do you want it?" I asked.

Win nodded at the wall by the closet. It wasn't until she let it go that I realized how much of the load she'd been carrying. She turned and walked back into the other bedroom. I sat on the bed, bewildered. Had I missed the clues Win had given me about work? I thought back. Yeah, I had. She complained with a light hand and I'd just dismissed it as sarcasm. I watched her pass the door with the chair.

Damn, Emily had created a monster. I didn't think Win would be as clear about her feelings if she hadn't worked with her. Here I was, stumbling along, trying to understand Win and trying to understand me. I was doing better with Win than I was grasping my own actions and motivations.

When she walked back down the hall, I got up and prepared to put the beds together. Had she bought linens? I stood at the doorway. Win was down on her hands and knees, waxing the plank floors.

I grabbed the floor lamp and set it outside. Then went back to empty the closet.

"I can't give the uniforms to Goodwill. Go ahead and burn them," Win said, without turning around.

I took the bunch and moved them into our closet. I went back for the caps and helmet. I'd have to find a place for those, so I dumped them in the living room. As I went through the dresser, I discovered a box in with the blankets. I opened it and saw Win's medals and framed commendations. Quite a stack of glory to be hidden in a bottom drawer. In so many ways, Win was a mystery to me.

CHAPTER NINETEEN

Win

I trusted Caleb had taken care of the tail. Gotten a plate and had the guy under surveillance. I wouldn't interfere, but I felt a bit uneasy. Wondered what the hell the tail was after.

Sarah had lunch waiting for me when I'd finished the floor. She seemed subdued. Thinking about what I'd said? I hoped so. If she couldn't leave her work at the office, then she needed to share the thoughts with me. Otherwise, what did I have left? Two small girls who needed to see their new moms interact with love. Argue but come to terms. Forgive.

"I probably came down on you too hard," I said, keeping my gaze on my soup bowl. "I was frustrated because I'd tried to say something a few times, but I felt like you ignored me."

"You're right, I ignored what you said because I thought I was right. I've realized I was just getting into the job deeper and deeper, trying to prove I was a good sheriff."

I raised my head, saw the tears coursing down Sarah's face. "Because you're gay?"

She nodded. "I wanted to prove to the people who voted for me that I deserved their vote."

"Why didn't you tell me that?"

"Because I didn't realize it." She reached across the table for my hand. "I never do. I just put my head down and plow ahead. I'm sorry. I'm trying to be more reflective about what I feel, but it doesn't come easy."

I entwined our fingers. "When did that happen, Sarah? Growing up, you never hesitated to say what you were thinking."

"No idea, but I promise I'll try and figure that out. I will, and if I'm not working hard enough on it, I'll be open to correction. I trust you, Win, with my life, with my heart and with my love. If I screw this up…I just couldn't take it." Sarah raised our hands, kissed mine. "Sometimes I feel so overwhelmed I just shut down. Maybe drift off, I don't know. But at the bottom of all this, I want to serve the people. I want to bring law and order that's impartial and fair. It's not easy."

"I know. I do know that. Let me help you with my expertise. Not as some crazy co-sheriff, but as a partner who can help. Occasionally."

She nodded. "On a limited basis. Is that okay?"

"For now. I told you, Sarah, I'm not a cowboy."

"Cowgirl?"

"Shit."

"Did you buy linens for the beds?" she asked.

"No. I was waiting for input. How about we put the beds up? Then we can go shopping. But first, I've got to bring in the mattresses."

"*We* have to bring in the mattresses," she said.

* * *

We didn't make love that night. Too tired from the shopping, or maybe the emotional turmoil. I hated fighting with Sarah, hated seeing pain in her eyes. Pain I caused. I'd dreamed last night of Sarah and me when we were kids. Free to say anything.

I ached to touch Sarah, to kiss her body. Just to hold her in my arms. But I couldn't. I pushed the covers back and got out of bed. Put on socks and my new robe, a Christmas gift from Sarah. As I padded out to the kitchen, I noticed the pile of my caps on the couch. I picked up the helmet. Battered as it was, it was a wonder I hadn't gotten any brain damage. Why had I kept it? To remind me of the danger of combat. To be careful.

Now it was combat of a different kind. To stay open to the woman I loved, not become defensive, not wound her. To be careful.

I let Des out and started the coffee. Looked at the helmet I'd laid on the counter. So many battles. So much blood. Des barked to get in about the time the coffee maker beeped. I let her in, poured two mugs full and walked back to our bedroom. I called Sarah's name softly.

Her eyes fluttered open and she squinted at the clock. "Couldn't we sleep in once in a while?"

"Sit up and we'll have coffee in bed."

She pushed up into a sitting position. "Oh, I'm sore, too much lifting yesterday."

I handed her the mug, settled on my side of the bed. "So what do you want to do today?"

"Go back to sleep."

"All day?"

"We could stay in bed all day. Uh, talk."

I turned to face her. "I dreamed about you last night. When we were kids."

Her eyes widened. "I dreamed about you. And Hugh. He said, 'That was a rookie mistake.' Only it wasn't." She sipped her coffee. "It was a dream, Win. Let me see if I can remember."

She closed her eyes, laid her head back. She had a beautiful neck. But if I did what I wanted to do, we'd never talk.

"That's what it was about," she said, opening her eyes. "There were crossed wires, dispatch gave me the wrong address and I ended up inadvertently making a drug bust, kind of out of the blue. When I told Hugh, he was snotty about it."

"Told you it was a rookie mistake?"

"Looking back on it now, I realize I scared him. I thought I was serving a warrant on check forgery. I knocked on the door, a guy opened it. They were cutting cocaine in the living room."

"Fuck it, I understand his scare."

"But that's when I stopped telling him stuff like that. When he died and I moved back home, Dad was sheriff. I couldn't share those kind of mistakes with him. Mom got sick and we didn't talk about work at all."

"You shut down."

She nodded. "I go to Dad now when I want advice or can't figure something out. But hell, it's taken a long time for me to get there. That first year after I was elected, I felt like Dad was looking over my shoulder, ready to criticize."

"To tell you you'd made a rookie mistake."

"Yeah. Now that I hear you say it, it sounds so silly."

I put my arm around her. "That's why you need to think about this stuff. To banish the hobgoblins, to dismiss the irrational fears."

"Irrational, huh?"

"Yeah, most of the time." I rubbed her shoulder. "Look, I've spent a lifetime not talking. Not about my missions, not about being lesbian. Silence was a valued habit. So was not examining what I was feeling. Now I've changed. I feel free for the first time in years. I'd like to see you feel the same."

"I'll try, I promise."

"Okay." It was the best I was going to get now. "How about you fill me in on those letters? Then we can go over to Nathan's, see what he's found."

"First," she said, putting her coffee on the nightstand. "How about we make up?"

CHAPTER TWENTY

Sarah

We walked into Nathan's in the early afternoon and I was floored to see Dad bent over a keyboard. "What are you doing here?"

He looked up. "Hired assistant to the Chief Hacker. Leastways with this job, I get paid."

I looked at Nathan who didn't appear the least chagrined. "We've covered a lot of territory trying to fill in the local picture." He punched a couple of keys and two monitors came to life. "This guy's been in steady contact with the group in Idaho. Also fancies himself a hacker."

"You hacked him?" I asked.

"Sometimes amateur hackers are the easiest to hack because they're so arrogant."

"Has he hacked either of us?"

"With the fire walls I've installed on Win's service and the sheriff's department, I don't think he stands a chance. But I'll keep checking."

"You have a picture of him?"

Nathan brought up an Indiana driver's license featuring a forgettable face. "I didn't really hack this, Sarah. I just combined your databases into mine."

That didn't make me feel any easier.

"Meet Joshua Leatherby, who's lived in the county the last six months. He moved here from Washington County. No arrests, no warrants."

"I've seen him twice, once at Rhomer's and once yesterday when I was getting the beds," Win said. "What does he drive?"

"A 2001 Dodge Durango, forest green."

"What?" I asked.

"He tailed us about halfway home from Rhomer's last week," Win said. "Yesterday, he followed me into town. We need to check with Caleb."

"You think he's triangulating?" Nathan asked. "Or planning something?"

"Both," Win said. "I think the first was a chance meeting. He was shopping for his own shit. But if he wants an exact location, why not just follow Sarah home from the sheriff's office?"

"Maybe he can't," Nathan said. "Maybe he works the same hours and can't get into Greenglen when Sarah's leaving."

"He works six days a week? Maybe he's afraid of Sarah picking up on him."

"I'm here, in the room," I said. Win glanced at me with a raised eyebrow. "I've been keeping an eye out for tails. Also for long, shiny reflections in the hills, as well as unusual people hanging around outside the department. Nobody's tailed me from work."

"I expect he figures you're on alert," Win said. "But if the opportunity presented itself, he must've thought it was too good a gift to ignore."

Nathan nodded. "I'm doing a deep search, but it may take a couple of more days."

"I can't pull him in for anything," I said, feeling weary.

"Mebbe Win an' me can do a bit of tailin', pick him up in the mornin', change off durin' the day."

"I go back to work tomorrow in Bloomington, Micah," Win said. "I won't be home until Friday night."

"Dang, I forgot. Mebbe I can talk to my buddies. Mebbe even work a three-man team."

"I have to be here some of the day, but count me in," Nathan said.

I began to tear up, then glanced at Win. Her face was set hard in anger. "I'll be okay, Win."

"You realize some of these militias are armed like the Taliban or Al Qaeda?" she asked, her voice hard. "That one person could set up on Foley's Knob and send an RPG into our home?"

* * *

Win was quiet on the ride home and I sure didn't know what to say. The image of our home blown to smithereens could invoke nightmares for both of us. I kept my eyes open, both on the rearview mirror and on the hills. I could tell Win was doing the same.

"They've used a rifle so far," I said.

Win nodded. "If they can't get to you easy, they'll go the easy route with a big boom."

"I've been driving into work every day. Once a shot's taken, there's not a lot of evasive maneuvers I can make." I turned onto Clayton Corners Road with no one behind me and no glint of a rifle barrel. It wasn't until I parked that I started to breathe again.

"Maybe Nathan can put a trip wire and camera on the path up to Foley's Knob," Win said as we hurried inside. She let us in and Des out, then leaned against the closed door. "I don't want to live like this. Always on alert."

I slipped into her arms. "I don't want to either."

"I'm terrified to go into Bloomington," Win said. "Maybe I can come home every night instead of staying in the apartment."

"We've got to live as normally as we can or we'll go crazy. At least I will. Maybe you're used to this kind of pressure. Are you?"

Win pulled me into her arms. "I have been. On foreign soil, not so much here." She kissed my eyelids. "I wanted to leave all this crap behind me. Live a normal life. Hard to do, sometimes."

"Your PTSD? You feel like it's kicking in?"

"Not yet, but I'll keep checking in with myself." She rested her forehead on mine. "Emily always asks the questions that go to the heart of my demons."

"I want to help, but I don't know what to ask or where even to begin. I can't help you and I feel so damn useless."

"You don't have to ask questions, just be here with me." She stepped back. "Nathan's going to contact Bill, find out who's got the heavy hardware for sale. He'll check Leatherby's contacts. I'm still worried about a sniper. I'd rest easier if I knew nothing heavy was coming our way."

I pulled her back into my arms and we embraced until Des barked to get in. I made quick work of heating up soup and making sandwiches while Win lit the fire. After dinner, we sat on the couch, afraid to talk about the situation, afraid not to.

"Maybe we should move to Vermont," I said. "Raise dairy cattle."

Win laughed. "You'd get your exercise."

"You think I'm getting fat? Do you?"

She felt around my middle, then lifted up my sweater to look and ran her hands around me. She raised an eyebrow.

"No! I have not gained more than five pounds since we've been together."

"Five?"

I swatted her. "You better watch it, or we aren't going to do much dancing."

"Which I would miss terribly."

"Maybe I can meet you at Ruby's Friday night, stay the night at the apartment."

"That might work—they wouldn't expect it. Besides, I love dancing with you there."

CHAPTER TWENTY-ONE

Win

Sarah handed me her civilian parka and a small duffel bag before she left for work. "Do I still have a clean uniform there?"

"I'll make sure you do," I said, examining her face. Tense, but not panicked.

She slipped her arms around me, nestled her head on my shoulder. "I want to go with you, be a faculty wife."

"That would be…interesting. You'd have to bone up on feminist philosophy." I stepped back. "Don't let this all get to you. We'll get this guy. In the meantime, look for a beat-up old Ford truck following you around."

"Dad?"

"Yes, would be my guess. Please realize this isn't a plot to diminish your authority." I dropped the bag, put the parka on top of it. Kissed her with a memory of last night.

"Whew," she said. "You always leave me weak-kneed."

We embraced and I savored the scent of her. "I'll see you Friday night. Stay vigilant. Concentrate on your job, Sarah."

In my mind's eye, I saw Des and me standing on the front porch in the cold, watching Sarah leave for work. I sighed. I saw my breath freeze and float away. How easily each of us can lose breath without the chance to watch it float to infinity.

I drove into Bloomington without incident, though it drained me to maintain the line between vigilance and hypervigilance. My phone rang as I was going up to the apartment. Micah. My heart did a flip. "Is Sarah okay?"

"She's fine, Win. Got to work just fine. No sign of a tail or anything untoward on the way. How'd you know I followed her?"

"I just knew it. Are you going to stay with her tonight?"

"Thought 'bout it, but reckoned she'd get her back up, say a 'no' flatter than a sheet of paper."

I grinned. "What if I call, ask her to request your presence until I get home? You know, so I don't have to worry."

"Ain't nothin' like a good guilt trip to get Sarah to do somethin' she don't want to do. Hope you get to concentrate on your teachin', Win. I'll stay in touch."

Micah was a sweetheart. I brought everything inside and hung her clean uniform in the tiny closet. I got my notes out for class. But before I started a quick review, I called Nathan.

"Anything new?" I asked.

"Morning Win. Sarah safe at work?"

"Yeah. Just heard from Micah. Are you working his detail?"

"You better believe it." His chair creaked. "I talked to Susan last night. The reservation is upset about a group of militia up to the north. So are some of the towns around where they train. I guess uneasy is a good name for the feeling. She said she'd talk to the sheriff, see if she can get any definite information."

"Uneasy people are good, means they're keeping a sharp eye out. What about the local picture? Anything on Leatherby?"

"I'll let you know if I find anything, soon as I do."

"Sorry, don't mean to push. I just hear a clock ticking."

"So do I. This letter writer isn't going to be satisfied with just making threats for much longer, or at least I get that feeling."

"It's a power-trip for him, Nathan. Don't be surprised if he keeps playing cat and mouse for a while longer. It's the people behind him I'm worried about."

* * *

I kept in contact with everyone over the next two days. Sarah in long talks at bedtime. Nathan and Micah via emailed updates. Bill puzzled me. He wasn't divulging much, which made me think McCrumb County was a small cog in a much larger investigation. At least that was my gut reaction. What? A militia uprising? Revolution? Fuck them all.

My students were glad to be back at work. Some had shown surprising enterprise by using the syllabus to work on what we were supposed to cover last week. I was glad of the distraction too. At least when I was in the classroom, I could only concentrate on the intricacies of the Tajik language.

We finished a little early Friday and on my way back to the apartment, I called Micah. It went to voice mail. Ditto Nathan. Ditto Sarah. My hand began to shake. The only other person I could think of was the institution named Dory, the sheriff department's primo dispatcher. I was relieved when she answered.

"Hi, Win."

I was expecting the standard spiel. Of course Dory had caller ID. "I've been trying to get hold of Micah and Nathan and Sarah. It all went to voice mail. You have any idea where they are?"

"In Sarah's office meeting with Caleb and John."

I took a deep breath. "I was worried. When they get out would you have Micah or Nathan call me?"

"Sure, hon. How're you doin'?"

"Hanging in."

"Sounds more like hangin' on. You take care an' I'll nab Micah the second he comes out."

"Thanks, Dory."

I continued my walk across the campus. Maintenance was still working on the sidewalks, Streets and Sanitation on the roads. I slung the courier bag across my chest, tucked the phone into my pocket and began the search for my gloves. I wondered if we'd ever see the sun again. Constant lowering gray skies were sapping everybody's energy, particularly mine.

I slipped and slid my way to my block. Then the tingling began. I looked around as unobtrusively as possible. Nothing. As I approached the doorway to my building, the tingle lifted the hairs on the back of my neck.

I was reaching for my keys when I heard a shot and the bricks beside my head exploded. I dove for the front entrance. Lay sprawled until I snaked my way to a safe corner. Waited. Remembered to breathe. Put my hand over my nose so I wouldn't send a plume into the still air. I shoved myself to a standing position. No other shots. This would be a waiting game. How long could a man aiming a rifle stand unnoticed in a public space?

I caught movement inside the hall. Double-teamed? I let a long breath out when the figure emerged from the shadows and I recognized my landlady, Mrs. Barrett.

"Get back!" I yelled. "Shots fired!"

She kept coming and opened the door. "He's gone. Left right after he fired. Figured you'd stay put until the cows came home if I didn't give the all clear."

I moved around the open door quickly and sheltered in the corner of the lobby. "Are you sure?" Dumb question. Mrs. B. was a former state trooper.

She pursed her lips, looked at me over her glasses. "Come on in. Let me clean off your coat and tend to your face."

I lifted my hand up. It came away bloody. I felt the sting on my cheek and temple. I hoped from flying bits of brick. I followed her into her apartment, a light, airy space sparsely filled with 1960s Scandinavian furniture.

"Give me your coat," she said.

I slipped off my bag and wiggled out of my parka. I followed her into her kitchen where she put it on the drainboard.

"First things first," she said as she reached into her pantry. "Sit."

I did, glad my shaking legs could rest.

She opened a first aid box and brought out some gauze. She wet it under the faucet and wiped my cheek softly.

"Do I need stitches?"

She shook her head. "Mostly I'm trying to get the brick dust out."

"You saw the shooter?"

"Yep." She moved back to the sink. "Too far away to see his face, so if you want to show me a lineup, won't do any good."

"But you know where he was standing?"

"Yep. You gonna tell me what's going on? Or should I just call the cops and let you explain to them?"

With Mrs. Barrett, honesty was the only policy. "Sarah's been threatened, there've been related murders and another shooting. My guess is that this is connected."

"Threats against that lovely woman? Those people in McCrumb County are a bunch of crazy hillbillies." She dried my cheek and temple and applied some salve. "Now, let's work on your coat."

My phone rang from one of the pockets as she lifted it. She jumped, more shaken than I'd thought.

I reached over and dug in the pocket. "Micah? I called about an escort in for Sarah tonight, but someone just took a shot at me. I'm okay. I don't think she ought to come in at all."

"Hold on, Win. Let me talk to her."

"Win! You're sure you're okay?" Sarah asked.

"He missed. Maybe wanted to scare me. I'm fine. I'll be home soon."

"Stay there. We're coming in—Caleb wants to find the shooter's position, see if we can't find a casing or footprints so we can make casts."

"That'll work, as long as you have an armed ride-along. Mrs. Barrett saw the shooter."

"Damn." I could hear her take a breath. "Vermont's looking better and better to me."

That's when I got really pissed.

CHAPTER TWENTY-TWO

Sarah

I felt like I'd been hit in the stomach with a baseball bat when Dad told me Win had been shot at. "'At' is the operative word, Sarah Anne," he'd said before he handed me his phone.

Dad, Leslie, Caleb and I hightailed it for Bloomington. En route I called their police department and briefed them on the incident.

The black-and-white landscape passed in a blur of gray as we sped northwest on mostly clear roads. Caleb was using siren and lights and we made it in record time. He slid to a stop in front of Win's apartment building and I dashed to unlock the door. I dropped the keys thanks to my shaking hands.

Win opened the door, I walked into her arms and hugged her as hard as I could. My relief at seeing her almost buckled my knees. I hung on to her until she loosened my arms. When I saw her cheek, I reached for it but Win intercepted my hand.

"I'm okay, really. Just a bit of debris. Stay cool, Sarah." She took me by the hand to Mrs. Barrett's apartment.

"Lovely entrance, Sarah," Mrs. Barrett said. "Siren and flashing lights. It'll give the neighbors something to talk about for weeks." She handed Win her things. "Good as new. Mostly just slush and salt, but

I sewed up a small rip on the parka. If you can find it, I'll buy you a new one."

"Thank you, Mrs. B. I won't even look."

A male voice's "um" behind us made us turn around. Caleb's big frame filled the doorway. "Ma'am, if you could point out where the shooter was standing…"

"Why don't you sit where you were when it happened," Win said. "You can guide Caleb from there." She dialed a number and handed her phone to the older woman.

Mrs. Barrett motioned him over and she pointed to two trees down the block. He nodded and headed out with Micah and Leslie, who stood waiting on the sidewalk.

She watched. "This thing on?"

Win nodded. "Just tell them when they're there. They'll take it from there."

Mrs. Barrett watched for a few more moments, then said, "Got it." She handed the phone back to Win.

We all watched as the three circled the trees at a distance, Leslie taking photographs, some with a ruler, others of the general scene. Caleb found something, lifted it with gloved hands to put in an evidence bag.

"Looks like they got the brass," Win said.

"You know where the slug landed?" I asked.

"They'll find it. It's going to be pretty deformed."

"You know, if your deputy would stand by the tree when they're done, I can tell how tall the guy with the rifle was," Mrs. Barrett said.

"You get that?" Win asked. We waited until the scene was documented. Then Caleb stood beside the shooter's tree. I shivered, even though I knew it was my chief deputy.

"About two inches taller," Mrs. Barrett said. "The man with the gun came almost level with that first branch."

Win thanked him and we watched as they started looking for the slug. They found it across the street. We thanked Mrs. Barrett and walked to the lobby.

"I've been thinking about this. We shouldn't change our plans," Win said. "We go dancing tonight."

"Oh, Win, no!"

"Listen to me, Sarah. Number one. I refuse to put our lives on hold or be controlled by those half-wits." Win turned to me. "Two. I was really looking forward to being on the dance floor with you. Have our own after-party. Somewhere not in McCrumb County."

I started to protest, then considered the intensity on Win's face. This whole messy business was taking a toll on both of us, no matter how hard we struggled to stay on an even keel. "Okay. If we leave early in the morning, we can see if anyone's tailing us. I'll have deputies standing by."

"In the meantime, can we leave the investigation to your team?" Win asked.

* * *

Win's hands around my waist, her body pressed close to mine and the slow beat of the music combined to send my libido into overdrive. I moved my hands from her shoulders to the back of her neck and pulled her into a kiss that continued to the end of the song.

"I'm getting the impression you want to go home," Win said with a grin.

"Um. I'd hate to be arrested for public lewd and lascivious behavior." I took her hand and led her to our table. "It's a good thing we're not driving all the way back home tonight."

Win shook her head. "Wild woman. Call your dad and tell him we're getting ready to leave."

With Dad and Caleb waiting at a diner next door I felt a little like a teenager being chaperoned. The plan was that they'd follow us to the apartment, check into a motel and follow us home in the morning. It was weird to have Dad babysitting me, but both he and Caleb had refused to budge.

I called and Dad's only comment was, "Makin' it an early night?"

"Only for dancing. Meet you at the door." I was blushing as we made our way out of Ruby's.

"See anything?" Win asked when we met up with them.

Caleb shook his head. "Walked the neighborhood about fifteen minutes ago. All quiet on the western front."

I raised an eyebrow. Caleb must be hanging around Dad too much and was picking up his literary habits.

They hustled us into Dad's truck, refusing to let me drive my own truck. Win sat on my lap in the middle of the cab. As unobtrusively as possible, I got my hands under her parka and around to her front. She made a noise deep in her throat and both men quickly looked out their windows. Dad gunned the truck forward.

When we got inside the apartment, Win pinned me against the door. "Don't ever do that to me in front of your dad. Or Caleb. I was mortified."

I shrugged and grinned. "I was just getting my hands warm."

"Your hands were already warm." She unzipped my parka and slipped it off. Put her hands under my sweater and kissed me with all the passion that had been building on the dance floor.

"Whew." My heart was beating faster and I felt myself melt into her arms. I took her parka off, we both slipped out of our boots and padded over to the overstuffed chair Win used for reading.

She pulled me down on her lap. "Before we get too involved to think, we should talk about this business. We've got to get ahead of these guys. We can't live like this. At least, I can't. My PTSD isn't back—yet. But without Emily available, I feel very vulnerable."

I examined her face. In the sharp light of the reading lamp she looked tired and thinner. "How do we do that, Win? Get ahead of them?"

"Set a fucking trap." She pulled me to her. "We can talk about it on the way home in the morning. I don't mean to ruin the mood 'cause I'm feeling romantic too."

"Romantic?"

She kissed me and moved her hands under my sweater. "Downright on fire for you."

CHAPTER TWENTY-THREE

Win

"Joshua Leatherby served two tours in the army in the nineties," Nathan said, looking up from his notes to the officers gathered around the conference table. "I don't think he liked taking orders. His service record is full of citations for insubordination. He was given a general discharge, came back here and had a series of low-paying jobs. Same problem, he didn't like taking orders. Two and a half years ago, he was hired as a shift supervisor at Zelcore."

"Who the hell did he know to get a cushy job like that with no experience in manufacturing?" Caleb asked.

"I ran all their employees and I couldn't find a connection," Nathan replied.

"Dad, you know anybody who works there?" Sarah asked.

Micah shook his head. "Only retired guys."

"I do," Caleb said. "A couple of them coach in the same baseball league I do."

"Make up a story," I said, leaning forward. "Maybe a bar fight and somebody thought the guy was Leatherby. You're just trying to get a feel for the guy, not haul him down to the station on such a thin ID."

Caleb nodded. "Sounds good, Win. I'll go real light."

"Anything else, Nathan?"

"Nothing from phone or computer records. We put a GPS tracker on his car—legally thanks to Bill. Nothing interesting so far—except he wasn't your shooter yesterday. His car was at work. He checked out."

Sarah sighed. "I was really hoping…"

"So was I," I said, looking around the table. "As far as we know, Leatherby isn't in electronic communication with whomever's behind him. So how do they talk?"

"Carrier pigeon?" Micah asked.

"Maybe." I grinned at him. "Who could he contact on a regular basis without raising any questions?"

"Pastor? Shrink?" Sarah guessed.

"Ain't got paperboys no more," Dad said.

"Bar or restaurant?" John piped in. "Or how about a co-worker or boss?"

"That's the problem nowadays," Micah said, leaning back in his chair. "Nobody much talks face-to-face. Used to be, you could stop an' chew the fat with 'bout anyone. Like mail carriers. Which brings me to the thought—wonder if Leatherby has a post office box."

"Can we check that?" I asked Sarah.

She nodded. "But realize, folks, he may not be using his real name. We'll have to get a warrant—"

"Why don't you let me talk to Millie down at the post office? Since she's postmistress an' all," Micah asked. "Unofficial-like. If it don't work, then you can get all the paperwork you need."

Sarah looked at me. I liked the "unofficial-like" so nodded.

I'd been taking notes and a couple of thoughts occurred to me. "Caleb, when you talk to the Zelcore people, could you find out if Leatherby hangs out with any particular co-workers?"

Caleb nodded.

"Nathan, would you get together with John? Cross-check the rolls of militias with the Zelcore employees? Maybe dig deeper on the militias since you have the warrant to do it. Especially the McCrumb County Rangers."

"What are you going to do?" Sarah asked.

"My own little project." I couldn't help but grin. "We need someone to infiltrate the Rangers, if they prove out. I've talked to Bill. We're going to get someone in place now."

* * *

When everyone but Sarah had left the conference room, I took her in my arms and pulled her close. She came willingly.

"Thanks for handing me the boss job," I said.

"It wasn't hard," she said, her head on my shoulder. "I know the county, but I'm not used to running an intelligence op like this and coordinating the higher-ups. This is getting serious."

"Will you tell your people thanks? For being so easy to work with, for being so good at what they do."

"I think they'd say the same to you, Win." She snuggled deeper. "It's nice to just stand here, in your arms, not caring if someone walks in." She looked up at me. "I don't regret coming out."

"That's what could be behind this," I said, stroking her hair. "Laura's lesbian. Don't forget the Brownes."

"Nor will I forget they didn't go after Laura directly, but people who were supporting her. For me, that's you," Sarah said, frowning.

"Plus Micah, Nathan and all of your deputies." At her panicked look, I lifted her face to me and kissed her. "All of us, standing around you, ready to protect you."

"At what cost, Win?"

"That's why I want to get one step ahead." I kissed her again. "Got a meeting with Bill's candidate."

"Where?"

"Bill's house. Out on Gilbert Road."

"Can I come with?"

I shook my head. "Stay here and attend to your paperwork. Monitor your minions."

She groaned.

"I'll be back to pick you up. As soon as I can."

* * *

I drove up to the brick house. Didn't see another car or truck. The front door opened and Bill yelled, "Park in the garage, Win."

I pulled into the garage and closed the doors after me. Bill, out of uniform and in jeans and a flannel shirt held the back screen door open for me.

"We're skulking again, aren't we?" I asked as I followed him into the living room.

"Yeah, and with good reason. These militias are a fucking pain. Bunch of civilians running around like they're special ops troops." He motioned me to a chair and sat in one opposite. "He'll be here shortly. Good man. Hope you approve."

"Your call. At this point, I'm grateful for any help you can provide." I told him what we'd found out so far. "Not much, but something."

"We'll see if we can't add to it," he said. He crossed his legs to telegraph a new topic. "How're you and Sarah doing? Any fights yet?"

"We had our first fight before we were married. We've had a few since." I shrugged. "But we always make up. Talk it out."

"I'll bet Sarah's a handful." He suddenly reddened. "I didn't mean it that way. No offense meant."

"None taken. She is a handful in every way imaginable. I've met my match."

He smiled. "Still in love?"

I nodded, unable to speak for a moment, overwhelmed by emotion.

"I'm really glad for the both of you. I worried you'd never settle down."

I heard a truck pull into the driveway. Bill got up, looked out the window. "He's here."

He walked to the door, opened it to a powerfully built man who was stamping the snow off his boots. He looked up.

"Nolan? Is it really you?" I stood up on shaky legs. He was one of the men medivaced from the village where Azar died. He held open his arms and I rushed into them. "Man, I'm so glad to see you."

"Yeah?" he asked with a shy smile. "I kept waiting for you to show up at the hospital."

"I went a little crazy." Understatement. "I went AWOL, didn't leave the village until it was rebuilt. When I finally left, you were already out of the hospital. Maybe on another mission? Or did they give you leave?"

"Leave. Just across the Ohio in Paducah." He hugged me hard. "I'm glad you're okay and I'm real sorry about Azar. She was a good woman."

I blinked away old tears. "Thanks, McBride."

"You look fat and sassy—you find somebody here?"

"Fat?"

"Okay, just sassy."

I held up my left hand. "Married somebody here. Well, we got married in Vermont."

"Who?"

"Sarah, the sheriff of McCrumb County."

"Oh god—the woman at the center of all of this. Guess we gotta get this one right." He hugged me again, hard and quick.

"Hate to break up this reunion," Bill said, settling back into his chair. "But we need to go over our plans."

CHAPTER TWENTY-FOUR

Sarah

I was almost through the stack of paperwork when Caleb tapped on the doorframe. "You think about taking two days a week?"

"Yep—even I voted for two days off. Have you got a schedule worked out?"

"Played around with it, but I was waiting for a 'go' from you."

"Go."

"You want Monday and Tuesday? Or the weekend?" he asked.

"You take the weekend—your kids have games, don't they?"

"Yeah." A big smile lit his face. "I'll get it on your desk this afternoon."

"Anything about Leatherby?"

"A little," he said as he sat across from me. "I ran into one of my buddies who works at Zelcore grocery shopping last night. I'm trying to take it easy, not call them and try to pump them over the phone. Bob said Leatherby doesn't hang with anyone, though maybe after work he does. He's got no idea how 'the jerk' got the job. I have a feeling we're going to be hearing more of that. He's not liked because he's a bully."

"Keep digging but don't push it."

Dad walked in without knocking and with a big smile on his face. "Millie sure is the nicest lady."

My eyebrows shot up.

"She's married, Sarah Anne, so wipe that smirk off your face." He laid a piece of paper on the desk. "A PO box under the name James McNab. Collects the mail once a week on Monday around noontime. Gets a letter once a week. No bills. Millie thought that was peculiar."

"So is Leatherby using the name McNab?"

"Ain't proven," Dad said. "But it's peculiar. Think we should keep an eye on it."

"Did Millie remember a return address on this once-a-week letter?"

"Nope." He rocked on his heels with a big smile. "But next one comes in, she will commit it to memory."

"Can she do that?" Caleb asked. "Legally, I mean?"

"Ain't against the law to remember somethin'. An' a conversation with a friend?" He shrugged.

"Be careful, Dad."

"You think the United States Postal Service is gonna come after me 'cause I talk to the postmistress of a small town? Pah! They got more pressin' issues to deal with."

"Like delivering mail," Caleb said.

I threw up my hands. No county laws were being broken. Federal? Hell, I was just a county sheriff.

* * *

I sent those details to Nathan, then I went back to paperwork but found myself checking the clock every ten minutes. My shift was almost over when I saw Caleb striding through the bullpen with Win at his heels. He put the new schedule on my desk with a flourish.

"I never thought I'd see the day," Win said.

Caleb grinned. "Me neither."

I scanned the duty schedule. "Starting this week?"

"Yep. So I won't be here tomorrow. But Sarah, just like always, you need something, call. All I have on the plate tomorrow is watching football. I recorded all the games I missed, so I got all day to catch up."

He saluted with two fingers and left.

"Ready to go?" Win asked.

I put my last file in the out-box. "You meet the guy who's going undercover?"

"Tell you about him on the way home."

On the drive, Win was quiet but a smile tugged at the corners of her mouth.

"So who?"

"Nolan McBride. He was on my team in Afghanistan when the UAV hit Azar's village."

"An old friend?"

"Yeah. More than a friend. The kind of brother I never grew up with." Win sighed. "It's hard to describe the bond a small team forms. With four of us, usually embedded in enemy territory, we got close. Fast."

I glanced at her. "How close?"

"Not like that, Sarah." Win frowned. "I said 'a brother.' But it sure was good to see him. First time since that night."

I suddenly felt so distant from Win's previous life, though she'd talked about it some. It chilled me to think what would have happened to her had she been captured by the Taliban or Al Qaeda, and that could've happened any day she was there. "So you think he'll do a good job?"

"The best. He's a genius at detecting lies. Summing a person up from one meeting. Knowing their weak spots as well as a quick assessment of their strengths." She glanced at the rearview mirror for the hundredth time. "When this is over, I want to invite him over to dinner. Have him meet you."

"Did you tell him about us?"

"That we're married, yes. He knew about Azar and me. I never realized how much his support meant." Her eyes went to the rearview mirror again. "Let's stop and pick up some calzones. Call dispatch, Sarah. See if there's a patrol car behind us. If not, get one."

I'd been watching the side mirror and called in. "They're on their way. Probably pick us up when we stop."

"Good. These guys know where we live."

"How do you figure that?"

"Where did they pick me up the last time?"

"But how could they find out?"

"County property records, open to the public if you pay the fee. You might want to inquire when you go back in." She made the turn into the parking lot. "What I was going to say is, since they know where we live, why the tail?"

"They mean business this time?"

"Or just shake us up?"

She pulled into a parking space in front of Duo's. We watched the truck pass slowly on the road. I couldn't make out the plate. "GMC, late nineties, black," I said to dispatch. "They drove on by, but I saw brake lights come on down the street. Don't stop them unless they initiate action, but get the plate number." I disconnected and looked at Win. "You go in—I'll cover you."

Win gave me a searching look, then nodded. "Won't be long. Don't initiate action."

"You too, except for food."

CHAPTER TWENTY-FIVE

Win

As I stepped out of Duo's with bags in hand, a sheriff's cruiser streaked by with siren and light bar going. It disappeared in the direction we had come. "What's going on? Deputy's going the wrong way."

Sarah took the bags and settled them on her lap. "Smart deputy. He got the plate and eyes on the driver. When the driver looked at him, he took off in the opposite direction with a splashy U-turn. I'm waiting for them to run the plates. Maybe this time, we'll get something concrete."

"We go home now?"

"Yeah. Deputy will turn around and follow us, or the truck if he's still there."

I saw our tail pull out and follow us for a mile or so, then turn off. "He's gone."

"He probably noticed the deputy behind him," Sarah said with a satisfied smile.

"When we get home, can we give all of this a break?"

"What? You don't want to think about it?" Sarcasm in Sarah's voice.

"No, I don't. I want us to eat in front of the fire and relax," I said, glancing at her. "You have to work tomorrow and go back to this full-time. I want us to have one stress-free night together."

"I have Monday and Tuesday off."

I checked in the mirror. "So you've got two days off if nothing breaks. Let's take this opportunity while we can."

"Win, are you sure your PTSD isn't coming back?"

"It never leaves," I said as I sought Sarah's hand. "I'm hypervigilant, but in this case, I have reason to be. Otherwise, I'm okay. We'll see how I sleep when I'm in Bloomington next week. I don't want to leave you, Sarah."

"I'll be safe. Dad and Nathan will shadow me and keep an eye out for nefarious folk."

I squeezed her hand. "I sure as hell hope so."

When we got home, I gave Des some exercise. She hadn't been getting the long walks she needed since this began. Tomorrow I'd make up for some of it with a hike to the top of Foley's Knob.

As we ate dinner, we talked about the girls' room, what we still needed and what I thought they'd like. Some of Sarah's questions stumped me. How could I describe the radical cultural changes these kids faced? After dinner, I showed her photos I'd taken in Azar's village. Interiors of the houses. Inside Azar's quarters. Sarah studied them intently.

"Where's the furniture?" she asked.

"They don't need tables or chairs because they sit on the floor. Mattresses are on the floor." I switched to the next image. "Azar's quarters were unusual because she had a fireplace and a small platform for the mattress. Her husband had built both for her out of a desire to make her comfortable. Some of the villagers said she lived in a mansion because the fireplace used more fuel."

"Mansion? It's so not."

I switched to a series of exteriors. "These compounds remind me a lot of the pueblos in New Mexico." I stopped abruptly when I saw a photo of Azar and me, my arm around her, smiling at the camera.

"That's Azar, isn't it? She's beautiful, Win. Her eyes…it's like you can see into her essence."

"I could." I swallowed. Turned to Sarah. "We Americans guard our eyes. Our souls."

"Do I do that?" Sarah asked.

"Not too much anymore." I closed the file, turned the computer off. "It's a struggle to stay open, isn't it? We're so afraid someone will see our demons and use them against us."

"Have I met your demons, Win?"

"Some of them."

* * *

Tailed by a deputy I took Sarah to work. I wondered how long we could keep this up. I knew the sheriff's department was stretched thin. So were Sarah and I.

"Is the guy following us on overtime?" I asked.

"Gal," she said. "Dad set up a schedule, asked for volunteers and we have coverage for the rest of the week."

"Not much time to catch the shooter."

"One step at a time, Win. One week at a time for scheduling."

I drove into the lot behind the building. After Sarah had unfastened her seat belt, I pulled her close to me, held her. "Be careful today."

"You too. I'm not even going to ask what you have on your agenda." She took a deep breath. "Trust."

I watched her go inside. All this protection wasn't going to save her from a sniper. I would've rather seen her in full battle gear.

I pulled out the burn phone Bill had given me and called Nolan. "Can we meet today?"

"Yeah, if it doesn't take too long. I have to start looking for a job today."

"At Zelcore?"

He laughed. "Where do we meet?"

I gave him directions. Told him I'd wait at the last turn. Half an hour later, we drove into the clearing and Nathan waved us into his cabin.

I made the introductions. "You know I trust both of you with my life. No doubts. But I'm placing Sarah's life in your keeping. Don't screw up."

I got two simultaneous hugs. "What've you got, Nathan?"

"Not much. Whoever's doing their network is one clever bastard, but I'm working on it. It just takes time."

"The clock's ticking." I told them about the tail last night. "What really worries me is the shooter. He's fired three times. The only reason he didn't kill the second time is because the sun hit the windshield. He's not using a sniper rifle, guys. Not sure whether he meant to hit me or not."

"You think it's military training or a long time hunting?" Nolan asked.

"Seems like if he's military, he'd being using something more sophisticated. The thirty-aught-six has limited range. Can't be broken down." I shrugged. "Nathan?"

"I agree, not that I know much about the military. But if anyone can make shots like that, they've been shooting that rifle a long time and are comfortable with it."

"Anybody like that on your lists?" I asked.

Nathan shook his head. "But I can get the DNR's records for deer hunting licenses. I'll cross-check. Maybe Micah can think of someone who's that good with a rifle. I know a few, but none of them are on the Ranger list."

"Remember Nathan, the ballistics match the Coeur d'Alene murder on the reservation in Idaho. This may not be a local guy." I ran a hand through my hair. "I can't understand why we can't get a better picture on these people."

"Maybe there's more to them than a local outfit," Nolan said. "I can show you some databases, Nathan. Maybe if we put our heads together…"

Nathan nodded and led Nolan over to a bank of computers.

"Shit man, I'm impressed." Nolan stood with his hands on his hips, examined the servers with interest.

"You're on your own, McBride," I said. "I'm going snowshoeing with Des."

"Wear a vest, Win," he said.

* * *

Back home, Des did her happy dance when I picked up the snowshoes. I angled diagonally across the road, Des still danced around me, woofed at the sky. The sun was out, casting short shadows across the field. Good to see details. I put the snowshoes on when we hit the soft stuff. While my target was the top of the Knob, I didn't want anyone picking up my tracks. I headed in the opposite direction across the field, then switched course to the woods. I backtracked through the woods until I came to a deer track up the Knob. No sign of tracks other than a rabbit and mice. I worked upward, wishing I'd brought my poles. I stopped as I breached the summit. Scanned the area. "Shit."

Someone had not only been here, but had lain in the snow. From the body print, I could see his head had been facing our house. Deep elbow prints. Hands holding binoculars? I took photos. Wished I had moved faster because the shadows had flattened as the sun moved across the sky. Still, with the zoom lens I could pick up some good detail.

The person in question had come up the other way. I sidestepped down through the trees, off-trail, looking for a clear print. Found one, laid a ruler down next to it. Irony because I'd bought it for the girls. I took the shot, then worked laterally across the Knob to where we hit the trail down.

Des had been so well-behaved at the scene, sitting and waiting for me, that I gave her an extra treat when we got back home.

I called Nathan. "Somebody's been scoping out our house from the top of the Knob. Any suggestions on how we find who?"

Nathan let out a long breath. "Cold weather, Win, with colder temperatures coming. The batteries for a camera won't last more than a day or two. I've got another solar powered one like the two I put in for you, but with the trees bare I don't think I can disguise it. Let me think on it."

"Think fast. I'll attach some photos to an email."

"Are you going to tell Sarah?"

"Yeah. I reamed her out for not telling me about the letters, so quid pro quo. The front of the house doesn't have large windows. A shot would be really tricky from the Knob."

"Tricky, but not impossible?"

"Impossible with a thirty-aught-six. Out of range. With a sniper rifle? No, not impossible. Especially when we went out the front door or at the bottom of the drive." I banged my fist on my desk. "We've got to get this guy. These people."

CHAPTER TWENTY-SIX

Sarah

My office was the last place I wanted to be. Snuggled in Win's arms in front of the fire, talking about the girls and planning for them, that's what I wanted. I was tired of the constant escort and weary of the danger behind my need to have one.

Dory intercepted me. "We ran the plate from last night but it don't match the truck. Supposed to be on a Toyota. Here's the info."

"Damn." I took the sheet Dory handed me. "I thought we'd finally caught a break."

"Your daddy's waitin' in your office."

Dad was seated on my couch, his long legs stretched out in front of him. "Mornin'," he said as he unfolded his body and stood. "Went back an' chit-chatted with our esteemed postmistress an' she pulled this." He handed me a folder containing one sheet. "Don't mess it up. I gotta return it."

I stared at the sheet. A color copy of an Indiana driver's license, the ID James McNab had used to get his post office box. Now we had a face to run, but it wasn't the face of Joshua Leatherby. "Doesn't seem like McNab is Leatherby's alias. What the hell is going on?"

"Dang if I know. Send that to Nathan an' let him sort it," Dad said. "I understand he has access to databases we don't."

I scanned the image, sent it to Nathan and returned the sheet to Dad. "Thanks for keeping after this."

"We got a bunch of puzzle pieces an' I know it's frustratin' right now, but they'll come together. You got a passel of good folk workin' on this." He hugged me. "Keep the faith, Sarah Anne."

I knew what he said was true—given enough time. But did we have enough time? I knew Win was worried about a ticking clock only she could hear, but I was beginning to listen for it.

My phone rang. Emily?

"You okay?" I asked.

"Getting better," she said. "Win gave me a damn good kick in the butt. Sorry I shut down, but I needed to, at least for a little bit. I'm calling about you two. I'm hearing rumors about you both being in danger and that you're taking it seriously."

"True on both counts."

"How's Win doing?"

"Fraying around the edges, but basically sound," I said. "But Em, this situation is taking its toll on both of us."

There was a silence. "That's what I was afraid of. Can you both see me this afternoon in my office?"

"I should check with Win," I said. "But let me accept. If you don't hear from me, we'll be there. What time?"

"Four thirty?"

"See you then."

I printed out the two photos we had and walked them up to the detectives' loft. John was going through some files and sighing. He looked up. "Hey, something new?"

I placed the photos on his desk and told him what Dad had found out. "We seem to have two men who've got access to the post office box, but only one visits regularly."

"I don't get it."

"I don't either. Seems like this is all smoke and mirrors," I said as I sat on the edge of his desk. "They look enough alike to be brothers."

"Maybe they are. Or cousins."

"Nathan's tracking McNab. I need to call him, see if there's any progress."

"Let me do it. I need to work with Nathan more. That is, if you don't mind?"

"Getting ready to take the reins, eh?" I said with a smile and thumbs-up. "Who do we have covering the post office tomorrow? No, never mind. It's your op."

"You want me to keep you updated tomorrow?" he asked.

"Only if it's a big break in the case," I said, running a hand through my hair. "If I get too curious, can I call?"

He gave me a big smile.

* * *

Win picked me up at four and we drove to Em's office with our escort unobtrusively tucked a block behind us.

"How'd she sound?" Win asked.

"Not her usual prickly self."

"You think she's prickly?" Win asked. "I'd say sharp-edged like a laser."

"You've definitely been working with her too long." I took Win's hand and squeezed it.

Em's office door opened as soon as we walked into the waiting room. "How are the two of you holding up?" she asked.

"Fair to middling," I said. "I'm getting really tired of looking over my shoulder."

"Win?"

"I'm angry. Guys like this play games, just like spooks. They rattle the target, keep the pressure on, push until someone makes a mistake. This time, Sarah is the primary target and we have to get them before we make a mistake."

Em was silent for a minute. "Were you ever a spook, Win?"

"No. I had the misfortune of working with them on occasion."

"Do you think these threats come from people who've had, uh, spy experience?"

"Possible. It's been methodical, done in increments of harassment. But anyone who's a bully knows the technique," Win said. "Are you joining the investigation?"

"God no! Professional curiosity is all." Em recrossed her legs. "What I'm trying to do is tell you Win, how amazed I am you've survived at all. Much less thrived like you are. I remember you when you first came home."

Win squeezed my shoulder and said, "Hard lesson. But I learned I needed help."

Em stared at Win. "Touché."

"What's this really about, Em?" I asked.

Em shifted her gaze. "One, I really wanted to check in with both of you and see how you're handling the additional stress. Fair to middling isn't good, and I'd like to see you both do better. Has the sex cooled down?"

Win snickered and I blushed.

"Are you taking the stress out on one another?"

"I don't think so," Win said. "We've had a fight or two, but I think it was more about boundaries and openness than just striking out to ease the worry and frustration."

"Sarah?"

"Win yelled at me for not telling her about the letters and I think she was right. I'm so used to playing everything close to the vest and she's helping me understand why I do that."

"You agree?" Em asked.

Win grinned. "It's pretty hard to talk about something when you refuse to think about it."

"That means you're developing an ability to ask the right questions on an emotional level," Em said. "Which leads me to my second point. I'm starting a group for veterans and I'd like you to lead it with me, Win."

"I don't do groups," Win said.

Em gave her that half-lidded stare. "I won't push, but I'd like you to really consider it."

"Yeah," I said as I turned to Win. "You've helped me work through stuff I never would've thought about unless you pushed me. You're good at it Win."

Win examined my face, then turned to Em. "You have a number three?"

"I don't, but my partner Marty does," Em said. "If you'll meet with her independently of our therapy sessions, she has something she'd like to discuss with you both."

"Sure," I said. "When?"

"How about now? She's in the waiting room."

* * *

Marty was as athletic looking as Em, though a few years younger and softer. Laughter came easily to her.

"I do counseling with students at the LGBT center in Bloomington and I've been hearing talk. We keep telling these kids it gets better, but I'm wondering if it ever does. Three students at IU have been stoned by so-called Christians citing Mosaic Law."

"What?" I asked, suddenly wide awake. "'Stoned' as in having rocks hurled at them?"

Marty nodded. "I couldn't believe it either, so I investigated. Three or four men, older—either grad students or from off-campus—threw not only rocks but quotations from the Old Testament. There was definitely that particular biblical slant to it. One of the other counselors there said it's part of a far right-wing religious movement that was popular in the eighties, then seemed to die out in the nineties. But with all the radicalism on the right, they seem to be resurgent."

"This is an organized group?" Win asked.

"I'm not sure," Marty said. "I don't know if these people came from one congregation or just got together to spew their hate."

"Have the cops done anything? Did you get to read their reports?"

Marty frowned. "These kids are just coming out and are so shaky. They didn't report the attacks."

"Oh man." Win leaned forward. "I'll talk to campus police when I go in on Wednesday. They may have heard something. This happened on campus?"

"Yeah, but the thing I can't figure out is how they got onto our kids. Like I said, they're just beginning to come out to themselves. Not even family."

"Surveillance," Win said. "They saw kids going in or leaving your building. Do you have any exterior cameras?"

"No. Bloomington's always seemed like a safe place. With the university, the population's fairly progressive."

"Not true," I said. "There've been attacks on a number of minority groups over the past ten years."

"Well, yeah," Marty said. "But that's been a lunatic fringe."

"Gay haters aren't a lunatic fringe?" Win asked. "Get cameras, watch for faces who loiter around the building or reappear on a regular basis. I'll hook you up with someone who can set them up and give you a good price."

"We don't have money to—"

"You want to wait until one of those kids dies?" Win asked. "We'll find the money."

Marty nodded, but looked more worried. "I've done some digging. These groups used to be called Christian Reconstructionists. If you Google them, you can find a number of entries."

"I'll look tomorrow." Win stood. "Talk to everybody at the center. Encourage them to leave in groups, not alone. Don't wait until the worst happens."

CHAPTER TWENTY-SEVEN

Win

"You should really think about doing the group with Em," Sarah said as I drove home.

"Uh-huh." I kept checking the rearview mirror. Our escort was fairly far back. I worried that another car could slip in and separate us.

"You're good at it, Win. You've helped me a lot, ever since our first kiss."

I glanced at her. "Because I love you." My gaze returned to the road and the mirrors. "But I don't love every veteran in McCrumb County. I get impatient with bullshit. Shut down. Emily would kick me out of the group midway through the first meeting."

"Talk about bullshit."

"I'm not taking time from the little we have together." I glanced at her again. "I don't want to do it. Not now. Not while we're under fire."

Sarah leaned back, closed her eyes. So much for surveillance from that side of the truck. We made it home without incident and our escort waited at the bottom of the drive until we got inside. I was still worried about the watcher at the top of Foley's Knob.

"Why are the shutters closed on the front windows?" Sarah asked as she hung her parka up.

"Because I found we had a watcher on top of the Knob."

"You what? When? When were you going to tell me?"

"Today. Now. Tonight we were supposed to concentrate on Emily. Not this." I went to the fireplace. Leaned my hands and head against the mantel. We were sniping at one another again. Shit.

"I'm sorry, Win. I didn't mean to—"

"I know." I turned to face her. "I don't want to fight with you. Understand, thinking of somebody stalking you makes me crazy. People stoning gay kids? Really crazy. We're both wound tight."

Des woofed at the door. Sarah opened it. Des licked Sarah's hands, whined.

"She's picking up on our tension, Sarah. Let me build a fire. Would you put some music on?"

Soon the fire was popping to the sound of Cris Williamson. We sat on the couch, feet on the coffee table, fingers entwined.

"You're right," Sarah said. "The tension's getting to me."

"Want to go to the dojang tomorrow? I'll give you a workout. Great way to relieve stress."

"I was hoping to stay in bed…"

"All day?"

"All morning?" she asked with a lift of her eyebrow.

I grinned. Sarah laughed. I realized it had been a while since I'd heard her laugh. The lines on her face softened and her shoulders relaxed.

"Without all this outside crap, we're doing fine as a couple." She turned to probe my gaze. "Aren't we?"

"You never leave the toilet seat up, so I'd say that's a really good sign."

She laughed again. "When have you ever had to deal with that?"

I pulled her to me for a long kiss. "Tonight, we forget there's a world out there. Tomorrow, we go on the offensive."

She reached up, stroked my cheek. "Tomorrow afternoon?"

* * *

"So what's our offensive strategy?" Sarah asked over lunch.

We hadn't made coffee until eleven that morning. Unless we stayed out of bed, we weren't going to have an offensive strategy. "While you were in the shower, I sent what info I had on the Christian Reconstructionists to Nathan. Wasn't much. I wish Bill would set me up with some of their databases."

"He won't?"

"He can't. I don't have security clearance anymore." I finished my coffee. "I asked Nathan to dig. See if we can find specific congregations in our area."

"How are you going to do that?"

"Language analysis of church websites." I sighed. "He's got a lot of work going. Glad your dad's lending a hand. There is news on one front. He's getting satellite images from Bill for Foley's Knob. We'll know if the watcher returns."

"Win, have you thought about how open the back of the house is?"

"When I designed this house, I was in the throes of paranoia. I scoped out all the surrounding places where someone could launch an attack. There's nowhere in the back. Not even with an RPG. That's why I put the big windows in."

"So what's on the agenda for today?" Sarah asked.

"Dojang?"

"I seem to have released a lot of tension last night, not to mention this morning."

I grinned back at her. "Then what about some cross-country skiing?"

"Really?"

"How about you find out if someone checked the records on this property."

"That's work, Win. This is my day off."

"And I'll check with Zoe, see if she followed the tip I gave her."

"What tip was that?" Sarah asked as her shoulders stiffened.

"I told her I thought the McCrumb County Rangers might be a good story. A while back. I didn't tell you because…I just didn't think about it again. Zoe hasn't got back to me."

"Do we have to go into town?"

"We have these wonderful new devices for talking to people who are far away, Sarah. They're called telephones."

"Smartass." Sarah stretched. "Two days off, Win. Two whole days of no paperwork, no patrol and no investigating. It's such a luxury, especially since you'll be gone for three days. I just want to talk with you and look at you and touch you."

I walked to her and held her. "If we get this stuff out of the way, we'll have the rest of today and tomorrow to just be together. Any way you want."

She looked up at me. "I know you think I'm just refusing to think about the danger. I know it's there. I do, constantly. I go to work in the morning and think I might not come home. That thought's with me every morning. You go to Bloomington, you might not come home. I know that, bone-deep. That's why I want to just be with you whenever we can."

"Carpe diem, huh?"

"Exactly." She slipped her hands under my sweatshirt. "I promise I'll go to the Recorder's Office first thing Wednesday morning."

"With photos of McNab and Leatherby?"

"Promise. I'll text you with the results. Okay?"

"If I get to call Zoe while you're doing the dishes."

"You push a hard bargain, woman," Sarah said with a grin.

"I've got another clause. We snowshoe on the property. Enough to get some real exercise. I need it, so does Des and so do you."

Des woofed on cue.

Sarah threw her hands up. "I surrender. Make your call, we'll go outside and play and then come in and relieve any tension that's left."

"Light a fire."

* * *

I called Zoe, but she was out of the office. "Call me," was the message I left. Frustration was what I felt. When I left for Bloomington, my head had to be in academic territory. I wanted to kick-start this investigation while I was here so Sarah and I could get back to a normal life. Not wait for a bullet.

As we trooped around my land, I kept an eye out for footprints that shouldn't be here. Nothing. Maybe I was right and nothing at the back of the house was vulnerable. But the thought would be there when I turned on lights tonight: *maybe I was wrong*.

On our return, I built a fire as Sarah made hot chocolate and Des settled in her favorite place in front of the fire. A light snow had started outside the big windows. Cozy. Serene. Why couldn't I stop waiting for the crap to hit? Because the threat was out there. Waiting.

Sarah brought two mugs and settled down beside me. I cradled the mug in my hands, relished the warmth. Idyllic. I wondered if Sarah was thinking the same thing.

She sighed, rested her head on my shoulder. "I wish we never had to go to work, but could stay here like this."

"This is making a memory, Sarah. I engrave the scene in my mind. Every detail. When things get rough, I pull up the scene."

"What's your favorite scene of us?"

"The first time we made love. You'd just opened the window because it was stuffy in your bedroom. You were naked from the waist up and the sun sculpted your breasts. You turned to me, looked so aroused. Scared at the same time. The breeze blew a curtain against your body, your nipples got tighter." I put my arm around her. "You looked ephemeral—like if I blinked you'd be gone."

"I remember." She sipped the hot chocolate. "I wanted you so bad and I'd thought the day would never come. I was scared, at least a little. I was a tad worried about the performance part, you know?"

"That you wouldn't come?"

She took another sip. "I think on some level I was worried fingers couldn't replace a penis."

"Wow. I didn't pick up on the penis thing."

She grinned. "You wouldn't, would you?"

I groaned. "Last thing on my mind. Was that all you were afraid of?"

"No." Another sip. "I was afraid I couldn't let go because…it was so new and…knowing you were a woman."

Always a big step, the first time. Because it was forbidden, this need to bring such a deeply felt bond to a physical destination. "But you came. Rather spectacularly if I remember rightly."

"And haven't stopped since." She tucked her head into my shoulder. "Drink up so we can make more memories."

"Do you have a favorite scene of us?"

"There are so many, Win. I start remembering one when I'm at work, get aroused and start blushing like crazy. I think Dory believes I'm going through the change and it's hot flashes. But it's not that kind of hot flash." She finished her cocoa and put it on the side table. "The most memorable was on the kitchen chair at Dad's house when you had me tie you up. I didn't know a woman could come so many times or so many ways. I could feel each one through your whole body. Your face was so open, Win."

"My surrender." I finished and handed the mug to Sarah. Watched her as she set it next to hers. "Do you think we've settled into a rut with our lovemaking?"

"If we have, it's a rut I don't mind staying in. Why? Do you want to do some other stuff?"

"No. I'm still learning your body, Sarah. I keep finding new places that turn you on."

"It's your touch that turns me on. Anywhere you touch me."

CHAPTER TWENTY-EIGHT

Sarah

Win disentangled our limbs, got up and walked to the fireplace. Her body in the low glow from the embers was so beautiful I almost got up to touch her. I watched her muscles ripple as she added a couple of logs and bent over to blow the embers into flame. Her ass was perfect, high and lusciously round. As the logs caught, she added another and turned around.

"Making a memory, Sarah?"

"Oh yeah. I envy your butt."

She laughed, settled next to me and pulled me atop of her. "I love your butt just like it is. And your breasts. And your belly. And—"

"No more inventory, please." I looked out the window. The snow had stopped as it grew dark. "Are you hungry?"

"For you? Always."

"I was thinking about dinner. I bought a couple of frozen pizzas for evenings like this. I can put one on and come back and snuggle."

"Frozen pizzas?"

"From Mama Mia's, guaranteed not to be cardboard crap by her son."

Win gazed at my breasts and sighed. "When you get food on your mind, there's no stopping you, is there?"

I put the pizza in the oven and set the timer. When I returned to the couch, Win had stretched out with one arm behind her head and one leg bent at the knee. In the soft light from the fireplace, she took my breath away. "Can we take some pictures?"

Her eyebrows shot up. "Naked?"

I nodded. "Something more tangible than memory. You look so gorgeous, like someone a Renaissance master would've painted, except you're too muscled for back then. Where's your camera?"

"Those kind of pictures can get people in trouble, Sarah. If they go on a computer, they can be hacked."

"Then we'll keep them in your camera."

"Which can be stolen, Sarah."

"Enough! Where's the damn camera?"

"Last cupboard in the hall."

I found it and returned to the living room. Win had sat up and wrapped both arms around her up-drawn knees. "No you don't, Kirkland. Back as you were, marine."

She resumed her reclining position. "I really feel naked, Sarah."

"That's the purpose." I took a couple of shots from different angles, then asked her to move in front of the fireplace.

She did so reluctantly. "Just don't shoot my crappy thigh. It's not romantic."

"Shut up and get sexy." I grinned at her, buoyed by her first discomfort at anything sexual. "You talk a good game, Kirkland. Now walk it."

I sensed an immediate change in her and when she threw back her head to laugh, I clicked off a shot of a beautiful woman relaxing into her sexuality. I took several more, then she grabbed the camera.

"Your turn," she said with a huge grin. "Is there any space?"

"I put in a new memory card. You can hide the card easier than the camera."

She motioned me to exchange places. I did, but I was so conscious of my sagging breasts and butt, I hid both as much as I could. She moved me into position. I knew I was beet red in the face, but that wasn't what she was focusing on. I realized what she'd been feeling and told myself to get with the program. I watched her move around me, lithe and smiling. I began changing positions on my own. I was on my back when the oven timer went off. "You get the pizza, I'll get the robes," Win said as she put the camera on the coffee table.

As we ate, Win reviewed the images, those of her rather quickly, lingering on mine.

"Shoot Win, you're a helluva photographer. I actually look okay."

"Look at this one," she said, going forward rapidly. "You, woman, look downright sexy."

I did, to my surprise. I thought it had more to do with my eyes than my body. "How about these as a late anniversary present?"

"I thought we weren't giving anniversary gifts," she said.

"Could you pull a couple of prints? I'll frame them. We'll hang them in the bedroom."

She smiled. "I'll work on it tomorrow. I couldn't figure out what to get you anyway. I mean, something that has meaning."

I thumbed through them again while Win got another piece of pizza. I couldn't decide which of hers I liked best. "Maybe two of each of us."

"Eat your pizza so we can make new memories."

After we finished and cleaned up, Win removed my robe and took my hands. "How about one photo of us together?"

"I'd like that."

She walked back to the cupboard and returned with a tripod. After she attached the camera, she moved the rig to face the fire and motioned me toward it. "Stand with your hands raised. As if my palms are on yours. A little lower."

I heard the sound of the zoom lens and she tinkered a bit more. "Hold on, we're almost there."

She shed her robe, stepped into the frame, her palms against mine, our lips straining to meet. After I heard the shutter, I pulled her into my arms for a long kiss. I thought I heard the shutter sound again, but ignored it as the heat grew.

Win pulled back. "Let's see what we got—if it's not good, we'll just have to keep practicing."

We walked to the camera and when Win showed me the photo, I gasped. The fire backlit us so that we appeared mostly in silhouette except where the firelight made rosy modeling along our bodies. "Perfect."

* * *

The phone got Win out of bed and moving at eight thirty in the morning. I followed reluctantly, showering first, then padding into the kitchen for coffee. Win was at her desk, phone still tucked into her shoulder while she took notes.

"Can you send me your files?" she asked. "Great. Zoe, if I get any leads from this, I promise you'll be the first to know. Er, the second. Thanks so much."

She turned toward me. "Zoe. She's been poking around in the Ranger thing. She might've found some good leads. I'd like to go over her notes, then send what I think is important to Nolan and Nathan. Zoe managed to talk with some of these goons and has transcribed their conversation."

"Can I have coffee before we talk business?" While it was brewing, I watched Win. Dressed in Marine Corps sweats and heavy socks, she was far from the firelight vixen of last night. But she was still beautiful.

After the high-pitched beeps, I took two mugs of coffee to her desk. She'd just opened a zip file from Zoe and was focused on the text scrolling down the screen. I kissed her forehead and put the mug on the desk out of reach of her elbows. "Good morning."

She looked up at me and snaked an arm around my waist. "Good morning. Quite a night, eh?"

"Why do I have a feeling we're not going to stretch last night into today?"

"We're already dressed?"

"That could change quickly." I looked at the screen and sighed.

"Pull up a chair. Let's do this together."

"Breakfast?"

She swiveled around to look at me. "Shit, you're resistant."

"My head's still in last night, I'll admit that. But I haven't had a cup of coffee yet and I'm hungry. Go take your shower and I'll fix breakfast. What do you want?"

She examined my face, then smiled.

"Then we'll go over this material together?"

"Cross my heart." The phrase "hope to die" flitted through my mind.

"Deal. This is an oatmeal day." She closed the file and put the computer to sleep.

Win shoveled in breakfast like she'd been starving. She looked up. "I guess I was hungrier than I realized." She grinned at me. "Once we get finished with work, I have a feeling I'll need to be fortified."

Fortified? "I don't, you know, come on too strong, do I?"

"Why would you ask that?"

I shrugged. "It's just...I never initiated sex before you. You'd tell me if you didn't want to make love, wouldn't you?"

"Honey, I have a headache?"

"I'm serious, Win. If you don't want to, you'd tell me. Wouldn't you?"

"Should that ever happen, I promise I'll be honest. But I hope you realize I initiate half the time. Same promise applies to you." She sighed and pushed her bowl away. "I can't multitask like you do. I take my full concentration and focus on one thing. Problems. You. It's futile to flirt when I'm concentrating on something else. That's just the way I am, Sarah."

I raised an eyebrow. "When do we print the pictures?"

"Uh…"

"Is there any way we can view them in a larger format?"

She laughed. "Shit, you're insatiable, Sarah. Not that I'm complaining."

"Are you sure? I get so lost in you, Win. I look at you and I'm off and running. I can't seem to get enough of you and each time I come I feel my love grow."

She wrapped me in a tight embrace. "I feel the same. Sometimes worry begins to nibble."

"I'd step in front of you if a bullet was coming, Win." I blinked away my tears and kissed her. "Let's go read, even if it's my day off."

CHAPTER TWENTY-NINE

Win

"Look at this from Zoe's files," I said. "This is a direct quote. 'We must treat homosexuals as the sex offenders they are.' A homosexual registry? Restrictions on where we can live? What jobs we can work? Fuck him."

"Who said it?" Sarah asked.

"Notation is just J. We'll have to ask Zoe who J is."

"Joshua or James?"

"Maybe. Let's not make assumptions."

"Win, this sounds like one of the ugly emails and letters the *Sentinel* got when Dad got into a verbal fight in the paper about gays. Ask Zoe if Lloyd kept them."

"So the anti-gay hate's been brewing for a while?"

"At least with this guy." Sarah frowned. "We need more context for this interview. Why don't you invite Zoe for lunch?"

I nodded and got on the phone. "She'll be here at one. With files."

"What do we have to feed Zoe?"

"You want me to go away? I thought we were supposed to work this together."

"It was just a question, Sarah."

"Ham sandwiches and split pea soup. Now keep scrolling."

I found a couple of other interesting quotes full of military lingo. I sent them to Nathan and Nolan. "These people are crazy. They don't even have a basic understanding of the Constitution. I would so love to tread on them. Specifically, their necks. Then ship them off to North Sudan."

Sarah glanced at me. Quickly transferred her gaze back to the screen. I meant it. I had little patience for "patriots" who didn't value democracy. I returned to scanning Zoe's notes. What really upset me was how many people in the county felt government was choking them. Or maybe it was a few who were really loud, really hard to tell from this crap.

When we'd finished reading both interviews and leads Zoe was following, I closed the file. "Disgusting."

"Welcome home, Win."

"I have a better appreciation for what coming out cost you publicly. Your bravery astounds me."

She shrugged. "It wasn't bravery, just inability to live a lie." She grinned. "Can we look at the photos now?"

I glanced at my watch. "Almost time for Zoe. Let's get lunch ready. Then, after Zoe leaves…"

Zoe arrived on the dot. We sat down to lunch and general conversation. Like why the hell she'd quit a lucrative career in broadcasting to write for a small town weekly.

"They told me how to dress, how long my hair had to be and pushed me to be provocative. Not just with my appearance, but with my copy. They wanted quicker investigations with less factual content and more insinuation." She stirred her soup. "I'm not that kind of journalist. I started looking for another job about two years before I left."

"But why here?" I asked. "Surely there are still some prestigious newspapers still alive."

"They may be alive for the moment," she said. "But I wonder how much longer they can hang on. It's all going digital and I think the general public believe everything on the Internet should be free."

"Not a good business model," Sarah said. "But I agree with Win. Why here?"

"Lloyd, our editor and publisher, is an old-fashioned journalist who wants old-fashioned journalism from me. Besides, where else would I get to investigate militias with the publisher's blessing? In Chicago, New York or LA, I'd have to do a specific beat. Here I get to cover everything from the Knights of Columbus to murder and get to know people in the process. You never know where a good lead will come from. Plus, the *Sentinel* is on firm financial ground because it's the only place for local news. Now, shut up folks and let me eat."

Back at the computer I pulled up her notes. Zoe sat next to me and Sarah stood behind me with her hands on my shoulders. "First question—who's J?"

Zoe put on her glasses. "Scroll back a bit. Let me get the context." She read the previous entry, then the section I'd marked. "J is for jerks. I'd stopped in at Dog's for dinner and a drink after work. Three guys sat next to me and I was only vaguely aware of them. Then one of them mentioned a meeting of the Rangers and my ears perked up."

"Did you recognize the guys?"

Zoe shook her head.

"Sarah, you have the pics?"

She went to get them.

"Did they have any identifiers on? Uniforms? Company logos? What kind of footwear? Anything you can remember would help."

Zoe closed her eyes. "No cop or military uniforms. One looked like a janitor or something, you know, gray overalls, but he kept his jacket on so I didn't see a logo. The other guy just looked…average. Jeans, work boots, flannel shirt, old bomber jacket. The third looked like an office worker. Gray suit, nothing real expensive, black loafers."

I'd been taking notes. "Great. Haircuts?"

"All short, but the one in overalls could've been a skinhead. He had a cap on."

"Tattoos?"

"Not that I could see. There could've been some on Overalls, but he kept pulling his sleeve down." Zoe opened her eyes. "I couldn't watch them overtly. I was taking notes, sneaking a peak."

"You did great. This is helpful. Really."

Sarah walked over with her laptop and pulled up the two photos. "Either one of these two at the table?"

"Both," Zoe said, without hesitation. "The one on the left is Overalls. The one on the right's Average Joe."

"Did they call the third one by a first name?"

"No. I think he intimidated them. Just an attitude I picked up on and I can't be specific. Sorry."

"They talked about FEMA camps?" I asked. "Like it was true?"

"Overalls and Average Guy did, even thought the Feds would use Camp Atterbury. But Office didn't say much. Kept trying to get back to the plan."

"The plan?" Sarah asked. "What plan?"

"I don't know. The only thing he said when they kept going on about other stuff was the plan would never work if they weren't properly prepared to take action. And that they were already behind schedule."

Sarah looked at me, her eyebrows raised in query.

Zoe checked her watch. "Gotta go. Here's the correspondence from the previous dustup." She laid a thick manila envelope on the desk. "This has been a delightful time and I hope to hell you get these guys for treason and…"

"Send them to North Sudan?" Sarah asked. "That's what Win wants to do."

Zoe gave me thumbs-up.

Sarah walked her out. When she came back in, she closed Zoe's file. "Pictures. Now."

* * *

Sipping her coffee, Sarah stood gazing at the photos I'd printed out yesterday afternoon. A slight frown furrowed her forehead.

"What?" I asked as I joined her. "You don't like the one you chose?"

"No, all three are…breathtaking. I was just wondering about when the girls come."

"Bahar and Dorri?"

She nodded. "I mean, is it going to traumatize them to have two moms? Then seeing these? You know they'll be in our bedroom unless we decide to lock them out."

"Are you getting cold feet?"

"No! I'm really looking forward to meeting them in person."

"We've got a lot of winter to get through. I vote we go ahead and frame them. Hang them in our bedroom for now. When it gets closer to the time, we'll figure it out." I wrapped my arms around her. "You could always hang them in your office."

I got an elbow in my ribs for the suggestion.

"They're Muslim, Win."

"Their family was Sufi. Lost their *turuq*—their teacher—when their village was destroyed. Right now, they don't have any religious affiliation. I've been looking for someone in Bloomington. It'd be a lot easier if they were Buddhist or Hindu." I picked up the photo of the two of us. "I'm going to blow this up to eleven by fourteen. It's so symbolic because of the way we were drawn together. I fought it until you overwhelmed my defenses."

Sarah touched my cheek. "You think the girls will roll with it, with us?"

"They're young. I worry more about static they'll get at school from local kids."

Her frown reappeared. "Me too."

"Take the mountain photo in the bedroom down and put it in the kids' room. I'm going to print some more shots from the Kush. I don't know if it'll make them feel more at home—or miss their homeland more."

"There's so much we're guessing at, Win."

"We'll muddle through—no, we'll do better than that. I can handle the Afghan side. Help them adjust to all of this. You've got the best credentials in the world—your own parents." I traced the line of her jaw with my fingers. "The most important thing for them is to feel loved."

CHAPTER THIRTY

Waterstone stood in front of the Transport Aviation hanger and watched the Eclipse 550 Twin-Engine taxi toward him. *Not what I would've chosen to lead a revolution, but still a spiffy little plane.* When it finally stopped, he picked up his duffel bag and walked toward the door on the side and followed the stairs being pushed to the door.

The white-haired senator motioned him to one of the plush leather seats as an attendant took his duffel. Fastening his seat belt, he surrendered to the softness as it engulfed him. He was weary, but it was dangerous to show any weakness to this man. The constant pressure of working with idiots and then the message that had sent him on a mad dash to Evansville were fast eating up his reserves.

The man maintained silence until they were in the air. "Your evaluation of Kirkland?"

"She's as good as her reputation. I think she's slower with this material because she's always used her language background to analyze intel, and now she's using English and is uncertain of her opponent, sir."

"So we should take her seriously?"

"Definitely sir."

"Weaknesses?"

"Her only weakness is her wife."

"Fuck it, Waterstone, carpet-lickers don't have wives. They're just a bunch of women who want to be men and can't grow one, so they strap it on."

"You asked me her weakness and the only one I can see is Sheriff Sarah Pitt. Together, they're a great team—one I wouldn't hesitate to deploy if they could be flipped."

"They're perverts." He signaled the attendant for drinks. "So what's your plan?"

"Put the sheriff in the crosshairs for real—the nasty letters are a waste of time. Shake her up with a few close calls, but wait until the assault to finish her off."

"And how is that plan coming?"

"If I could bring in a small team, we'd be ready to go within the week. With the Rangers? At least a month, maybe more—that is, if you want a successful endgame."

"Oh, I do. We have further plans for McCrumb County because we've found a high-value target. Ever hear of Ridley Forge?"

"The storage depot for VX gas? Hasn't it been deactivated?"

The senator shook his head. "I want all obstacles, including these women, out of the way." He stood and walked to a cupboard. When he turned around he held several large sheets of paper rolled together. "When you get back to camp, I want you to pick a small team of our best. Build this as a mock-up, work up a plan to successfully implement theft of the gas."

CHAPTER THIRTY-ONE

Sarah

Wednesday, bloody Wednesday, with enough paperwork on my desk to last until the next election. I ripped through as much as I could, then slowed down and concentrated on the active case files. Precious little news on the Rangers and I felt as if we kept coming up against walls that we couldn't get around, jump over or tunnel under. Win and I had made more progress than my whole department and that was depressing.

I made a note to contact Nathan and find what he'd discovered from our new leads. Then I remembered my promise to Win and check about a search on her land. The third thing on my list was to call Dad and see if he'd talk to Dog. In the years since he'd retired, the two had become friends instead of cop and biker bar owner. I glanced at my watch. The courthouse was open and I could question Kay Castle, our Recorder of Deeds. I pushed the files to the side of my desk and grabbed my parka.

"You going somewhere?" Caleb asked as he grabbed his jacket.

"Are you?"

"Yep, wherever you are. So, where are we going?"

I filled him in on the watcher on Foley's Knob. "Nathan's getting sat images, so if he returns we can nab him. But Win had an idea we might be able to fill in a blank if the guy has made a deed search."

"Good thinking," he replied. "I talked to one of the other guys I know at Zelcore. He said Leatherby is universally hated. He thought Leatherby must have pull with somebody in management and pretty far up at that."

I wondered if Mr. Office from Zoe's trio could have a management position at Zelcore. As we paused at the courthouse door, I told him about what Zoe had overheard at Dog's and that I was going to send Dad on a discovery mission. "Do you have a reason to be here, or are you just my shadow."

"Have a couple of warrant requests, but please don't leave until I catch up with you."

I sighed. I didn't think there was a ghost of a chance someone would take a shot at me in the heart of Greenglen, but with crazies it was better to play it safe.

I opened the Recorder's office door and her receptionist popped up from behind the counter. "Hi, Sarah. What can we do you for?"

"Kay in?"

"Sure, go on in."

I tapped on her door and opened it. She looked up and smiled. "What havoc are you investigating this time?"

"Department business." True, but not the whole truth. I explained what I was looking for.

"Yeah, a couple of weeks ago," Kay replied, tapping a pen on her blotter. "He said he was a developer and researched a lot of deeds in that area. Pain in the ass, issued orders like a damn general."

"Name?"

She brought a file up on her computer. "Greg Hall."

"You don't by any chance ask for a driver's license?"

"Yes, and we copy them for the paper file. Let's go out and look."

I followed her to a bank of filing cabinets. "Someday we're going to get all of this computerized." She sighed as she opened a drawer, flipped through the folders and finally pulled one out. She took it over to the counter and skimmed through a series of stapled requests. She handed it to me.

From Zoe's description, I suspected I was looking at the copy of Mr. Office's license. "I'll return it, Kay. But first, I need to run this guy down. Thanks."

* * *

As I returned to my office, I kicked myself for having put this on the back burner so I wouldn't have to think about it. John could've followed up. We'd be two days ahead of where we were now.

"Dollar for your thoughts?" Caleb asked.

"Inflation bites, doesn't it?" I stopped, stamped my boots on the sidewalk. "I should've had John move on this because we'd be two days ahead of where we are now."

Caleb gazed at the sky. "Why didn't you?"

"I…"

"Couldn't delegate?"

I nodded. "I keep trying to let go and loosen the reins. This'll be a lesson for me I won't forget."

"I know you trust our people, so why not delegate?"

I started walking again. "I think it goes back to when I was first elected. We had so many of Mac's people and I didn't trust any of them."

"With good reason," Caleb said. "But most of them are gone and the ones still here seem to have turned the corner away from Mac and toward good policing."

"Maybe it's just habit now. Protecting the department from people who'd abuse the badge. I'm trying to change. Besides, Win is saying the same thing. Loudly."

Caleb held the station door open for me. "Old habits die hard, but drunks can get sober."

"Okay," I said as I stepped inside. "Can you run this Illinois license and send it to Nathan. I want to go out there and see what he's come up with."

"Who're you taking with you?" Caleb asked.

I groaned, inwardly I hoped. "I'll see who's free."

"Leslie," he said with a smile. "She finished up the forensics and is awaiting your call."

I shook my head. "Can't win, can I?"

"Don't even try, Sarah. I'll call Leslie."

I called Nathan and he said to come on out. By the time I hung up, Leslie was waiting for me by the door.

"You know where Nathan lives?"

"Somewhere in the woods," she said. "I assume you can give me directions."

"I don't even get to drive?"

Leslie grinned. "Orders."

As we headed out of town I glanced at Leslie and wondered how her search for a girlfriend "tried and true" was coming. I realized I was shy about asking. Hell.

"So how's the dating scene?"

She glanced at me. "Pretty barren for a while. But I've met a woman who's…interesting. Do you know Deborah Voran?"

My eyebrows popped up. "Lawyer? About my age?"

"Yeah. You think she's too old for me?"

What the hell did I know? Maybe a fifteen year or so age difference wasn't important. Still, it was quite a gap. "How'd you meet her?"

"You do think she's too old for me. But she's smart and funny."

"And good looking."

"Yeah, there's that too." Leslie grinned. "She said a group of professional women, all lesbian, have dinner once a month in Bloomington. She got bored, came over to Ruby's. We, uh, connected, talked like we'd known one another for years. We've gone out twice since. Once to the movies, once to dinner. It's been nice. Different. I've decided I like real dates."

I glanced at her. She was busy scanning the road ahead with a small smile tugging at her mouth.

"Deborah's a good woman. She took off for Harvard Law School after graduation from IU. Came back to take care of her mother a couple of years ago. She talk about her life and times in New York?"

Leslie shook her head. "I get a feeling something traumatic happened there. With a lover. I want to ask her, but…"

"It's not your business unless she tells you." It had been a hard lesson for me to learn, but I had. Mostly. Not that Win had been less than open with me, but I had a good imagination that ended up driving me crazy. "Em says to leave the baggage behind unless you need it to understand where you are now."

"But if there's trauma, shouldn't it be out on the table so I don't tramp all over a sore spot?"

What the hell did I know? "Honestly, Leslie, this is so new between you two and if there's pain in her past, I wouldn't expect anything on the table right now. You need time to build trust." I turned to look at Leslie. "How serious is this for you?"

She frowned. "I don't know yet. I'm going to dinner at her house Friday night. We'll see how that goes."

"Turn right at the next drive and slow down or you'll miss it." I wondered if Leslie would be on duty and ready to concentrate on work Saturday morning.

* * *

"I think you're up against a well-organized group that knows how to hide," Nathan said as he sat at the console. "First, Joshua Leatherby. I went back in the BMV records, just to see if I could find a change of address." Two Indiana license photos appeared on one of the monitors—of two different men, same name, same address, same everything.

"How can this be?"

Nathan pulled up two more licenses, again, two different men, both with the name James McNab. "At a guess, the men we now know as Leatherby and McNab got rid of the two original men and assumed their identities. I can't find any other record of either name. They've disappeared off the map."

"But how, Nathan? These men had to have friends, family, at least people who knew them."

"Both were unemployed loners. Both lived off by themselves, no close neighbors." He swiveled his chair to face me. "I'm running both through all my databases, but I haven't got a hit yet. It would help if we could pinpoint the time when the real identities went missing. Any chance of getting a deputy on a door-to-door in the area?"

"That might tip our hand. How about Dad? I was going to ask him to talk to Dog." I told him what Zoe had uncovered. "He knows how to keep below the radar."

Nathan nodded. "Call him now. I'm getting frustrated, Sarah. This should be a cinch and it isn't. That tells me they've got expertise."

"Expertise in what?"

"Covering their tracks, assuming new identities." He shook his head. "They had to have scouted the area to find both men. How did they find them? They couldn't have been lucky enough to stumble on them by accident."

"Staking out the unemployment office?"

"Maybe. Could you have Lloyd send me the want ads from that period?"

"How about Zoe? She's been on the trail of the Rangers."

"Cool."

"Let me make two calls. I promised Win I'd let her know what's going on. Have you made any progress on the third suspect, Greg Hall and that Illinois license?"

He glanced at another monitor. "Still running the initial check."

I hit Win's speed dial symbol and waited for her to pick up.

CHAPTER THIRTY-TWO

Win

"Any chance these guys could be skinheads?" I asked.

The chief of campus police brushed his mustache. "Not unless they wore wigs. From the description I have, all of the men were shaggy-haired. Let me run you a copy of the complaint, Professor."

"Please, call me Win. I'm an adjunct, not a professor."

He grinned. "I can never tell with academics." He shrugged as he got out of his chair and left the office. He came back, handed me a file. "You say there were two more attacks? They didn't report them?"

"You have to understand, these kids are fragile. Just coming out to themselves, from conservative families, conservative areas. They've been hiding from themselves long enough that they know what kind of shit's going to hit the fan if they come out. They're not going to put their names on a public report."

"You won't give me the names?"

"No. I'll encourage them to talk to you, but that's it." I scanned the report. Nothing new but a partial tattoo. "A snake tattoo?"

"He thought it was a rattlesnake, but only saw a part of it."

Interesting. I'd have to go back and talk to kid. I wondered if it was like the "Don't Tread on Me" rattlers. I closed the file. "We've put in surveillance cameras at the LGBT center. If we find anything interesting, I'll shoot the pics to you."

"Anything we can do to help, holler. You're married to Sarah Pitt?"

I nodded. It felt weird to hear her called by her previous married name.

"Had an opportunity to work with her last year on a drug case, and she's one helluva cop. Anything I can do to help, I will. I mean it."

We shook hands in the vestibule and I headed to my apartment. Make that, lonely apartment. It'd be less lonely with Des, but I'd left her with Sarah this time. Figured she could use a bodyguard while she was home alone.

I walked in the door and started emptying my pockets, discovered I'd left my phone off all day. Three voice mails from Sarah—"Call me," "Call me," "Please call me," and a text that read "Turn on your damn phone, Win."

She picked up on the first ring. Her voice sounded strained. "I was beginning to worry."

"Sorry. I always turn it off in class. Then I went to see the campus police." I told her about the one new clue to identity. "That may tie them into the some of the other hate groups."

"Nathan thinks we're up against a highly organized national group with military expertise. I'm waiting to hear from Dad."

"I hope he's careful. I don't like the sound of this 'highly organized group with military expertise.' We could be talking about a nationwide network ready to make mayhem."

"I know, me too. But he's a master bumpkin and I don't think he'll make waves."

"Still. These are mean bastards. I want Micah to be grandpa to our kids."

I could hear the intake of her breath.

"Can I talk to Des?" I asked.

"You want to talk to the dog when you're talking to your *wife*?"

"Yeah." I tried to keep the grin out of my voice. I made kissy sounds when Des woofed into the phone and made sweet-talk.

"Hell's bells, you should see her tail going. It's a wonder she isn't propelled across the room." Sarah's breathing came down the line for a moment. "I love you, Win. I miss you something crazy."

I swallowed hard. "Two more days. That's all we have to wait. I love you, Sarah. Please stay safe. Please."

* * *

I called the LGBT center the next morning and asked if they could round up the three students for an interview after my classes. They'd let me know. I wanted to see if I could shake any more details from them. Gently. I didn't need to add to their trauma.

On the walk across campus, I called Bill. "Anything new?"

"Morning, Win."

"Good morning, General. Sir. Anything new?"

"It's a good thing you're not in the Corps anymore." Papers shuffled. "We're really hamstrung. FISA courts have gotten so much flack from a certain political party, they're not granting many warrants these days. Still, some patterns are becoming apparent."

"A nationwide network?"

"Yeah. I'm not even going to ask how you figured that out."

"Have you heard from Nolan?"

"Briefly. He's installed at Zelcore, getting the lay of the land."

"I wish I could talk to him. Figure he's safer if I don't."

"You're right. But maybe I can find a way to arrange a meet. Let me work on it."

"I'd appreciate it." I paused on the sidewalk outside the building. "Does a rattlesnake have something to do with this?"

Silence.

"Like the "Don't tread on me" snake?" I asked.

More silence. "Jesus, Win. You're still running your own ops, aren't you?"

"I asked a simple question, Bill."

"Maybe. We need to schedule a meeting. Soon."

"Weekend. When I'm back home."

"Does this meet include Sarah?"

"The letters that started all of this were aimed at her. She belongs in this investigation. It could help save her life, Bill."

"Okay. I'll give you a call Saturday. Maybe we can meet at Nathan's. Let you know."

I spent the day speaking Tajik, keeping my mind on teaching. Not that I didn't worry about Sarah. We needed a briefing from Bill. A real one. When class was over, I talked briefly with Sarah. And Des. I knew she thought I was crazy, but Des and I had bonded early on. I needed to reassure her doggie soul that I'd be back this time. Maybe she needed to reassure me too.

I also met with two of the kids who'd been attacked. Shook out a few more details. The third kid had left campus. Quit school. Shit. I couldn't let the haters win. I just couldn't.

It wasn't until I was almost back in McCrumb County Friday night when I picked up the tail.

CHAPTER THIRTY-THREE

Sarah

"Where are you?" I tried to keep my voice calm and in charge, but I knew Win could hear the panic.

"It's okay, Sarah. I called dispatch first thing. Two units are close. Heading my way with sirens. I need to put you on speaker."

I could hear the click as she set the phone in its holder. Then a crunch of metal and an oof from Win. "What's going on?"

"They're just getting a bit pushy," Win growled. "Fucking bullies. They're going to be sorry they ever started this."

"Are they trying to run you off the road?" I heard the screech of brakes and then the collision of metal against metal. "Win!"

"I'm okay. The other guys aren't. Deputy's almost here."

I heard a door open and a siren drawing closer. Then voices, one of them Win's cussing. Where the hell was she? Was she hurt? What the hell was I doing here fixing dinner, and with the fire burning cheerily in the fireplace? I should've picked her up. I shouldn't have let her go to Bloomington.

"Situation's under control, Sarah. Guys are in the ditch with their truck. Both deputies are here. They'll take them in. So, as soon as photographs are finished, I'm on my way home."

"What—never mind. How far away are you?"

"Bastards crunched my truck good, but it's drivable. Fuckers." She slammed a door. "Give me forty-five minutes. One unit's taking the suspects in, the other's escorting me home."

"Hurry home, Win. Be safe."

I paced with Des at my side until I heard her truck on the drive. With weapon in hand, I eased back a shutter and watched her truck pull in. I was waiting for her at the door, Glock tucked in my waistband at my back. She stepped inside with a grin and said, "Honey, I'm home."

Des must've thought her new name was "honey" because she swarmed Win.

"You scared the bejeebers out of me." I pulled her into my arms, relieved to feel her body close to mine.

"You want to talk about this now? Or eat dinner? I'm starved."

"Just let me hold you for a while." I felt her hands on my back.

She stepped back. "Uh, I think you ought to disarm before you end up with a bullet in your ass." She took off her parka and shoulder holster, and I slipped the Glock in a drawer.

"I guess we should eat, but can't we talk about what happened while we eat?" I started dishing up the lamb stew.

Win started to put together the salad. "Not much to tell. I picked them up close to the McCrumb County border. Don't think they followed me from Bloomington. They had one headlight misaligned. I would've noticed it if they'd been behind me the whole way." She grinned. "Now they've got no headlights."

I carried the bowls to the table and went back for the Italian bread. "So, what happened?"

"As soon as I picked them up, I called dispatch. Then I called you. Either we hit the section of the road they'd planned or they thought I was on the phone too much. They hit the back of my truck. You heard the rest."

"I heard brakes screeching and a collision—what did you do?"

"You ever had an evasive driving course?" Win asked.

I shook my head. "Just the pursuit classes."

"We'll sign you up for the next one."

"Who's 'they' and where's it offered?"

"If I told you, I'd have to kill you," Win said with a grin. She got serious again. "I don't know if this is related to you or the bullies I've been looking for in Bloomington."

"The LGBT center? They followed you? Who are these guys?"

"I'll call the center in the morning. Have them send the surveillance stream. See if anybody was hanging around when I left. See if either of the two creeps from tonight were there." Win broke off a piece of bread and sopped up the remainder of the stew. "We can see if they match our three brigands."

"You don't know?"

"I really didn't get a good look at them. Their faces were still in the airbags. Then the deputy took over." She looked up at me. "Couldn't you make me a reserve deputy or something? I have a carry permit. I've never felt so impotent in my life."

"You'd have to know all the statutes and procedures."

"You'll give me the test?"

I smiled at her. "Which test?"

* * *

Win was still in the shower when our escort showed up in the morning. Even though Des's tail was wagging, I followed the deputy's exit from the squad car before I put the Glock back in its holster and opened the door to a very sleepy Leslie who accepted my offer of coffee with exaltation.

"I gather it was a good night," I said as I handed her a mug.

Leslie blushed bright red. Nodded.

"Are you okay to drive?"

Leslie nodded again.

"You came here directly from Deborah's?"

Still not looking at me, she nodded and took a gulp of hot coffee.

It was interesting for me to see such a self-possessed young woman so discombobulated. Must've been one hell of a night.

Win entered the kitchen in a partially open robe, saw Leslie and quickly pulled it to her. "Uh, morning, Leslie. I'll grab coffee. Go change."

As Win rapidly retreated down the hall, I switched my gaze from her lovely backside to Leslie. Leslie was watching Win. I sighed and sipped my coffee.

"She's stunning," Leslie said. "Not that you aren't—but I get to watch you at work."

It was my turn to blush. "I didn't know we had that kind of relationship, Leslie."

"Oh, we don't. It's appreciation. Like looking at a great painting." She ducked her head again. "Shit, you understand what I mean, don't you?"

"I've never thought of myself as a painting."

"Oh, man, I'm just digging myself in deeper, aren't I?" She leaned against the counter. "It's not just your body I like to watch, it's the way you handle yourself—issue orders, solve problems. Stuff like that."

"I'm glad I'm not just a sexual object to you." Since she was still looking into her mug, I didn't disguise my smile. I didn't think it was possible, but she reddened further.

Win walked in fully dressed. "I suggest we go directly to Nathan's. He's pulling all the threads together. But he asked we hold off until ten. I think he had a late night."

"Okay, I'll tell dispatch. Leslie, go to bed—first door on the right. Try and get some sleep or you'll be a zombie today."

She finished her coffee and headed toward our bedroom. "On top of the comforter, Leslie," I said as she hesitated at the door. She saluted and went inside.

Win took my belt and pulled me to her. "What's going on?"

"She was appreciating you, specifically your body, and I gave her a hard time."

Win smiled. "Nice to know there's still something to appreciate. If she told you that, it means it's harmless." She kissed me. "While I do admire your body, it's not in that pure sense. Not disinterested. Very interested."

CHAPTER THIRTY-FOUR

Win

Sarah had been tempted to leave Leslie at home, asleep. Not a military attitude. If you chose to play through the night, you also chose to suffer the consequences. I'd smacked Leslie hard on her foot and hustled her out of bed. Handed her a travel mug and her coat. "Work's calling," I'd said. "You need to build up your stamina."

She blushed as red as Sarah said she did. I laughed. Pushed her out the front door. "I'm driving Sarah's SUV. She's riding shotgun. Finish your coffee."

By the time we got to Nathan's, Leslie was a bit more awake. When I walked in, every monitor in the place was alive. Chomping data in a two-hundred-year-old cabin. Enough to throw anyone into a psychotic state but he seemed to see it all as a whole.

He sat down at his console. "A few things are coming together, but there're still a lot of holes. These are the two punks from last night, Win. Recognize them?"

I studied the mug shots, tried to imagine their faces without the battering they'd taken when their truck ended up in the ditch. "The one on the left looks like McNab."

"That's what his license said. The kid on the right is Kenneth Salie. Twenty-two. Sealed juvenile record, but he's had a couple of arrests for battery in Bloomington." He tapped a key and the arrest record came up.

"That's outside Ruby's," I said. "We need to check, but I'll bet those were drag show nights." I copied down the dates. "Where does this guy live?"

"Used to live right outside of Bloomington, but his current address is in McCrumb County. It's an RD number not far from Logan Station."

"Interesting," Sarah said. "Not far from where Leatherby and McNab live, a damn nest of vipers."

"That may be truer than you know, but let's wait on that stuff." Again, he tapped a couple of keys and a younger version of the real Joshua Leatherby came up. Complete with his arrest record from Kentucky.

"You found him," Sarah said. "Shit, look at that rap sheet—he didn't stop at battery. I bet with the B & Es he was stalking. Have you found any of the victims? Done any work on them?"

"The women seem to have disappeared, Sarah. Could've married outside the area, but there's no further trace of them. I didn't want to hack Social Security unless there's real need."

"I don't know what we could get from them that would help this investigation," Sarah said. "I wonder if McNab came from Kentucky too."

"When I found Leatherby, I searched. Nothing."

"How do you do that, Nathan. With your own face recognition program?" I asked.

"Yeah. It's a little more, um, agile than the government program." He grinned up at me. "Enhanced a bit with what Bill gave me." He hit another key. "Here's the stream from the LGBT center. We got two hits." They popped up. "Salie and an as yet unidentified man."

"Unless Salie wore a wig, my money for the attacks is on the unidentified man," I said. "At least from what the victims told me."

"Am I just really thick this morning?" Leslie asked. "I have no idea what you're talking about, or who."

I put my arm around her shoulders. "Thick, probably. But I bet you haven't heard most of this. To try and do a simple rundown, we got onto Leatherby and McNab when we were trying to figure out who was writing the letters. But that's not really who they are. They took over the identities of two local men who have since disappeared. We just found Leatherby's real name: William Robert Underwood, probably known as Billy Bob. We're still searching for McNab's real name and where he came from. Okay?"

She nodded, taking notes furiously.

I told her about the attack on the students from the LGBT center.

"The unidentified one, the longer-haired guy, could be one of the stoners?"

"Gives a whole new meaning to the word," Sarah said with a grin.

"Yeah," I said. "I think we'd better start calling people by the names they're known by in the county or we'll all be confused. Anyway, we have one more suspect. Greg Hall. He went over the plat map that contains my land. We tracked him through the Recorder's Office. Anything new on him?"

"I think that's an alias," Nathan said. "But I haven't found a trail to his real name. Still working on it."

"Wow, I had no idea," Leslie said. "So you think the three guys, Leatherby, McNab and Hall, are connected here in the county. Then the two mug shots could be connected to what's going on here—and might be connected to the stoning in Bloomington?"

"Succinct and well done," I said.

Sarah's phone buzzed and she walked over to the window to take the call. "We need to get back to the station," she said as she stuck the phone in her pocket. "When are you available to continue this, Nathan?"

"Anytime, just let me know."

She gave him a hug, then went to put her boots on.

When we got back in the SUV, Sarah turned around to the backseat. "You tell Deborah if she keeps you up all night again, I'll come gunning for her." She turned back around and a big smile lit her face.

I looked in the rearview mirror. Leslie was mortified and fire engine red yet again. "If Sarah gives you any static, just let me know. She's not going gunning for anybody but the bad guys."

"I'll talk to you at home," Sarah said, smiling primly and folding her hands in her lap.

* * *

The smell of burning diesel fuel and tires made me think about Iraq. I shifted my attention from the horrendous mangle of eighteen wheelers, trucks and cars. I scanned the nearby hill just off the interstate for snipers. I could shift the focus from protecting troops to protecting Sarah.

We'd sped to the station, dropped off Leslie so she could pick up Vincente and the crime scene van. We switched to a squad car and Sarah turned on lights and siren. Floored the gas pedal. We'd seen the smoke rising on the interstate from a half-mile away. I'd helped where I could. Got people out, carried them to safe areas along the highway. Now all the first responders in southern Indiana were here. I was left to wonder what Nathan hadn't told us. Something about vipers would be my guess. Vipers?

We left midafternoon. "Back to Nathan's?"

She shook her head. "I've got to begin paperwork on the accident. Try again in the morning?"

"I'll call him while you slave away." Ask him about vipers.

I did and he was noncommittal. "There's more stuff coming in, Win. Let me try and put it together. We need as complete a picture as possible or we won't know what we don't know."

When we finally both got home, I let Sarah work on dinner while I built a fire, and to get rid of the stink of burning diesel fuel, showered and changed clothes.

I walked into the kitchen. "Smells good. Except for your *eau de feu*. What can I do so you can go shower?"

She sniffed her sleeve. "Casserole's in the oven with about twenty minutes to go. Put the bread in ten minutes before you take the casserole out. Make the salad. Okay?"

"Sir, yes sir."

She grinned and smacked my butt. I almost delayed dinner right then, but the smell on Sarah's hair and clothes was too strong for desire to overcome memory.

"Do you remember Deborah Voran?" Sarah asked as we ate.

"Went to high school with us?"

"IU too, except you left. She went to Harvard Law, joined some important firm in New York and came back home a couple of years ago to take care of her mother."

"You're asking me about her because?" I stopped before I took another bite. "She's Leslie's new heartthrob?"

Sarah nodded.

"You don't like her?"

"No, I like her a lot and was glad to see her come home. She works for a local firm now. I'm just thinking about the age gap."

"That's their business, Sarah."

"Not when it cripples my CSI's abilities. I've never seen Leslie anything but bright and bushy-tailed."

"I'd say that young woman was suffering from over bushy-tailness," I said. Tried not to laugh. Unsuccessfully.

Sarah sighed, then a small smile formed.

"When we first got physical, you were off on sick leave. Otherwise somebody might've complained about your attention to duty."

"Some? Damn, Win, I still have trouble concentrating on work when I think of you."

"I'm glad," I said with a smile. "Means we're still cooking."

"Her woolgathering could be dangerous."

"Can you change her schedule? If Deborah's still working, she only has weekends off. Remember our five days together? How much better it is when you take two days off?"

"Oh yeah, to both. But the CSIs set up their schedules together. Vincente has a family and Leslie offered to take weekends since his kids play sports."

"Early shift on Saturdays? How often do teams play on Sunday? Or don't you want Leslie devoted to anything but work?" I watched her as I finished up. "She's not you, Sarah. Not yet. You're struggling right now to find some kind of balance. It'll be harder when the kids get here. Help her find balance now."

* * *

When I woke the next morning, Sarah was gone from our bed. I smelled coffee brewing, bacon frying. The clock said it was five thirty. I thought about staying in bed, ambushing Sarah when she came to wake me. Then thought about being a responsible adult. I got up.

She glanced at me as I walked in, poured me a mug and kissed me on my forehead.

"Who's your escort this morning? Leslie? You want to prove to her you can have a healthy sex life and still be raring to go to work the next morning?" I asked.

"You are my escort," she said. "Leslie worked until about an hour ago on the accident scene."

"Talk about a zombie. I'll bet Deborah doesn't get any loving today."

"Win!"

"So why are we up this early?"

"I woke up and knew I couldn't get back to sleep, so I did what my mom used to do. Cook."

"What are you worrying about?"

"What the hell I'm doing! How am I going to be a mom when I can't even guarantee when I'll be home from work?"

"Ah." I untied her robe and slid my hands underneath. "Let me tell you from experience. It doesn't matter if a mom's there or not—if she's not loving you."

"You make absolutely no sense."

"Think about it, Sarah. May not make sense to you now, but its wisdom will come to you in time." I moved my hands to her breasts. "Now, let's eat before I carry you away. Don't want to burn the bacon."

I watched her scramble the eggs. Drank my coffee. Sarah was fighting a battle I couldn't join. She had to decide for herself how much she wanted to put into being sheriff. How much she wanted to put into building our family. How much guilt she could deal with either decision.

We were about to leave when the trip wire at the base of the drive pinged. We both drew our weapons, stationed ourselves on either side of the door. Sarah peeped out the window. We heard the soft purr of a car and a door slam closed.

Sarah holstered her Glock. "Company of the friendly variety." She opened the door and stood back until a wiry woman came through.

"Sorry to visit this early, but I didn't want to come to the station because it might give me a bad rep with my clients."

They embraced. Then Sarah turned toward me. "You remember Win. Deborah Voran."

We took a moment to introduce Deborah to Des.

"Jesus, Win, you haven't changed a bit," Deborah said, straightening up. "Since this is the first time I've seen you together, congratulations on your wedding."

"Thanks," I said. "But I didn't think you even noticed me in high school. We sure didn't travel in the same circles."

"No, you were one of the Three Musketeers. I was jealous as hell— you guys seemed so close, so solid. The crowd I ran with would stab me in the back on the slightest whim. Damn good thing I didn't realize I was lesbian then."

I grinned. All of that was true.

"So, what're you doing with my deputy?" Sarah asked.

"That's what I came for, to apologize. It was our first time and she surprised me with her, ah…"

"I get the idea," Sarah said. "You only have weekends free?"

"Pretty much. I don't always work at the firm during the week, but if I don't keep up, I'm not prepared for court or meetings. Why?"

"I'll see if I can get Leslie Sunday off—but no guarantees. Police regs don't take into account affairs of the heart. It is an affair of the heart, isn't it?"

Deborah nodded. "It's early yet and things might not gel. But Leslie's...like a soft wind in spring. I never expected...well, you know."

Sarah looked at me. Smiled. "No, I never expected to fall in love with a woman, and surely not this woman."

"So I'm forgiven?" Deborah asked.

"Just don't let it happen again," Sarah said, all sharp edges now. "Leslie needs to be alert when she's on duty, and if she's not, it could get her or another officer wounded or killed— which is a hell of a hard thing to live with."

Deborah nodded. "The other thing I wanted to tell you is some of the women in our dinner club are getting threats like those you've gotten."

"How do you know about that? Not through pillow talk?"

"No! Judge Wallington. I gather he'd heard something and I thought it was common knowledge."

"It's not, so don't repeat it. These women got letters? How can I get hold of them?"

"I'll gather them up and drop them off to you. Okay?"

"Quickly, please," Sarah said.

"How many women?" I asked.

"Six at least."

"Well hell."

CHAPTER THIRTY-FIVE

Sarah

I walked Deborah to her car. "I meant what I said about Leslie—don't put her in jeopardy. She's got a bright future ahead of her with the skills she's developing."

She turned and examined my face. "Not everything's about the job, Sarah. I learned that the hard way."

I waited for her to continue.

"Lizzy and I were together nineteen years and eighteen of them, work came first for both of us. When she got sick, my priorities shifted. Now my only regret is that they shifted so late. My only consolation is that we had such loving times that last year."

"I'm sorry, Deb, I didn't know. We really lost contact, didn't we?"

"Priorities, Sarah." She opened the driver's door. "Leslie's really opened some windows in my stuffy old house. I hope they stay open. I hope I've learned how I want to live my life. If I think our enthusiasm is putting her in danger, I'll change my behavior—but I won't change my hope for something long-term for us."

"All I can say is that I hope you find what I've found with Win."

She grinned. "Love, ain't it grand!"

I was frozen by the time I got in and headed straight for the coffeepot. "Deborah's a tad giddy."

"We should have them over for dinner some night," Win said as she refilled her mug.

"Leslie's my deputy and I can't invite her to dinner."

"Why not?"

"Because I'm her superior at work. It'd be seen as favoritism."

Win looked away. "Well, we could have all your deputies and significant others over in shifts. Of course, Deborah may not want to accompany Leslie as her significant other. It doesn't look like she's out in the county. Personally, I'd like to reconnect. She seems very different from the driven snot I remember from high school."

"Driven snot?" I asked. I'd never thought of her in those terms.

"Ms. Perfect." Win shrugged. "Just an idea. Doesn't matter."

Win was pissed. Did she feel this was another incursion of my job into the life we were building? Was it? Did I keep all my deputies too distant?

Our ride in was silent, Win staring out her window. As we walked into the station, I picked up my messages, walked into my office with Win trailing and closed my door.

"This is new territory for me, Win. Give me a break and let me think about it."

"Don't take too long."

"Dad always had the department for a cookout in the summer, but I don't remember him inviting deputies over for dinner."

"Skip it, Sarah. It's not important." She slumped on the couch and yawned.

"Don't do that, Win. Don't shut me out."

She sat up straight. "I marched into your territory and I'm sorry. I hereby formally withdraw." She gave a big, noisy sigh. "I just want us to have a community. A broad community, not just Micah and Nathan, though I thank our stars every day for them. I want our kids to have a community here. Plenty of aunties they can go to when they're mad at us."

Sometimes Win took my breath away with her sheer beauty, inside as well as out. She'd been thinking about the kids, I'd been thinking about departmental decorum. "Maybe dinner at Ruby's could be a start."

She turned on her high beam smile. "Atta girl."

* * *

My preliminary interstate accident reports were on their way to the state police, so we headed out to Nathan's. I'd handed the keys to Win as a peace offering, or maybe just so I could try to wade through the swamp of my feelings. I felt pulled in two directions and couldn't see how I could just walk away from the duties I had sworn, both to the office and to Win.

Maybe I was just being Sheriff Drama. I sighed, leaned my head back and closed my eyes.

"You're supposed to be riding shotgun," Win said. "Not napping."

I straightened up. "I was thinking."

"Sarah, you don't have to make any black-and-white decisions. Not all at once. We'll take the challenges as they come. Together." She took the turn at Nathan's drive and pulled into the clearing. "Let's use these opportunities to grow closer and stronger. I told you a long time ago—I know 'sheriff' is in your DNA. So we have to learn to live with it. We can, you know."

"I'm trying to compromise, but I feel like I'm in a booby-trapped jungle, Win. I take one wrong step and I'm swinging upside down."

"I'll come cut you down. Promise." She squeezed my hand. "Let's go get the skinny from Nathan."

Nathan stood in the doorway as we got out and by the time we'd walked inside, he was already seated at his console. "Lots to report, some of it speculative. Let's go because I really need to strap on my snowshoes and get away from this stuff.

"I printed out everything I could find on our local suspects—there, box on the table. I'll just highlight and you can go through the details on your own time."

Nathan looked weary and I wondered how long he'd been at this without breaks or sleep. The printed files took up half a banker's box. "Will do."

"First, I found Greg Hall, our third impostor. Born Aloysius Brennan in Moscow, Montana. Moved to Algoma, Idaho when he was in eighth grade."

"Grew up in Idaho?" Win asked.

"Yeah. Kind of a wild child, got sent off to military school for the last two years of high school. Did a tour in the army, but didn't re-up. Hooked up with a militia a few years ago. It's all in the file." An image of a snake, coiled and ready to strike, came up on the monitor. "But the thing I've been working on is a group called 1776 Corps. I got onto them from some emails they sent Greg—encrypted—that he stupidly forwarded unencrypted. Orders from them and copies of all that is in his file." He retied his hair at the nape of his neck. "I think there's a hell of a lot more to this group, but the digging is hard. They've got layers of safeguards. I'm going to back away for a bit."

"Go snowshoeing," Win said.

They knuckle-bumped and looked at me.

"All right. We'll take the files, go over them and tomorrow, Win, we'll go hit the trails. In the meantime, Nathan, please be careful. If you've exposed something hidden…subterranean, you could be a potent threat to them. You want to come stay with us?"

"Not necessary Sarah, but thanks. This place is wired better than Win's and I have backups for the backups."

"You have a defense system for an RPG?" Win asked.

CHAPTER THIRTY-SIX

Win

We got back to the station without incident. I could tell the constant vigilance was taking more of a toll on Sarah than she was willing to admit. She shooed me upstairs to the detectives' loft with the files.

"Can I do anything to help?" John Morgan asked when I dumped the box on an empty desk.

I filled him in on what Nathan had done. "We need to collate these. See where these guys intersect—places, contacts. All of that."

"How do you want to do it, Win?"

I thought a minute. Didn't want this stuff on a computer, no matter how secure. "You have a free whiteboard?"

"Low tech on purpose?"

"You got it."

He went to get one. As he rolled it into place, he asked, "Where's Des? I've still got a couple of treats I've been saving for her."

"She's at home on guard, hating it. But I just want some protection that's not dependent on electricity." I rolled my shoulders. "If this wasn't a real threat, I'd be in deep shit."

"You were a marine—you came back with PTSD? Or shouldn't I ask?"

"Screaming case. I got help. It's better now...but I have to stay aware of it."

"This stress can't be good for you, with Sarah at the center of the threats." He crossed his arms. Rested his butt on his desk. "Maybe I shouldn't have said anything. I don't mean to pry."

"I appreciate your concern. You have a question, you ask it. I can deal with that. If it's too much, I'm real good at telling people to butt out." I grinned at him. "I'm as worried about the stress on Sarah as my own. At least I recognize mine."

"She does have a tendency to power through things. Sometimes I wonder how she does it."

"So do I." I pulled the first file. "Let's start on these. A sense of progress lessens my anxiety."

Sarah didn't show until quitting time. We'd filled the board with names, dates and places, all connected with lines and arrows. She frowned as she looked at it. "All of these guys were in Idaho?"

"At one time or another, probably a training camp. We need to ask Nathan's contacts if they know where the camp is."

"And what they know about it?" Sarah asked.

"Yeah. But I bet it's not much. They run these militia camps like an army base—hard to get in or out."

What I didn't say was that if our guys had been trained in one of these camps, we had a bunch trouble on our hands.

*　*　*

When we got home, I dug out my burn phone and called Bill. "Thought we were supposed to meet yesterday?"

"Not possible."

Why not? I didn't ask because I knew I wouldn't get an answer. I told him what we'd uncovered and asked him about 1776 Corps.

"We've been tracking them about ten years," he said. "Potentially nasty group, but so far they've managed not to break any laws."

"Any way I can get your files on them?"

"No, I just can't because your security clearance went bye-bye when you left." He breathed a heavy sigh. "I know I've done it in the past, but Congress is on our butt. How about I shoot them to Nathan?"

"Fine. Uh, any chance you could provide Nathan with some extra security?"

"You think he needs it?"

"Just a niggle, Bill. But if I'm hearing you right, if they discover he's been snooping their patch..."

"See what I can do, Win. I suppose you don't want him to know."

"My first inclination is to say no, I don't. But when you get everything set, I think you'd better tell him. Avoid unforeseen consequences."

"Roger that. One more bit of business. I was going to set up a meet with you and Nolan. How does Bloomington sound? Thursday night?"

"Fine. Where?"

"There's a bar on the outskirts, the Olive in the Bottom."

"Sounds like a great place for the nineteen-fifties."

"It was a dive back then, worse now. But a very empty place early. I'll get there around five, you follow at five thirty and we'll wait for him."

"Do I have to come on to you like a cheap hooker?"

"Well, that'd be fun. How about a clandestine affair?"

"In your dreams. See you then."

"Who are you coming on to like a cheap hooker?" Sarah asked, walking into the living room in sweats. "Do I need to hear about this?"

"Bill. Undercover meet with Nolan. I don't have to be a hooker."

"I can't imagine you as a hooker."

"I'll take that as a lack of imagination on your part. Or do you mean I'd be a high-class call girl?" I held my hand up. "Never mind. Build a fire and I'll change. Then we'll snuggle."

When I returned, Sarah was coming from the kitchen with two beers.

"I can't imagine a more perfect place and time," I said as I settled on the couch. I took the beer and pulled Sarah down on my lap. I buried my face in her chest. Held her tight. "Heaven right here and now."

"What's wrong, Win?"

"What?" I released my tight hold. "I can protect you when you're in my arms. Like I'm protected in yours."

She leaned back. "Is the stress getting to you?"

"Is it getting to you?"

Sarah leaned into me. Whispered in my ear. "Yes."

I rubbed her back more. Up and down, up and down. "Don't try to power through. John said that today. That you power through the rough stuff. But that just means you push the stuff down."

She slipped off my lap and picked up her beer. "You've seen horrible stuff and so have I. All I know how to do is keep after the perpetrator until I put him behind bars. Prepare the best case I can for the prosecutor. Is that powering through?"

"Yeah." I slipped my arm around her shoulder. "You never think about the energy it drains from you, trying not to think about it. Not remember it after it's over."

"I can't dwell in the past, Win. There's always something new on my plate every day I go to work. Gotta keep on truckin'. If I dwelt with the images I've seen, I couldn't function. I can't bring that stuff to the surface."

"Don't box both of us up in silence, Sarah. Just promise me you'll talk to me when you feel the pressure."

She leaned her head on my shoulder. "I can try, but no promises."

"We can't live in fear. It's moments like this that sustain us." I wrapped my arms around her and kissed her. "There's this beautiful Persian word. *Jaaneman*. Used like 'sweetheart' or 'darling.' In a kind of basic translation, it means 'soul of me.' That's who you are to me. My soul."

CHAPTER THIRTY-SEVEN

Sarah

I tried to lie quietly at Win's side and to pretend I was asleep. I watched snowflakes drift down outside the window, a slow waltz in white on black. I contained the feelings I'd accumulated as a cop in a small subterranean room of my psyche. If I didn't, I was terrified of my actions at the next incident, the next crime scene, the next time I had a criminal at the end of my Glock.

I had to contain the anger, the rage and the pain in its underground chamber or I'd never be able to pick up the Glock again. Talk about the pressure, Win? Sure, I could do that. But what caused the pressure-cooker? I had to keep that small room locked and guarded. I had to.

As the sky began to lighten, I fell asleep, finally worn out by my interior battle.

When I woke, the sun was high in the sky and I felt befuddled. I slipped into my sweats and walked into the living room. Win worked on her computer, totally engrossed until I moved into her peripheral vision.

"What time did you finally fall asleep?" she asked without looking up.

"Any coffee left?"

"Thermal carafe on the counter."

Mug in hand, I moved behind her to see what she was working on. I sipped and tried to focus on the screen, but Win was scrolling too fast for me to follow. "What's this?"

"Some intel on 1776 Corps that Nathan sent."

"This is my day off, Win."

"You just woke up." She stopped scrolling. "You want to hear what MCIA dug up? Or should I wait until Wednesday after class to call you? Tell you what these reports say?"

"Stop with the sarcasm, Win. Let me get some coffee in me, and breakfast too."

Win took my free hand, laced her fingers through mine. "Coffee, food, back to bed—is that your plan for the day?"

"Sounds good to me." I leaned down and kissed her. "Doesn't sound awful to you, does it?"

"Go shower. I'll make your breakfast."

When I settled down to eat, awake after my shower, I watched Win across the table. The frown lines on her forehead told me she was distracted by the train of thought I'd interrupted.

"You hear anything from Micah?"

"He said he was taking it slow and didn't want to ruffle feathers. It's a pretty closed community down there and, according to Dad, it's way too easy to step in shit and track it all over the county."

Win's frown deepened. "What about Deborah? Anything from her?"

I shook my head.

Win let out a gusty breath. "No wonder they're ten steps ahead of us."

I returned my attention to eating. I wasn't getting involved in policing, at least not this early in the day. Win had cheered when I told her about taking another day off and now, it seemed, all she wanted me to do with it was work.

Win took her mug to the sink, rinsed it out and returned to her computer. I couldn't figure out if I was angry with Win or myself. I wanted the pressure off, the threat to end. So why the hell couldn't I make the effort to work with her, even on my day off?

I figured I could at least call Dad, see if he'd made any progress. I'd just hung up the dishtowel when the warning system beeped. I grabbed my Glock and took up a post by the shutter. I eased it open and waited.

"All clear," I said when Deborah's vehicle pulled into the clearing. Des didn't even get up from her place in front of the fire.

I opened the door for her while Win put away her weapon. "Morning. What's up?"

Deborah walked in, a large manila envelope in hand. I reached to take her coat. "I can't stay, but I knew you'd want these. I called all our dinner club members and found out most of them had received these damn letters. That's almost thirty women, Sarah."

"Damn." I took the envelope.

"Can you make a list of those who haven't?" Win asked.

"Sure," Deborah said. "Can I drop it off on my way home? I'm due in court."

Win nodded. "One quick question—how formal or informal is this group? I mean, do you take anybody who wanders in? Do you pay dues? Have officers?"

"No dues, no officers," Deborah said. "But membership is only by invitation. A lot of these women aren't out-out."

"If you get time, can you make us a membership list? Think about why those particular women didn't get threats? You know, haven't attended in a while or left before dessert."

"Why don't you just come for dinner?" I asked.

"Uh, I'm expected home for dinner tonight," Deborah said.

"Shit, Sarah," Win said. "Screw favoritism—this is work."

I took a deep breath. "Why don't you call Leslie and ask her to come too."

"Wasn't exactly what I had in mind for tonight, but if we can make it early?"

"Five?"

Deborah nodded. "See you then."

* * *

"Okay Win, I surrender. Tell me about this corps—like the Marine Corps, right?"

"Spelling-wise, yes. Intent, no." She opened the file. "You don't have to do this now. Seems like one minute I'm pushing you to leave work at work, the next I'm pulling you into this mess. Sorry for the mixed message but I'm used to dealing with intel as it comes in."

I put my hands on her shoulders. "I trust your judgment, so let's get to it. Maybe we'll get some playtime later."

Win pulled me onto her lap, kissed me and smiled. "We get through this and you can take a nap. You need it before fixing dinner."

"Nap time for both of us?"

She grinned again and brought up the file. I felt the heat of her hand on my stomach and found it hard to concentrate on the screen. I laced our fingers together and began to read the reports.

Forty minutes later, Win closed the file. She bit her lip and frowned. "I'll bet there's a hell of a lot more we don't know than we do. They remind me of an octopus with tentacles reaching all over the country. It's squirted its ink so we can't see anything more than the outline."

Win sounded weary, so I put my arm around her shoulders. "Octopus? I thought you would've used the snake as an image."

"You're a genius." She picked up the phone, then put it back down. "Maybe I need to do a little reconnoitering first."

"For what?"

"Sarah, these guys need money. Think of the American money behind Shamsi's acquisition of weapons. Fuck, it might be the same group. That's another thread we need to find.

"But the question is, how is the group funded? Is it personally financed by some billionaires like the Koch brothers? Or do they make money? How? Ask their followers for contributions? What other support systems do they have? There's got to be some. Finance, media. What I'm wondering is if they've used snakes as some part of the names or logos."

"How the hell do you begin to look for that?"

"Hell if I know." She shut the computer down. "Let's go nap on it."

* * *

I could see Win's mind was still puzzling through those questions as we made dinner. I surrendered to slicing, dicing and chopping. I didn't even know where to begin to discover this kind of national conspiracy. Or was there one? Could what we faced simply be a local backlash to local politics? Was Win used to looking for complicated plots and so she saw one here? Yet Nathan seemed to think the locals were receiving orders from…someone, somewhere else.

A car came up the drive at exactly five. I watched Deborah reach for Leslie's hand as they walked to the front porch. I wondered if she'd feel so free if I was the old Sarah, the straight Sarah. If she'd even have told me about the letters.

"Hey," Win said as she opened the door. "Let me take your coats."

Deborah unwrapped her scarf and unzipped her long, quilted coat. "Smells delicious in here."

Leslie handed her uniform jacket to Win with a little bob of her head.

"You want to eat first, then talk?" I asked.

"I'm starving," Deborah said. "Missed lunch today. Okay with you, Leslie?"

"Sure." She ducked her head.

Win slung an arm around Leslie's shoulders. "Weird, huh? Having dinner with the boss."

Leslie grinned. "You better believe it."

"Remember, she's a woman just like you. Puts her uniform pants on one leg at a time."

Saved by the oven timer, I blushed and turned to the kitchen to get everything on the table.

Win opened the wine and poured three glasses. "Who's driving?"

"I am," Deborah said. "One glass is okay, isn't it?"

Win nodded as I pulled the casserole in all its bubbling, golden cheese glory from the oven. Conversation was general as we ate, but I could see Leslie was still uncomfortable. I grinned at her. "Boss is a pretty good cook, eh?"

She grinned back. "Super. Best lasagna I've ever had."

"You're lucky I didn't cook," Win said. "All I know how to make are Middle Eastern dishes. Mom and I had a continuing war when I was young. Resulting in my banishment from the kitchen when I was eleven."

Leslie eased into being a tad more comfortable.

As we sat in the living room with coffee and I tried to sum up what Win and I had discovered so far.

"Those letters resembled Sarah's," Win added. "But I'd bet they weren't put together by the same hand. There are physical differences—when you get back to work, Leslie, take a good look at them. The cuts are different. Letters not so meticulously put on the page. But there's no physical threat, only threats to out the women."

"The language is very familiar to me," I said. "Came directly out of the bible of the Reverend Manfred Brown of the Family Praise Tabernacle."

"That kook who tried to out you?" Deborah asked.

"Yeah. The question seems to be if he's the one who sent the letters or if someone copied his style to avert suspicion from them."

"I'm so fucking tired of this anonymous band of cretins," Win said, leaning her head back. "At least in a war zone, you mostly know who the enemy is. Your job is to blow them away."

I rubbed her arm. "I think the whole department's equally frustrated. The Brownes are dead. We've had one deputy wounded.

Win's been shot at. We seem to be on a constant state of alert and I can't figure out why these people are spacing their attacks far apart."

"You answered your own question," Win said. "Stressed-out deputies make mistakes. Let their guard down. Hypervigilance can make you crazy."

I took her hand and rubbed it with my thumb. "Which is why we need to find these guys and nail them ASAP."

"We've got leads," Win said. "No proof. Which is frustrating as hell."

"The thing is, there've been attacks on three students who are members of the LGBT center in Bloomington," I said.

"Which we can tie to the antigay group active here in the county—"

"We can tentatively tie them in, Win" I said. "Which is the problem we're encountering with the whole group. We have an idea of what they're doing, but—"

"No idea of the endgame," Win said. "So you come up with the list of women who weren't targeted?"

"Yep." She got up, rummaged in her bag and handed me the list. "I think I figured out why. This whole group left a meeting right after dinner to catch a film."

"How long ago?"

"Last month."

"It could've been anyone there or outside," Leslie said. "Someone who got onto the group one way or another, or an employee of the restaurant."

"The letters started a couple of weeks ago," Deborah said. "Some of the women are really nervous because the only person they're out to is their lover. Well, except for the group."

"Same tactics," Win said. "Get people nervous. Looking over their shoulders. Sow distrust."

"For women just coming out, believe me, it could be terrifying," I said.

"If you want, I could come in a couple of hours tomorrow and start on this new batch," Leslie said.

"Oh no, you don't. Anything else I can do, ladies, let me know," Deborah said as she rose. "It's time for us to go."

CHAPTER THIRTY-EIGHT

Win

Deborah turned to me as I helped her on with her coat. "Those photographs of you two in the bedroom are absolutely gorgeous. Did you hire a photographer?"

"No." I wasn't going to embroider. Sarah would probably kill me if she knew Deborah had seen the photos. "It's been nice seeing you again, Deborah. Let's do this again. Maybe meet for dinner at Ruby's after things quiet down."

"You're on, Win. I told Sarah before, I always envied you two and Nathan when we were kids. It seems the trust you built when you were younger is paying off now."

"Sarah's always had my back." I leaned forward. "Just make sure you've got Leslie's."

Deborah nodded. "She's a real treasure in my life that I sure didn't expect. I'm not going to do anything to screw that up."

Sarah got Leslie's coat. Looked at her chest. "You don't have your vest on. Please tell me you didn't leave it at the station."

"It's out in the car."

"Go get it."

Leslie opened the door, dashed to the car. Was back inside in a blink.

"You can't wear the uniform without it, even when you're off duty," Sarah said. She turned to Deborah. "Make sure she wears it. Remember what we've been talking about tonight. All deputies have a target on their back until these guys are behind bars. *Every* deputy."

"Thus spake the sheriff," I said. "It's a hard line to walk, Leslie. We discovered a watcher on the top of Foley's Knob. Hasn't been back as far as we can tell, but with a sniper rifle, he'd be able to take you out the moment you stepped out of the car. Or stood on the porch."

Leslie paled. "I didn't know about the watcher. I won't take chances, Win. Honest."

As the brake lights came on when they hit the bottom of the drive, I turned to Sarah. "So, was that awful?"

"Uncomfortable at first, but not as bad as it could've been. Thanks for taking care of Leslie, helping her relax." She put an arm around my waist. "Leslie's good people. I don't want to scare the bejesus out of her, but I really want her to stay safe."

"That's the line we all have to walk right now." I pulled her close. "There's a light at the end of the tunnel, Sarah. We'll get them."

"Before they do more damage? Before I lose a deputy?"

Before I lose you? "We will."

* * *

The call came as we were slipping into sleep. A deputy had run off the road on a bend. Heading for the hospital in critical condition. I started to dress while Sarah marshaled her forces.

"Is Mike Bryer on the way?" Sarah asked. "Good. I'll head for the hospital. See that they look for a sniper's nest. Maybe it's too dark for him to have policed his brass. Look for anything, Caleb. We've got to stop this."

When she hung up, I took her hands. "You're sure this is an attack? Not just an accident?"

She nodded. "The deputy called dispatch for help and said he heard a shot before he lost control of his unit."

"Okay." I wanted to hold her. Soothe her. But she wasn't in a mood to stand still. I could feel the rage radiating from her. "Let's go."

I drove Sarah's SUV. She'd installed a rack that held two rifles. One of them was a .30-30, the other a Mark 12, my favorite sniper rifle. If anyone attacked, we'd be properly armed. That is, if we weren't lying in a ravine unconscious.

"I think we're going about this the wrong way," I said. "I think we need to view these guys as fanatics—just like the insurgents in Iraq or Afghanistan."

Sarah turned to face me. "You want to call out the National Guard?"

"No. Dealing with insurgents, we gathered intel. Names, locations, travel patterns. Identified couriers. Intercepted communications. When we could, we disseminated false information. We had to be on the offensive."

"Well, we've done some of that, Win."

"Not enough. We need eyes on the guys we've identified all the time. Can I ask Bill for help with that? You don't have enough deputies to do the twenty-four-seven coverage. He does."

"You think he would?"

"He's been tracking some of these guys for ten years. If he can swing it, he will."

Sarah settled back in her seat, began to scan the highway again. "Go ahead and ask." She was quiet. Alert. She sat forward. "Eyes—that doesn't mean drones, does it?"

I shrugged. "It means whatever he needs to do the job. People on the ground, surveillance in the air. I have no idea what he has available domestically."

Sarah groaned. "This isn't Afghanistan, Win."

"No. But some of these dipsticks want it to be. Read all that background material Nathan gave us on the militias. Sarah, they're insurgents, want to overthrow the government of the United States beginning with local law enforcement."

"Local lesbians too?"

"Hell if I can figure that one out." I turned onto the road that would take us to the heart of Greenglen. "I don't know if the religious fanatics are simply being used by people with a bigger plan or if they're instigators. Still haven't heard back from Nathan on the religious radical right."

"He's been busy, Win."

"I know. We need more resources. We need people who can infiltrate. I need my security clearance back."

"You're not thinking about reenlisting, are you?"

"Never."

CHAPTER THIRTY-NINE

Sarah

We spent the night at the hospital, Win stretched out on a couch sound asleep, while I tried to help Larry's wife keep it together. They'd only been married a couple of years and she was expecting. I refused to go where my mind wanted to—what if it was Win undergoing major surgery? I kept glancing at the couch and making sure she was still with me.

They'd finished the surgery around five in the morning, saying he'd live though his recuperation would be lengthy. We left when Jenny could see him. He was still too groggy to question.

I woke Win by calling her name and she amazed me by opening her eyes immediately and was fully awake two seconds later. "How do you do that? Sleep soundly and wake up alert?"

"Lot of battle practice. You grab sleep when you can, wake up fast."

At the station, Win curled up on the couch in my office and was asleep again instantly.

News began to come in and I wanted to go to the scene, but at the moment, I was more useful coordinating the investigation. Maybe Win and I could go out there in the afternoon. I wanted her input as a sniper. My wife, the sniper. That fact never failed to shake me as much as having a wife.

The bullet was found in the tire, the same .30-06. When the sun was up, Caleb found the shooter's location and brass. Both were on their way in with Leslie, who'd been called out early. I was glad I didn't have to see Deborah today, though I understood with every fiber of my body why she'd be pissed.

Leslie gave a little salute as she headed upstairs, but she looked grim. I had to look at crime scenes, Leslie had to process them. Zoe called in for details and a statement. I gave her my answer: too early.

When first shift came in, I reminded them to vary their patrol routes. "Don't just do it one end to other one day and then reverse it the next. Do not stick to the same pattern in any way. Period."

Win woke at eight, stretched and asked if I wanted breakfast. "I can run over to Tillie's Heart Attack Grill."

"Get me whatever you get," I said with a grin. She was perfectly awake, full of get-up-and-go while I was beginning to wilt. After we ate, I gave Win the files on the other two shootings and she busied herself with them.

Mike came in about ten o'clock with a full scene reconstruction. "Shooter had to know when Larry would be on that stretch of road because all the signs from the nest said he came, he shot and he left. All within a matter of a half hour, hour at the max."

"I'll have to ask Larry how he varied his patrol. I tried to explain that we couldn't afford to be predictable and now, maybe they'll listen. Talk to Mark. As head of patrol, if they don't mix it up, his head's going to be on a shiny platter."

"Will do. In fact, I'll help serve him up. Unless Larry didn't pay any attention to the directive, my question is still how the hell did they know when he'd be on that stretch of road."

"Did you check the patrol unit for a GPS tracker?" Win asked.

"Jesus, I didn't even think about that. As soon as it gets to the garage, we'll start looking."

"If she's finished with the lab work, take Leslie along," I said.

An hour later, Mike called. "We found a GPS tracker. You need to tell folks to check their patrol units before they take them out. This one was on the back wheel well on the passenger side."

"Roger that. Any prints on it?"

"Cleaner than Doc's table before an autopsy."

I told Dory to put out an alert to first shift. "Make sure they check them right now, not their next break or whatever. Now."

"You changed tactics, they adjusted," Win said. "Typical insurgent behavior. They'll find a way around most things you do. Maybe you start finding GPS trackers before patrol goes out. They wait until a unit stops for a coffee break. You adjust, they readjust."

"We've got to get ahead of them, Win."

"I'll call Bill as soon as we get home. My burn phone's there."

I nodded. "You think they've got the skills to hack our communications system? Email and phones?"

She shrugged. "That's Nathan's bailiwick. If anyone can put up enough firewalls and stuff, it's him."

I put my head down on the desk, cradled by my arms. "Damn. Damn them all to hell."

Win put her notepad aside, walked up behind my chair and leaned over to rub my shoulders and neck. "Relax Sarah. We're not going to solve this with a magic snap of the fingers. We'll get there, we will. No doubt in my mind. Relax."

"Are you trying to hypnotize me?"

"No. Your shoulders are so tight I can barely get the muscles to move." She stopped and walked around to the front of the desk. "I think it's time to go home. You have anything else to do here?"

"Not really, but—"

"Good, gather your stuff. We'll stop at the hospital, you can talk to your deputy. Then home and a nap. I will brook no arguments. Move."

* * *

I woke up when Win rubbed my shoulder and it took me a moment to focus. The fire was burning in the fireplace and I found myself on the couch covered with a quilt. I yawned and sat up.

Win brought a tray and set it on the coffee table. "Chili, your mom's version." She handed me a bowl, took the other one. "We'll eat, have dessert and go to bed."

"What's for dessert?"

"Anything you want."

I smiled in response to her leer and tucked into the chili. "Oh, wow. This is exactly like Mom's. I followed her recipe exactly and it never tasted like this. What'd you do?"

"Added cardamom. It needed a little zing." She tucked her legs under her, grabbed a piece of garlic toast and dipped it in the chili. She looked up at me. "What?"

"I love your gusto."

"Eat." She dug into her bowl while the fire snapped and crackled. "I talked to Bill and he's willing to help out. He's got two guys he can put on our most probable suspect right now. He'll fly in six more, but it may take a day or two."

"How come so long? And how come so many?"

"The rest of team is out of the country. They work in two-person teams for continual surveillance. So which one of our miscreants would you like to cover first?"

"I'd like to line them all up in front of a firing squad and whoever survives, we cover."

"I don't think anybody would survive a firing squad, Sarah. For what it's worth, Greg Hall may be the best bet to go higher up in the organization. If you want the shooter covered, Joshua Leatherby."

"I'm not even going to ask how you figured that, but let's go with Leatherby. Should I call Bill?"

"Yeah. You know where Leatherby lives. Now eat."

When we finished eating, I called Bill, gave him the specifics and told him I'd send him the file in the morning. "Thanks. This whole thing is getting to all of us and we're already stretched so thin."

"No problemo, little lady." He laughed and laughed as he hung up.

"He called me 'little lady,'" I said as I handed Win the phone.

"Then laughed? Term of affection, Sarah." She sat beside me, put an arm around my shoulders. Her thumb traced the patch on my uniform shirt. "I feel better about this op since we've deployed more eyes."

"This isn't Afghanistan, nor is this a military op. As law enforcement, we have to uphold the law."

"We're at war, whether you recognize it or not. So far, we've suffered two dead, three injured."

"Three?"

"Don't forget Major Laura Wilkins. She was one of the first casualties." She wrapped me in her arms and pulled me close. "Laura was alone but we have each other. We'll fight this together. During lulls in the action, we'll make love. Celebrate life. Our lives. Together."

CHAPTER FORTY

Win

My internal alarm woke me at four, before sunrise. Cocooned in blankets with Sarah's body close to me, the last thing I wanted to do was get up and head for Bloomington. I nuzzled her neck. She smiled in her sleep. I slid out of bed, trying not to wake her. Went into the bathroom where I'd laid out my clothes last night. I peeked into the bedroom when I was ready to leave. Sarah hadn't moved. Her face looked relaxed in sleep. Wish I could see her like that when she was awake.

I placed a note on my pillow, kissed her forehead. Got the rest of my gear and went out to my truck. I fired her up, headed down the drive with the lights off. I didn't turn them on until I hit the road to Bloomington. Nothing in the rearview mirror, nothing up ahead.

Teaching that day meant putting the burden of the lesson on the students. We struggled through the day. At the end of class, I gave them a Tajik saying. "Anyone know what it means?"

No one did, though a couple tried. "It means 'my thoughts are elsewhere' and I apologize for that. See you tomorrow."

When I got back to the apartment, I prepped extra hard for the next two days. I missed Sarah. I missed Des. To keep my mind off the ache, I took a volume of Rumi off the shelf and began to read. It made it worse. I exchanged it for the legal pad I'd used to jot down facts about the current war in McCrumb County. I couldn't concentrate. I had to be here to teach, I wanted to be home at Sarah's side.

I got into my cold bed, turned the lights off and waited for Sarah's call in vain. That became apparent when I opened my eyes and the sun was easing into the sky. I looked at the phone. Three messages from Sarah. I called her.

"You forget to turn your phone on after class or should I have panicked?" she asked.

"Not funny, Sheriff Perfect. Truth is, I fell asleep waiting for your call." I could see the smirk on her face. "I'm giving a talk about staying safe at the LGBT center tonight. Thought I could review their security tapes when I'm finished." I pushed myself up to rest against the headboard. "They're showing a great film tomorrow night. Think you can come in?"

"Um. I wouldn't mind leaving the county behind for a night."

Precisely. "Why don't you have Leslie escort you and maybe bring Deborah along. We can stay the night here. Get an early start Saturday morning."

"Good movie?"

"Great movie."

"Let me ask Leslie. I'll text you back."

"Sounds like a plan." I cleared my throat. "Miss you. Stay safe, Sarah."

"You too, please. Des says she misses you too, so much she's given up small rodents."

I heard Sarah take a deep breath, then she disconnected. I knew in my heart Sarah was lying. Des could never stop thinking about chasing small furries.

* * *

The talk went well, though I wasn't sure the students bought my plea to keep their heads up and out of their phones while walking around. Sometimes I cursed mobile technology.

The meeting with Nolan and Bill produced little new intel. Nolan was settling in, would go to a meeting of the Rangers tomorrow night. "They've got something in the works," he'd said. "I'll let you know as soon as I know what."

The following evening, I'd headed to the LGBT center film night. I had my arm draped over the back of Sarah's chair in the media room.

The film had just started. Twenty minutes late because there were some short comments by the director and actors first. Now the room was lit only by the reflected light from the screen.

I caught some movement in my peripheral vision. Turned my head slightly and saw several males move to lean against the back wall. One of the guys had a bat sticking out from beneath a coat.

I leaned over to Sarah. "Don't look around, keep your eyes on the screen. I think we've got trouble forming. I'm going to the john where there's a door to the hall. Put your phone on vibrate. I'll text. Are you and Leslie armed?"

Her eyes were wide when she turned to me. She nodded. "What kind of trouble?"

"Four young males in the back of the room. One has a baseball bat."

"Oh, hell."

"Shhh. Could be a gay young man carrying a bat to protect himself. I'll let you know." I gave her shoulder a quick squeeze. "Stay safe, Sarah. No heroics."

I got up, sprinted to the ladies' room. Once inside, I banged a stall door. Tip-toed over to the door to the hall, eased it open. Saw another ten guys waiting in the hall. The swastika tattoo on one guy's neck gave proof to their intention.

I texted. *Get ready for attack. 10 in hall. When it starts, you & L slip behind them. I follow them in.* I hit send.

I followed that up with flushing a john while I called the campus police chief. Told him what was going on and to approach silently. I ran water. Walked back to the door to keep an eye on them. I thought a couple more had joined the group. What were they waiting for?

Then I saw him. Down the hall at the exit. A guy in his late twenties, early thirties. Turning off the flash, I slipped the phone out the door and clicked off a couple of shots. I looked at the results. Not great but maybe Nathan's software could work more miracles.

I typed *now* and put a finger over the send icon. The guy by the exit looked at his phone. He nodded to the group. I hit send. He opened the door and swaggered out.

I pulled my Glock, waited until a majority of the men were swarming into the media room. Sprinted down the hall, caught the last one in by his hoodie. His head had a hard meeting with the doorframe. He slid to the floor.

I pushed into the room, weapon in the ready position. The mob wielded bats. A couple had heavy chains. Women scattered. The men attacked the projector and the flat-screen TV in the corner, yelling all the gay slurs they knew. A few bodies got in the way of their wild swings and tumbled to the floor.

Sarah and Leslie had moved to either side at the back of the room. She nodded when she saw me. "Police!" Sarah yelled. "Don't move. Put down your weapons."

The fuckers paused, wide-eyed and cornered. I assumed the stance, aimed my weapon at the bastard who seemed in charge. We locked eyes. "Give me a reason to blow you away. Please."

He dropped his bat. The clatter seemed very loud in the now silent room.

"Hands on top of your head. Now," I said.

"That means all of you," Sarah said. "Drop the weapons. Kneel down, keep your hands linked on the top of your heads."

"You can't do this," one of them said. "We have the right to free speech."

Sarah flashed her badge. "And I have the right to fire if I think your actions threaten anyone." She stared him down.

I heard feet pounding in the hall and stepped back to see if they'd sent reinforcements. Thank the stars it was campus police.

The chief glanced at me, nodded. "What's happened?"

"Flash mob with intentions of mayhem. Property damage. Oh hell, I don't know the civilian lingo."

His men began cuffing the creeps with plastic restraints.

Sarah walked up and holstered her weapon. "Glad to see you, Chief. You can begin with assault and battery, throw in resisting arrest."

"That what happened to the guy in the hall?" the chief asked.

"I came up behind him. Must've scared him. He turned to run, but instead took a header into the doorframe." I held up my hands. "Scared rabbit not used to violence unless he was creating it."

The chief shook his head. "You looked mighty fierce when we made entrance. Think I woulda taken a header outta here too."

I grinned. He was going to buy the story. Besides the damage to the equipment, several women were on the floor, being administered to by those unharmed. I searched for Deborah but didn't see her.

CHAPTER FORTY-ONE

Sarah

This was not the way I'd imagined our night would go. Bloomington PD sent their patrol wagon and took all the felons to their jail. Win and I had just finished up with our statements and were waiting to go home. Leslie and Deborah sat across from us, held up by Leslie's participation in the bust. Leslie had told Deborah to get under the chair and stay there until it was safe. She'd stayed put until Leslie had gone over and lifted the chair away.

"This is giving me a whole new appreciation of the law," Deborah said. "I'm damn glad I went into corporate law."

"It was a good bust," I said. "It would've been better if the campus police had been there to stop the melee because I don't have jurisdiction. But I'm still a sworn officer of the court. I couldn't do anything else but intervene."

"I have no standing whatsoever," Win said. "But I do have a carry permit. It's just lucky they backed down."

I glanced over at Win. Did she view tonight as just another op? Another opportunity to get the adrenaline going? The other side of my brain asked another important question: what would you have done if she hadn't spotted them early?

The chief walked up to us. "Thanks for the heads-up, Win. Bloomington will file the charges and handle the arraignment. Lets us go back to patrolling for drunks and rapists. My thanks to all of you—it could've been so much worse."

"How are the women who were hurt?"

"No life-threatening injuries, though a couple of women have broken bones." He rubbed the back of his neck. "You all are free to go, but please be safe on the way home. Whoever instigated this isn't going to be happy."

"Keep me in the loop?" I asked.

"Of course, Sheriff."

As we walked into the clear, cold night, I looked at my watch. Nearly one a.m. "Are you driving back to Greenglen?" I asked Leslie.

"Yeah. All I can think about is going to bed," she said. She blushed a bright red. "To get to some sleep before I fall on my face."

"Why don't you two come over to my apartment?" Win asked. "I've got a sleeper sofa. Get a few hours of sleep before you hit the road. We can caravan tomorrow morning. Safer, Leslie."

This was definitely not what I had in mind for tonight. After the usual protestations about putting us out, Deborah and Leslie said okay. When we walked into Win's studio apartment, Deborah let out a small gasp.

Win turned to her. "We need sleep tonight, not sex. Sorry." She went ahead and prepared the pullout. She even managed to find two pairs of pajamas. "There's a new toothbrush in the vanity drawer. Go."

Deborah grabbed Leslie's hand and tugged her to the tiny bathroom. They shut the door.

Win sat on the edge of the bed. "I thought this would be a good time tonight. Can't tell you how sorry I am."

"It's not your fault. It's those pricks who think they're the devil's gift to this world." I sat beside her, put my arms around her waist and leaned against her. "I have so many questions about tonight, all jumbled up."

"That's why we need sleep, Sarah. You've been up almost twenty-four hours." She kissed me. "I don't have any more pajamas."

"I'll be glad to sleep naked as long as you're next to me."

"Getting from the bathroom is going to be tricky. A nude dash?"

I giggled. "You have T-shirts and I have clean underwear here. Sorry to spoil the fantasy."

"You're my only fantasy and I'm living it."

* * *

We left at dawn, with Leslie and the civilian behind us as we escorted them to Deborah's. I told Leslie to take the day off since she was exhausted. Besides, Deborah was still shaken, both by the violence and seeing her lover draw her weapon. A day in bed would do them both a whole bucketful of good. Win and I would have to wait until tonight.

We walked into the station and I sighed a breath of relief. "How do you want to divide our tasks?" I asked Win.

"I need to get hold of Bill, let him know what happened. Then I want to send the pics I shot last night to Nathan. See if he can identify the older guy who left before the fun started. Why don't you check and see if the IDs on those kids have come through? Run them to see who and what we're dealing with."

"Do you really think this has something to do with what's going on here? The letters, the shootings?"

Win nodded. "I haven't told you what Bill and Nolan said yesterday. I was going to do that last night after the film. Didn't get that chance, did we?"

"Soon. Let's get started on the housekeeping and then we can talk." I kissed her and then headed upstairs to the detectives' loft.

John was at his desk and looked up as I entered.

"Morning," he said. "Know anything about these arrest jackets? Came in from Bloomington PD?"

"Yeah, they're from our adventure last night. A bunch of kids attacked the LGBT center."

"Attacked?"

"With baseball bats and chains. It was well organized and orchestrated."

"Skinheads?"

"Maybe. Would you run the names through our databases? Put together a file on each?"

"You got it. Want me to send them to Nathan too?"

"Not yet. He's got enough to do right now. Thanks, John."

I went back to my office where I found Win asleep on my couch, her phone clasped in her hand. I lifted her shoulders and sat down, holding her head on my lap.

"This is nice," she said as she opened her eyes. "We can nap until something comes in."

"You sent your stuff to Nathan?"

"He's running it now. Now hush, lean your head back. Doze off, Sarah."

Win's eyes were already closed.

Strangely enough, I did. I wasn't used to catnaps and found it difficult to wake up when Win shook my shoulder. "What? What's happened?"

"Micah's here to report to the sheriff," Win said.

I squinted. Tried refocusing. "Dad?"

"Reserve Deputy Barrow reportin'." He was smiling. "On the assignments that you give me. 'Member?"

Win was already standing with a smirk on her face, so I pushed myself to my feet. "Talk to Dog and poke around the area where Leatherby and McNab live. I'm awake, Dad, so report away."

"You never could catnap, Sarah Anne," Dad said as he sat in the visitor chair. "Even when you was a kid, took hell and high water to wake you if you fell asleep daytime."

"Report, Dad?"

"Dog recognized them guys, said they come in 'bout ever' two weeks. Same time, sit in the same place, eat the same food. Talk a lot, eat fast. Always pay cash. Just so happened, Dog said he wouldn't object none to a little electronic eavesdroppin' at that table."

"He just brought that up out of thin air?"

"Yup. Thin air."

"Shit." I mumbled it, but from the look he gave me, not quietly enough. "I'll have to run it by the prosecutor's office, but it sure would help to hear what they're up to ahead of time."

"Think that'd be a right good idea. Did some door-to-door canvassing—"

"Dad! I told you—"

"I was careful, Sarah Anne. Collectin' for the Blue Otters—"

"Blue Otters?" Win asked. "A sports team?"

Dad grinned. "Reestablishing otters here. Started on the Little Blue River, now we're workin' on the Big Blue. Folk know I'm a volunteer. Don't raise no suspicions. Anyways, finally tracked down Bucky Boone, old snoop worse 'n me."

"Bucky Boone?" Win said. "You've got to be kidding."

"Buckminster St. Clair Boone. I didn't name him, so stop lookin' at me like that. Sure as the devil it's hard to deliver a report in this here office."

"Sorry," Win said, trying to wipe the grin off her face. "Continue, Deputy."

Dad cleared his throat. "Bucky is the kinda man who hears all the gossip in the county. The one interestin' item he heard was that the old Messinger farm been bought an' turned into a facility for paintball nuts. Also said he don't think paintball requires explosions or real rifle fire."

"Explosions? Rifle fire?" I thought I hadn't heard Dad right.

"Training camp?" Win asked.

Dad looked at Win and nodded. "That's what I reckon. Bucky did too. Thought it was some dang fool militia playin' brave."

I closed my eyes and took a deep breath. "Win, let Bill know. See if we can get regular satellite images. I'll call Kay and have her pull the plat map and deed. It'll be interesting to see who bought the place. Anything else?"

Dad shook his head.

"Good work. I doubt if Bucky would've talked to us, even if I'd thought to question him."

CHAPTER FORTY-TWO

Win

We stopped to eat on the way home because we'd left the station late. While I was out with Des, she'd started a fire.

"Isn't there a TV series called *The Walking Dead*?" I asked as I sat next to her on the couch with two beers. "'Cause I think you've been watching it too much."

"Very funny," she said. "I'm so tired I'm afraid to go to bed because I won't be able to get up in the morning."

I put an arm around her. Drew her to my shoulder. "At least we made some progress today. Thanks to Micah."

"Yeah. Thanks to MCIA and Nathan, we've got satellite images, safe com links and a bunch of other stuff—and one old man with a gift of gab hands us two solid leads. Go figure."

"Make you feel like a failure?" I asked.

Sarah stiffened, stayed quiet for a long time. "Yeah."

"Don't. You're the one who sent him out with the assignment because you knew he had the contacts to get answers the rest of your investigators couldn't. Smart thinking, Sarah."

"How long can I rely on getting answers because Dad's out in the field? I should be able to do it myself."

"Fuck the 'should.' Let go of the perfect sheriff image." I rubbed her shoulder. "The perfect law enforcement officer doesn't exist. I bet Micah would be the first to tell you that."

"Dad was pretty damn close when he held the office."

"As much as I love your dad, I wish he'd never been sheriff. Then you wouldn't have anything to live up to."

"That's not right. He gave me an example to follow."

"Shit." I looked her in the eye. "Quit. Before you know it, you'll expect me to be perfect too."

"You are."

I laughed. "Wrong. No matter how hard I tried to be the perfect command officer, I wasn't. What I learned is, nobody is. The smart officers learned from their mistakes."

"I'm just so tired, Win."

I put both arms around her, pulled her head to my chest. "I could say things will look brighter in the morning, but you'd probably hit me. It will, Sarah. You just need some sleep."

"Yeah, yeah, yeah."

"Can I help you get ready for bed?"

"Not if you want me to sleep. I wish we had a Jacuzzi."

"Me too. But when I was building, I thought it was a luxury item." I ran my hand through her soft, fine hair. "I love you, Sarah. It tears me up to see you like this. Not be able to wave a magic wand and make the bad stuff go away."

She raised her sleepy gaze, put a hand on my cheek. "I know that and I can't tell you how much your support means to me. But I feel like I've turned into a whiner and I can't tell you how much I hate that."

"Yeah, me too." I grinned.

Sarah burrowed into my chest. "I've been trying to delegate."

"Delegate the worry. When it gets to be too much, hand it off. To me. To Caleb, to John, to Micah."

"That's easier to say than actually do," Sarah mumbled.

"Emily's back at work. Go see her. Ask her to teach you some meditation techniques."

I thought she nodded, but her head was still pressed to me.

"I wish you didn't have to go to Bloomington this week," she said as she raised her head. "It scares me."

"This is the last week before spring break."

"Spring break? In the midst of winter?"

"We can celebrate the hope of spring."

* * *

In the morning, I let Sarah sleep in, called the station and put the coffee on. Took Des out for a good romp because she had so much excess energy. Cabin fever. Maybe today would be a good day to bring her with us, more stimuli with more people instead of being alone in the house. I'd have to trust Nathan's security setup.

I had a cup of coffee while I went through the week's tapes my system provided. Nothing but a couple of deer had disturbed our bastion. I hated living this way, in another war zone right here at home. But Sarah's safety was worth a trip to the paranoid side.

Around eight thirty, I took a mug of coffee in to Sarah.

She sat up, still groggy. "It's light out. What time is it?"

"Um, I called the station, told them we'd be late." I sat on the bed, felt the desire I hadn't expressed last night. "Drink your coffee."

She got hold of the mug, took a deep drink. Looked at me over the lip. "What time did you tell them we'd be in?"

"I didn't." I arched an eyebrow. "What do you have in mind?"

"I'm awake now. I wasn't last night—I don't even remember hitting the bed."

"Do you remember scattering your uniform behind you on the way in here?"

Sarah blushed. "No. Everything?"

"Yep. Take a look."

She peeked under the covers. "Should we take advantage of my nakedness before I shower and get dressed?"

"That was my plan." I stripped off my sweatshirt and pants. Climbed under the covers. I held her close. "Are you sure you're awake?"

"If I wasn't, I am now." She demonstrated by pushing me on my back. Stretched out on top of me. "I love you. You're the only thing that's keeping me sane."

We walked into the station at ten, Des stopping to greet each deputy. Once in her office, Sarah turned to me. "I don't mind working late today since we've got the next two days together. Do you?"

"You better believe it, Sarah. I want to pick up where we left off."

She laughed. A slight blush crept above her turtleneck. "We'll see." She turned to her in-box. Lifted a bunch of files and opened the first.

I hadn't touched base with Nathan in a while so I called him. "Anything new?"

"Did you get that packet I sent about the Reconstrustionists?"

"No. When did you send it?"

"Yesterday afternoon. Guess you haven't been online. Okay, here's a summary. Three small churches are spouting the same rhetoric. I managed to find my way into their membership lists, then ran them through a bunch of databases. A number of their members had arrest jackets and those are awaiting your attention."

"I'll pull them up as soon as we get home. Anything on the shots I sent you from Bloomington? The guy who was leaving?"

"Not a good shot, Win. I got four possible hits and one of them is the guy calling himself Leatherby. I discounted two more since they're incarcerated. The last was John Louis Underwood."

"Underwood. Related to Leatherby, AKA William Robert Underwood?"

"Younger brother. I sent you his jacket too. He's not a pleasant character—violent and just plain mean."

My heart sank. We didn't need another violent player. "Thanks, Nathan. You must be working on this full-time. We'd be lost without you."

"I just set the parameters and let the computers play. Besides, Sarah's my sister. I love her too."

"Thanks brother-in-law. You're one swell guy."

When Sarah got through her pile and looked up, I told her the news.

"I'd like to take a look through all of that. You think Leatherby's younger brother is the ringleader of those sonofabutts at the LGBT center? It's looking like one ugly conspiracy to me. You get the same read?"

"Seems possible. We need more data. What's the status of the bug at Dog's?"

"Won't know until tomorrow. Courthouse is closed on weekends, if you haven't noticed. I'll submit the paperwork tomorrow—ah, no I won't. I'll leave it for Caleb." She leaned back, closed the first file. "Kay's out of town, so we can't check the deed on Messinger's farm until tomorrow either."

"Does that mean we can go home now?"

"No. It just means I get to turn my full attention to all of the other misdemeanors and felonies in McCrumb County. Take a nap, Win."

CHAPTER FORTY-THREE

Sarah

It was almost five and already dark when we were finally ready to leave. I could see it was still snowing, not a blizzard but a steady wall of white that had begun around noon. I wondered if the plows had been out yet. If not, it was going to be a long drive home.

The dispatcher waved me over. "Sarah, we got fender-benders all over. You're gonna have to wait 'til Unit Five clears this one up and comes in for your escort."

"How long?" I asked.

"Forty, fifty minutes."

Win sighed behind me.

"I think we'll go on. With the snow coming down, we should be close to invisible."

"Ma'am, I can't in good conscience let you go. We have standing orders."

Which I gave. I glanced at Win and she was watching the snow, hands shoved in her pockets and shoulders slumped. She and Des had been patient all day. "Patch me through to Unit Five, please."

I talked with the deputy and he described a smash-up of three cars and a truck, all with angry drivers. I knew he'd be there until the tow trucks had pulled apart the mangled vehicles and their drivers. "Skip the escort assignment and concentrate on getting that mess cleared up."

I hung up. "Nobody else close?"

"Nope."

"Then we're going. If we wait a couple of hours, driving's going to be more dangerous than a sniper out there."

"I don't know, Sarah," Win said. "It's the least likely times that are the best to strike."

"Thanks, Win. You want to camp out here tonight?"

She shrugged and zipped up her parka. Des woofed. I turned to dispatch. "As soon as we get out of town, I'll call and keep an open line with you. Okay?"

He gave me a disapproving look, then nodded.

We walked out the back of the station, Win checked the truck for GPS trackers and I fastened Des into her seat belt in the backseat. With Win driving, as soon as we hit city limits, I dutifully called dispatch. "I'm just going to keep this line open. Is that going to screw up your incoming?"

"No ma'am. I'll keep an ear open too."

The plows hadn't been out and although Win had engaged four-wheel drive, she kept her speed slow and approached curves even more slowly. The windshield wipers thumped and squeaked at a slow rhythm.

"Shit driving," she said, her eyes scanning the terrain on either side of the road. "Though I like the way this car handles."

"Truck," I said.

She said something under her breath, but I thought it was best to ignore her muttering. My Escape was a small SUV with all the advantages of Win's truck and much better gas mileage. The wheel jerked in Win's hands and a fraction of second later, I heard the retort of a rifle.

"Fuck it," Win said. "Least likely time."

She held the truck to a controlled skid that kept us in the middle of the road.

"Shot fired, shot fired. We're—"

I heard another shot and the back of the truck flipped out to the side. We began to fishtail. "Another shot. We're heading off the—"

We hit something at the side of the road. The airbags deployed. The force of it slapped my head back. I couldn't see, just felt the truck tilt, then slam into the ground on its side.

When my airbag deflated, I tried to focus. I was hanging by my seat belt. I could hear Des whining in back. I still clutched the phone. "You still there?"

"Got help on the way. You okay?"

"Yeah. Win's not moving. I see blood. Get an ambulance out here. We're on—"

"Know where you are, ma'am. EMTs are on the way. Was this our shooter?"

"Somebody shot, twice. Win had us in a controlled slide…"

"Stay put and keep the line open. Understand?"

I looked around my seat. Des hung from her seat belt, unable to find purchase on the seat. I reached my left arm back to help her and felt a fierce pain in my wrist. I kept pushing on Des's chest until she found a way to sit on her own. I heard a door slam outside and drew my weapon. The shooter come to finish the job? The hell if I was going to go quietly.

"Sarah?"

It sounded like Caleb's voice. "Identify yourself."

"Chief Deputy, Sarah. I'm coming down. Hold on."

* * *

Muzzy from pain meds and lack of sleep I sat beside Win's bed. A cast replaced my watch so I watched the second hand on the wall clock. Win's surgery had ended hours ago and she should be awake by now. Her forehead was bandaged where her head had broken the driver's side window. She looked so pale. I held her hand fiercely, sending her love and what energy I had left. Dad called for hourly updates, frustrated that the snow kept him confined on the farm. Nurses had been in and out, taking vitals and giving me kind words.

"How's Des?" Win asked.

I stopped breathing and looked at her. Her eyes were open and focused. I squeezed her hand. "She's okay, a little sore around her ribs."

Des had risen and most gently put her paws on the edge of the bed. She licked our entwined hands, then stepped back with her paws still held up until she was away from the bed.

"What's my damage?" Win asked.

"Broken fibula in your left leg and a hell of a whack on your head. Gwen got the plastic surgeon in to stitch you up. Again." I hit the call button with my free hand.

"Your arm?"

"Wrist got broken somehow. How do you feel, Win?"

"Somewhere between shit and euphoria. They give me pain meds?"

"Yeah, you should float for a while. Caleb said we were lucky to get out alive. Haven't heard from the crash team yet, but I heard two shots. Did you?"

Win closed her eyes. "I remember the controlled skid—shit, I was in the groove and we would've been fine. After that, it gets fuzzy. Did I lose control?"

"There was a second shot and my guess is he hit another tire."

The door opened and Dr. Gwen Cody strode in. "You finally end your beauty nap?"

Win gave her a glare. "When can I get out of here?"

"When I sign you out." Gwen turned to me. "Is she making sense?"

"As much as she ever does," I said as I squeezed Win's hand again. "Yes, she seems lucid. Doesn't remember much after the second shot."

"That's to be expected." She checked Win's chart and nodded. "Your MRI doesn't show major damage to your thick head, but we're keeping you for observation. You've had head injuries before and we need to look for a cumulative effect." She went through a list of questions and a few neurological tests.

I could tell Win was getting rebellious, which was a good sign. "You think we'll be able to go home tomorrow?"

"We'll see," Gwen answered. "If she starts to look like a raccoon, don't worry. But if she starts experiencing blurry vision or slurred speech, give me a buzz right away. You both need some sleep." She walked to Win's side. "Your night's going to be interrupted by pushy nurses who will want to assess whether you still have a functioning brain. Be kind to them and don't throw anything."

Win muttered. I assured Gwen we'd be nice. I found it was easier said than done as a parade of nurses walked in the door every hour.

Win slipped into disturbed dreams during the nursing interims. This shooting had the power to shove Win back into her PTSD and I desperately didn't want that to happen.

I blamed myself. I should've waited or had a plow truck lead us home. Why did I have to be so fucking impatient? My fault. Win had warned me. All my fault.

Once, during the long night, Win wakened and squeezed my hand. "I love you. I always will, *Jaaneman*."

CHAPTER FORTY-FOUR

Win

To execute our escape from the hospital, Micah borrowed an Explorer. He'd rigged the truck so the nurses could prop me up in the back. Caleb and another deputy were in a patrol unit in front of us. Leslie and Vincente followed us. Damn big production.

"You have your CSIs close so they don't have to travel to the scene?" I asked without turning to the front.

"Yup," Micah said. "Never know what disaster lurks where you gals are concerned. Good idea to have them close to get the investigation off an' runnin' real quick."

Sarah snickered. "Behave, Win."

We got home and they extricated me. Slowly. Having two tall guys and one short trying to pry me out was something like a rerun of the Three Stooges. Once I'd pushed myself out, it was crutches to the door and a lot of helping hands. I don't think I'd ever felt so relieved when I was finally settled on the couch. Des was the only non-hoverer. She jumped up next to me and snuggled in. I interpreted her snort as, "Maybe now I can get some sleep. Everybody go away."

I heard Caleb at the door. "Sarah, stay home for a couple of days. Please. I'll let you know every detail of the investigation and that's a promise. Just get some rest and take care of Win."

I didn't hear her response. Micah was the last to leave. He built a fire and put a casserole in the oven. "Think you can take it out okay, Sarah Anne?"

I didn't hear her response to that question either. Micah came over, leaned on the back of the couch. "You need anythin', holler." He patted my shoulder. "That was way too close. Let's not let it happen again."

Finally, the place fell silent and Sarah settled on my other side. A fire burned brightly and my two favorite girls were next to me. If my head didn't ache so much, it would've been heaven.

"How are you feeling?" Sarah asked.

"Tired. How's your arm?"

"Achy. Damn, what a pair we are." She laid her head on my shoulder. "I can't believe they got us, especially not with the snow coming down like it was."

"Hush. We're not talking about it now. Let's just be grateful for breath, for the winter outside and the warmth in here."

* * *

I couldn't keep Sarah from thinking about the ambush. She'd be quiet, watch the firelight then bring up a new theory about how they'd found us. Finally, I pushed myself up, grabbed my crutches and announced it was time for bed. Along with my pain meds.

Walking with crutches was like cross-country skiing: once you mastered it, you never forgot how. The nurses had done a good job fitting them to my frame. I swung down the hall without a hitch. Getting us settled in bed was another matter. My left leg had to be elevated, so did Sarah's left wrist. Des settled on her bed with a luxurious sigh.

By the next morning, and before coffee, Sarah was on the phone to Caleb. I let Des out and thumped my way to the coffeemaker. Looked for somewhere to lean my crutches where they wouldn't fall. Got everything ready, then realized I needed to get water. Shit. I one-crutched it to the sink and back. Cinch.

While the coffee brewed, I tried to figure out how I was going to shower. A trash bag over the cast was one solution. Holding my leg outside the shower was another. Asking for Sarah's help was the easiest. The most enticing, but she had a cast to keep dry too.

Just like Sarah, I kept mulling it all over in my mind. With the snow falling so thickly, I hadn't had a chance to spot the shooter before the shot. How the hell had he seen us so clearly? How had he known we were coming? Only a skeleton crew had been on duty at the station. Had someone there inadvertently told someone we were leaving? Shit. Here I was, doing what I'd told Sarah not to do. It was too soon. I needed distance. I'd slept soundly last night, thanks to the pain meds. But I knew I had to watch it. Closely. Or I'd slide into the demon cave again.

"I was right, there were two shots," Sarah said as she walked into the kitchen. "Same ballistics as the other shootings. What I can't figure out is—"

"Can you help me shower?" I asked.

She stopped pouring. "Yeah, sure."

"I don't want to talk about the ambush now. Can you understand?"

"So no updates—for how long?"

"Until I ask you for an update. Okay?"

She set the mug down, put her arms around me. "Whatever you say. But you know I can't let this go. Is that okay?"

"As long as you don't go back to work tomorrow. We both need time to heal physically. You push too hard and you'll do permanent damage. It's really hard to keep you reined in."

"Do we have to stay reined in when you shower?"

"No." I kissed her. "Just careful. Soap plus water equals slippery. Neither of us can afford to fall right now."

"Does that mean we have to stop showering together when we're sixty-five?"

"Ask me when I'm sixty-five." I pulled Sarah close. I hoped she wasn't thinking what was running through my mind. *If we make it to sixty-five.*

CHAPTER FORTY-FIVE

Sarah

"I think we'd better move this to the bed," I said. Water beat down on us and formed rivulets on Win's beautiful body. "We're both going to end up on our asses."

Win sighed, then licked a drop from my breast. "Okay. Wipe the floor and then hand me my crutches."

I toweled down the floor and then I toweled down Win, with different towels of course. She was pretty much at my mercy, but I didn't press forward. I needed to remember what Win had said, not to push too hard. Not physically, not job-wise. I knew it should be my mantra, but right now all I wanted was to feel Win's body as close to mine as possible. Getting both of us settled so we wouldn't injure an already injured limb wasn't easy, but not impossible.

"So, pain meds before or after?"

Win smiled, snaked her hand behind my neck. "You're the only high I need, Sarah. Ever."

We spent the rest of the day in bed, mostly sleeping, but with interesting intervals. When night fell, I slipped out of bed and threw on my sweats. Des whined her "I really need to go out" whine, so I let her out. We'd planned to go grocery shopping today, so dinner fixings were minimal. We'd demolished Dad's offering. I closed the fridge and leaned against the counter.

"Go ahead and call for pizza," Win said, poking her head around the corner. "We just can't have beer with it."

"Why not? We're not driving, or are you afraid I'll fall out of bed?"

"Call. I'm starving." Win thumped to the fireplace and started twisting up paper for the first layer.

I found my phone and realized I'd left it off all day. There were about ten messages from Caleb. I went ahead and ordered the pizza, stuck the phone in my pocket and walked down the hall to the bathroom. I went down the list of text messages. Interesting. Kay had come through with the plat map for the old Messinger farm. At six-hundred acres, it was a mix of woods and fallow fields. It had been purchased by the Cobra Investment Corporation. Caleb had sent the purchase information to Nathan. Good.

He'd walked the paperwork for the electronic listening device over to the courthouse and presented it to the judge himself. Judge Hoffman was thinking about it. Thinking about what? Springtime? Going fishing? Caleb should've taken it to Judge Bergman. Well, it was in the works.

I sank down on the couch next to Win and leaned against her. She felt tense, muscles tight. From pain? I snuggled into her until she put an arm around me.

"I need to bring in more wood," I said, appreciating the warmth from the fireplace. "We're going to have to switch chores around."

Win didn't say anything.

"Are you okay?"

"Yeah."

"Are you feeling pain?"

"Some."

"Why don't you take a pain pill?" I thought back over the day. I couldn't remember Win taking any pain meds.

"I don't want to get hooked."

"You're in pain! Hell, how are you going to heal when all your muscles are so tight and all you can think about is hurting?"

She turned away, directed her gaze outside. "I've had pain meds sneak up on me before. That's not going to happen again, Sarah."

Win was using her stubborn voice. "Okay, I understand. But can't there be another path? I'll monitor you and you do the same for me."

She didn't answer and kept looking outside.

"How can we make love when I know every time I touch you, I could hurt you? I can't do that. We'll have to abstain until the doctors say it's okay."

"Is this extortion?"

I didn't answer.

"Maybe one after we eat. Okay?"

I started to kiss her, then drew back. "Maybe."

* * *

The next morning at breakfast, both our phones rang. Win sighed. "Emily," she said.

Mine said Nathan. I walked into the living room. "What's up?"

"Got some interesting stuff to share. Can I come over?"

"Sure. Give us time to finish breakfast and get dressed?"

"Be there at ten."

As I returned to the kitchen, I heard Win say, "About two? See you then."

"Em's coming over?"

Win nodded as she poured coffee.

"So is Nathan."

Win looked alarmed, forehead all scrunched up.

"I'll work with him, you can take a nap." I held out my mug for a refill.

"No. You need to keep up with the investigation. That's your job. I'll take a pain pill and go to bed. That is, if you okay the pill. We can talk the issue over with Emily."

When Nathan arrived, Win was already in bed. He looked around, raised his eyebrows.

"Win's in bed trying to recuperate. What've you got?"

"I sent all the details to Win's computer—can I power it up? I know her password."

He sat in Win's chair, then accessed a file. "The company that bought the Messinger farm is Cobra Investment Corporation. They're incorporated in Alexandria, Virginia. Their board of directors and major officers are interesting. Look at this."

A graphic showed the officers who served in similar capacities for several other corporations as well. Rattler, a security agency; Viper, telecommunications; Diamondback, an electric grid management company, and Anaconda, a media conglomerate.

"Weird, but I don't get it, Nathan."

He sat back. "If you were going to forment revolution, what would you need to disrupt government?" He held one finger up. "A paramilitary entity like Blackwater or whatever they're calling it now. And one that owns a training camp like the one in Idaho."

"The same camp that we traced our locals to?"

"Exactly. Plus, all of these corporations have either their corporate offices or major regional offices in the same areas as each other—Virginia, Idaho, California and New York. Plus, the instructions for the flash mob at the LGBT center came from Rattler. I don't think I would've found that connection if I didn't have an end point to check."

"The snake names are chilling, not separately but put together."

"Yeah, especially when you consider the logo for 1776 Corps is a copperhead. The Copperheads were a Civil War group of northerners who tried to undermine Lincoln and the Union effort. And, though I can't prove it yet, it looks very likely that one of these entities is the one who paid Shamsi for the drones and missiles."

I shivered. "Have you sent this to Bill?"

"Yeah and he said it filled in a lot of blanks. They're monitoring."

"Good—I really don't want to take on a national conspiracy. But what the hell do we have to do with all of this? Insurrection in McCrumb County?"

"Bill thinks this could be a test of their black ops capability."

I saw red. Two dead, a bunch of injured for a damn test for a fucking fascist revolution? "This is real?"

"This is real."

CHAPTER FORTY-SIX

Win

Sarah's voice lifted me from sleep. She sounded impatient, her voice loud and insistent.

"What?" I croaked. The green numerals of our bedside clock said 12:32.

"I thought you'd like to get up, clean up and eat before Em comes. Maybe present a human face to her."

"You're crabby, aren't you? What'd Nathan say?"

"You don't want to know—remember? Are you getting up or should I try this again at one thirty?"

Cranky, all right. "I'm up."

When I finally made it into the kitchen, she'd made a salad with all the detritus the fridge held. Delightful. "We need to go grocery shopping."

"I called Dad with a list. Are you going to Bloomington tomorrow?"

I shook my head. "I called yesterday. There's no way I can get around campus on crutches with all the snow. Not to mention the stairs to the apartment, or the fact that I can't drive my truck."

"Good."

I blinked back tears. I'd never seen Sarah in such a snit. I needed her with me, holding me. Not a small Vesuvius ready to erupt at any moment.

By two o'clock, I'd built a fire and settled at one end of the couch, my bad leg resting on a pillow on the coffee table. Sarah was in our bedroom talking on the telephone. Emily's arrival got her off the phone, but her head was still attending to sheriff's business. When she sat next to me, I asked her for some time alone with Emily. Her eyebrows shot up, her mouth tightened. She went back to the bedroom, slammed the door.

"What's going on?" Emily asked.

"I don't know. Nathan came over this morning. Whatever he found out upset Sarah. A lot."

"You don't know what it is?"

I shook my head. "I needed to back away from the investigation. I asked her to not talk about...sheriff stuff. For now."

"You feel that precarious, Win?"

The tears flooded down my face. "I failed her. I didn't protect her."

"Just like Azar?"

I hadn't even thought of that. I told Emily so. "I think it's brought up the IED attack in Iraq. The way the car lifted up, like the Humvee. Maybe a leg injury from both."

The fire popped and I flinched. Good going, Win. Emily was examining me with the half-staff stare. I felt like I was back at the beginning of therapy.

"What feelings does that attack bring up for you?"

I knew what she was asking. I couldn't say it. Not yet. "Luck. Being at the wrong place at the wrong time. There's nothing you can do about an undetected IED."

"Nothing?"

"Nothing. You either make it out or not."

"So you're at the mercy of chance?"

I nodded. I wiped my sleeve across my face. "You do your best. Sometimes that's not enough. People die."

"Why don't you just spit it out?" Emily asked, her voice soft.

The tears began again. "I feel so fucking vulnerable. Not only can't I protect Sarah, I can't even protect myself. All my fucking training. All those years in war zones. I can't stop one guy with a fucking rifle."

Emily sat down beside me and put an arm around me. Let me cry it out.

"Shit," I finally said.

Emily handed me a couple of tissues and squeezed my shoulder. "I think it's time to hear from Sarah. Can you do that?"

I nodded and blew my nose. Emily got up. I heard her knock on the bedroom door. Voices. When I opened my eyes, Sarah was sitting down. At the other end of the couch.

"What are you feeling about the ambush, Sarah?" Emily asked.

Sarah's mouth was still a tight line. "Anger. No, rage."

"Interesting," Emily said without inflection. "Why the anger?"

"It shouldn't have happened." Sarah looked out the window. "I was tired. I wanted to get home so I didn't wait for our escort."

"It was your fault?" Emily asked.

Sarah nodded. "Win wanted to wait and she warned me. I did what I always do—figured I could just do it and plowed ahead."

"That's not true," I said. "We both wanted to get home. It should've been safe, even without an escort. An escort couldn't have stopped the shot."

Sarah turned to me. "I thought you were dead. You were unconscious and bleeding. I could see the shattered window. I thought the second shot hit you."

Her tears began to roll down her cheeks. I reached my hand toward her. She scooted over, put an arm around me.

"I understand why Win doesn't want to talk about this case, but I need her to help me," Sarah said as she pulled me closer. "I'm feeling so overwhelmed."

"You're quite a pair," Emily said. "Wonder Woman and Xena."

"Which one am I?" I asked.

Emily just stared.

"I'm sorry," Sarah said. "I should've asked if you could listen to what Nathan told me. I was just pissed because I felt like when I needed you, you were back in Afghanistan."

"Iraq," I said. "I'm sorry too. But I needed time to sort, to understand the trigger, the feelings underneath." I took her hand. "And to come totally clean, I resented your job. We should've been concentrating on healing. Instead, I felt like you were riding off with your posse."

Sarah stiffened. "I don't know any other way to cope—honestly, I wish I did."

"Ah, I love the human side of Wonder Woman and Xena," Emily said. "You both have to talk about this stuff or you won't stay together. Period. Sarah, I know how much being sheriff means to you, but you've got to find a way not to bring home all the pressure. Put aside time for family that's inviolate and do it now before the kids arrive. Ask your dad how he managed it."

Sarah looked miserable. "I had a few years under my belt as sheriff before Win shook my foundation. I didn't have any reason not to be fully engaged. In fact, I had every reason to clean up the mess Mac left. I'm still trying to find my way and, evidently, doing a lousy job of it."

"You'll learn as long as you make it a priority," Emily said. "You don't need to go into investigative details, but tell Win what worries you. Or that you're worried. Ask for her help, but if she says she can't, accept it. Take the opportunity to rest *in* Win. Because she's feeling vulnerable right now doesn't mean she's weak. She's the strongest woman I know. You know in your heart she'll never abandon you."

Sarah took a deep breath. Touched my cheek. "Sometimes I get so lost."

"I didn't handle this very well either. I just knew I had to shut down for a bit. I should've explained."

"Sarah, when you get back on a regular schedule, make an appointment," Emily said. "I still have to sign off on your after-action clearance. Same goes for you, Win. Make an appointment. We'll talk about what this dredged up." She stood. "I love you both and I'll do anything I can to help you stay together. Don't be afraid to call."

* * *

We sat on the couch for a long time after Emily left, simply breathing together. Sarah rose to put another log on the fire. She leaned into me when she sat down again.

"It's not all your fault, Sarah. We both built the wall. I'm sorry. I just felt very fragile."

"Personally, I think we've been under so much pressure, it just made it easier not to talk."

"Only for you." I said with a grin. "Now, tell me what news Nathan brought."

"Let me show you."

I lumbered to the computer after Sarah. I read Nathan's file, asked questions as I read. By the time we finished, my head hurt. "I assume Bill's on this."

"Yeah. If this is a nationwide conspiracy it isn't really our concern and I sure as hell can't deal with it. But Nathan said our felons are getting their orders from high up and that includes the Bloomington crowd."

"So they are connected." I went back over the file. "You're right, we need to concentrate on the local cell, or maybe cells. We need to know what progress Nolan's made with infiltrating the McCrumb County Rangers. I hope to hell he's okay."

That thought had been floating around the periphery of my thoughts, trying to get my attention. I'd kept saying *overload*. It worried me that Nolan was out there by himself. No backup, no safe word. That had been his preference. I needed to talk to Bill.

"If you feel like talking about this—do you?" Sarah asked.

"Yeah. I understand why you were so livid. You don't like your patch being used for a test run."

"Exactly." She put both hands on my shoulders, kissed my neck. "Why do you think they didn't finish us off?"

"It's a way of saying, 'See, we can make you dead anytime we want.' Hubris. Making us even more nervous. Beware of the snake—it can strike at any moment."

"They sure as hell are succeeding, Win."

"Keep it steady and sure. That's the only antidote."

"You have any idea what they'll do next?"

I took a deep breath. "If I were planning the op, I'd attack."

"Attack what?"

"The enemy's headquarters. Send in a few RPGs, do a quick raid. In and out. Not engage in battle, just hit as many people as I could. Throw them way off-balance."

"Oh hell and damnation."

CHAPTER FORTY-SEVEN

Sarah

Back at work on Wednesday morning, I called Caleb in first thing. As I recounted Win's thoughts, I watched his jaw drop. His response echoed mine. "Oh, crap."

"Let's get everybody on the same page—on high alert. Have Mark keep SWAT close even if we have to rearrange patrol. We need to get the team together, go over possible attack scenarios. I'll feel better if we have a plan."

"Jesus H. Christ." Caleb's jaw still hadn't returned to its normal position. "This is unreal."

"I know. But would you rather be prepared or just ignore the whole thing as impossible?"

"If they attacked, they must know it'd be all-out war."

"With whom? As far as they know, we have no idea who's been sniping, much less that there's an active cell in the county. From their perspective, they do a quick attack and disappear back to their regular lives. We're up shit creek."

Caleb ran the back of his finger against his mustache. He nodded. "I'll check our armory, see what we have available. Make sure everything's ready to go. What else?"

"Find a way that we can monitor our building cameras constantly and make sure they have a wide enough view we can see trouble coming."

He nodded. When he got up, I thought his legs were a tad bit shaky.

I called Willy and told him what was up.

"This Win's idea?"

"Yeah."

"Then we better go full-out. Is she at the station?"

"No, she's recuperating at home."

"Any chance we could meet there? I'd really like her input."

"Willy, she may not want to be involved. The ambush brought back some of her memories from Iraq. I'll call and ask. If we meet there, what do I need to bring? Floor plans for the station?"

"Yeah, definitely floor plans. I'll see if Google Earth has some shots of the square. We need to know where they could set snipers."

"Let me call Win." I called home and explained what Willy wanted. "But if you don't think you can handle it, say so. I hired Willy because he had this kind of experience."

"Maybe I wouldn't feel like such a failure at keeping you safe if I helped. This is not something I want to do. But I can't let you twist in the wind."

"You're sure?"

"Positive."

We set a time, I asked Caleb if he'd come and we headed out around two. Caleb drove, our escort of two deputies up ahead and I had a rifle in my hands. My wrist ached and if I admitted it, I was tired.

When we got home, Win had cleared the dining table and pulled up chairs. The computer was on and the fire lit. I hated that war entered Win's sanctuary, but she looked alert and ready to go. She motioned for me to follow as she went into the kitchen.

"You want to serve snacks?" I asked.

"No, and what kind of question is that? I talked to Nolan," Win said, leaning toward me and keeping her voice down. "The Rangers are planning an op. Against the station. They haven't set a date or time yet, but Sarah, it's coming."

"I kept telling myself this was an exercise in vigilance, nothing more."

"Yeah, right. But you can't tell these guys anything is sure. It could blow Nolan's cover. Just say Bill's picked up some chatter."

I nodded. I strode into the war room knowing Win had my back.

* * *

My head was full of options and alternatives, plans and counter-plans. Win had talked with Bill and he was going to provide fortification for the most exposed areas at the station. Bullet proof glass and steel plates for dispatch and the complaint desk. We couldn't do much about the building itself because it was too old and we didn't have a fortune to spend. Before the economic downturn, the commissioners had talked about building a new station by the jail at the edge of town. This was the first time I thought it was a good idea. We needed a bunker.

We'd worked until five and then the contingent of law enforcement trudged out of our home. I tried to relax on the couch, watching the flames dance. Win had brainstormed us to a good defensive plan with minimal threat to our people. To me, minimal wasn't good enough. I wondered if our old station would go up in flames like the logs in the fireplace. If they used grenades or incendiary devices…

Win sat down next to me and let out a long breath. "How you doing?"

"Fair to middlin'," I said. "You? Was this too much for you?"

"It's what I used to enjoy most. Planning ops." She lifted her cast onto a folded-up towel on the coffee table and grunted. "As long as I don't have to be there, it's okay. Except I'd like to be there, at your back. I don't think I can do that, Sarah."

"I don't want you there, I want you here at home safe. If you were there, I couldn't think about anything but protecting you."

"Shit. We're screwy, aren't we?" Win gave me a hug. "I've set up a video conference with Emily for tomorrow."

"Hey, good idea."

"What option do I have? I can't drive my truck. First time I've ever wanted an automatic transmission. When do you get your new car?"

"Truck," I said. "When the insurance money gets here. They seem to believe I was using it for work."

"Bullshit. You need to get a lawyer on it."

"Already did. Deborah's sicced a guy in her office on it."

"You didn't tell me."

"Sorry Win. It wasn't on purpose, just one of those annoying things that got lost in all of the other stuff. Honest, I called Deborah and let it go."

Win took my hand. "We've let a lot go, haven't we? Cooking, cleaning. All the small comforts of life."

"Cleaning? That's a comfort?"

Win nodded and rubbed her thumb over the back of my hand. "This is the first home I've owned. Taking care of it gives me such great pleasure. It makes it real. Something to give thanks for, like I've survived. Like I give thanks for you."

Win took my breath away. Even in the smallest things, she found solace and maybe healing. "I never thought of it that way, but I will."

I put my arm around her and she leaned into me. I wished this moment could go on forever. The pop and roar of the fire, Des asleep at the end of the couch and my woman in my embrace. All of us safe and at peace. No matter the storm on the horizon, this was a moment of profound calm. I relished it and hoped it would sustain me, give me the courage to walk into the station with calm and certainty that we could face whatever came.

CHAPTER FORTY-EIGHT

Win

After Sarah left for work, I started crying and couldn't stop. I was terrified for her safety. At the same time, I knew I couldn't get near a weapon without blowing all the fuckers away. Armed or not. Already down or not. The razor's edge between fear and rage. I was scared to move.

Before my video chat with Emily, I went in and washed my face. There was no way I could tell her what was going on. Not over an unsecured link. I almost called her to cancel.

At our appointed time, I booted up the computer and brought up the link. Emily appeared on the screen, then leaned forward. "How are you?"

"Uh, not great."

"What's happened?"

"Um, some unexpected news, I guess." How could I let her know the threat to Sarah? To everyone at the station?

"Hold on a minute." She disappeared from the screen. When she came back, she said she had an emergency and would have to get back to me later in the afternoon.

Get back to me? I closed the link, pounded the desk with my fist. How the hell could she abandon me now? Fuck her! Damn if I'd ever go to her again!

My phone rang. I picked it up. Emily. "What?"

"I figured you couldn't say much, afraid somebody was eavesdropping. Right?"

"Yeah."

"I have one more client to see, then I'll come out. Can you hold out an hour and a half?"

Thank the heavens. "Yes. I'm so sorry. I don't want you to have to drive out here—"

"Can it, Win. I'll see you soon." She hung up.

I started crying again. Des padded up, put her head in my lap. I buried my face in her fur. She stood patiently until I pulled back, then went into a frenzy of licking my face dry. She woofed and went to the door.

"You've already been out. I can't play, Des."

She woofed again, stubborn dog. I got my parka, put it on. When I stepped out onto the porch, I was greeted by sparkling snow and warmer temperatures. I couldn't do much hiking, but at least I made a circuit of the clearing.

When we came in, I realized I felt better. "Thanks, Des. Good idea."

She woofed and settled down on her end of the couch.

Emily eventually arrived, looking worried. She settled in the chair, with me on the couch, upright. I explained the plot we'd discovered, how scared I was that I'd lose Sarah.

She shook her head. "Jesus, Win. How do you guys manage to land smack-dab in the middle of these 'situations'? Never mind, shit happens."

I closed my eyes. Took a deep breath. "When I woke up in the hospital, I immediately thought of the hospital in Germany. That I was at Landstuhl after the IED explosion. Brought back all those feelings of losing control."

"Of being impotent?"

"Of course."

"And how does that connect with what you're feeling now?"

"They're exactly the same. I feel like shit and there's nothing I can do."

Emily leaned forward. "Is that true? That you can't do anything?"

"I've been working on intel, trying to figure out what those fuckers want."

"What realization have you come to?"

I leaned my head back. Thought about the snake brigade and the hate they spewed. "They want revolution, to overthrow the government—national, state and local. For Sarah, there's a solid threat to her life. Not just to Sarah, to all her deputies. We've already seen two attacks on them, one on us."

"Okay, I get it and it's damn scary. You've created the role of Sarah's protector. Don't you feel she can protect herself?"

"Overwhelming force against a county sheriff? Odds are they'll succeed."

Emily shifted in her chair. "Why doesn't she call in the National Guard? Or, if this is a national plot, turn it over to the FBI?"

"She can't do anything without tipping off the conspirators we're on to them. Remember, it's nationwide. Fuck it." Des moved over to me and laid her head in my lap. I dug my hand into her fur. Rubbed the spot beneath her ear. "The more agencies involved, the more chance there'll be leaks. That would be disastrous—cause the snake brigade to go further underground where we can't track them. Sarah's damned if she does, damned if she doesn't. She's got MCIA behind her. That's enough for now."

"And you?"

"I may have a savior complex, but this is a real threat, Emily. The thing that scares me so much, if I'm there, I'd take all the bad guys out. Not stop firing until they're all dead."

"You're afraid you'll lose control?"

I nodded. "This whole collection of crackpots makes me furious."

"Why?"

"Why wouldn't they?" I leaned back and took several deep breaths. "They buy the propaganda blindly, whole-assed. Government's evil, ready to take all their rights. Ship them off to concentration camps. Their religion's the only true path. They always think in black and white, don't bother to listen to reason or facts. They see the world through the cockeyed lens of their own beliefs, religious or paranoid."

"So they're a bunch of twits. Why would they force you to lose control? How, Win?"

I had no answer, just a bubbling rage. "I will not allow those fucking idiots to hurt Sarah, to take her from me. I will kill every fucking one of them until there's no more threat."

My hands shook. I felt tremors that began in my stomach, pressed outward through my body. My chest was so tight I could barely force the words out. "I love Sarah so much. If I lost her...my soul would die."

The tears started to flow again. I couldn't get my breath. I felt Des get down. Then Emily sat down and put her arms around me. I gave up. Let her pull me to her shoulder. I cried until I was weak. She handed me some tissues.

I blew my nose a couple of times, wiped my eyes with my sleeve. Leaned back utterly exhausted.

"So it's not just protecting Sarah," Emily said quietly. "It's about protecting you too."

"I guess." I was too tired to argue. "I've never felt the depth of love I feel for Sarah. I can't lose her now."

"You shouldn't have to," Emily said. "But you know, have known, Sarah's wearing a target on her back for every crackpot and criminal in the county."

"She never signed on for a dirty bomb or international arms dealers or a national conspiracy to overthrow the government of the United States. But the bottom line is, this is just a fucking test run for these pricks before they do it nationwide."

"I understand your anger, Win. We just have to figure a way to contain it."

"Good luck."

"I don't think it's a good idea for you to be in the thick of the action," Emily said after a long silence.

"So glad you agree with my assessment."

"But you won't be able to stay home, not without exploding."

"I know." I leveled an elbow onto the arm of the couch, let my head sink down to my hand. "Screwed either way."

"Oh, Win. This isn't the end of the world. It's just a very dangerous situation. You're a trained sniper, aren't you?"

"Yeah. I could take lead sniper and pick them off while they mass outside."

"Would you?"

I leaned back. "No. Not before they'd done anything. But if they came out firing…"

"Would you shoot to kill?"

"That's what I'm trained to do. At this point, I honestly don't know."

* * *

When I finally pulled myself together, I asked Emily if she'd stay for dinner. She said yes with two conditions. "You lie down and get some rest and please, call me Em."

"You're lucky I don't call you Dr. Peterson. Or Doc."

I stretched out on the couch, my leg elevated correctly and a pillow under my head.

"Those are gorgeous photographs of you and Sarah," she said. When I jerked up, she laughed. "Where do you think I got the pillow? They're really beautiful and go to the heart of your relationship. Try thinking about them as you fall asleep."

I did fall asleep, quickly. Deeply. Without dreams or nightmares. When I woke up, I heard voices in the kitchen. Smelled the unmistakable fragrance of lamb roasting. The fire burned brightly. Magic elves?

Sarah walked in and sat down. I scooched over, took her hand.

"I'm glad you got some solid sleep. You've been tossing around a lot at night."

"Have I kept you awake? Is that why you're so draggy?"

"Draggy, eh." She leaned down and kissed me. "You invited Em for dinner and then let me cook after a full day of work, with a bum wrist, while you take a nap."

"I love you." I pulled her into a long kiss. "I'm really scared, Sarah. This whole op could go horribly wrong."

"Em told me a little bit of what you said, she didn't spill the beans or anything. But a sniper position might be a good place for you. When it goes down."

"I've been racking my brains, trying to think of another way to nail them. Before they put their plan into action. If there's enough evidence, conspiracy should be enough to put them away."

Sarah smiled, touched my cheek like a feather. "Conspiracy is one of the charges we'll file when we get them. They'll go away for life with no opportunity for parole."

"Is it worth it?" I took both of her hands in mine. "Putting them away for good? With your life in the balance? Your deputies' lives?"

She looked me in the eye. "Yes."

"Shit."

"I can't live with this festering in my county, Win. No matter how tempting it is to nip it in the bud, if these guys get out of jail in five years, it'll be much worse. They'd have five years of tutoring by other felons." She squeezed my hands. "Besides, arresting them before they strike would show our hand, just how much intel we've collected and our sources, including Nolan. We need to protect him too."

"I know. But I need to protect you, Sarah."

CHAPTER FORTY-NINE

Sarah

Tension ratcheted up over the next week, both at work and at home. Everybody at the station was jumpy and when Vincente dropped some boxes on his way down the stairs, every weapon was drawn. He apologized profusely, then dropped them again when he tried to set them on a desk in the bullpen.

Win was having nightmares and neither one of us was sleeping soundly. One good thing happened. When I went to the Ford dealer to talk about a new truck, he gave me a loaner until the insurance money came through. That gift allowed Win to get into town twice for sessions with Em. We were each due back at the hospital for follow-up treatment and hopefully lighter casts. Win complained periodically about the weight of hers. "I don't know why the hell they had to put this thing on. They're still in the damn dark ages." Then she'd thump down the hall on her crutches.

I agreed. My left arm was getting downright muscular. Besides, I was scared I'd strike out at a dream opponent and do real damage to Win. Even Des picked up on how stressed Win was and followed her around the house constantly. So far, they'd avoided getting tangled up.

Win had updates from Nolan every two or three days. It looked as if D-Day would be next week, when Win was supposed to be back in Bloomington teaching. She couldn't take more time off, but I wondered what the distance and the worry would do to her. I didn't think I'd seen her so fragile since she'd come back into my life.

"Can you relax?" I asked.

"When this is done."

"Win—"

"I can't stop now. I know. It's not healthy. Emily's made that perfectly clear."

"Then—"

"Not open to negotiation, Sarah. Let me be on high alert now. When it's over, we'll go down to West Baden for a week. Soak in the hot springs. My treat."

If we made it that far. I couldn't go much longer like this and neither could Win. The strain affected every part of our life together, even at home, even in bed.

I pulled into the hospital parking lot and dropped Win off at the door. By the time I got inside, Win was already closeted with the orthopedic surgeon. I would've twiddled my thumbs, but the damn cast made it too hard. While I waited, I went over our plan. Bill had come through with a steel grate he had welded over the back door, as well as steel plating to protect the lower portion of the complaint desk and dispatch. He'd install the bulletproof glass above both the night before the attack, assuming we'd have that much advance notice. The bug in Dog's was only feeding us information that we already had. Our best source, hands down, was Nolan, Win's friend who was putting his life on the line for us.

The door opened and Win maneuvered her way out with a grin on her face. "New lighter cast. Yes! Your turn. Good luck."

The surgeon waved me in and had me sit on the exam table. He had the radiographer x-ray my wrist. "Great new digital system," he said. "No waiting." He moved the unit aside. Took my hand and examined the cast. "You've been boxing? Or doing martial arts?"

"What?"

"This is so banged up." A machine beeped and he went over to it, then stuck the film on a light board. "Hmm."

"Please tell me you're taking this damn thing off because it's making me crazy."

"We'll take it off so we can put a new one on," he said as he gently turned my hand over. "Your wrist is healing, but you need to protect it more. Looking at this cast, you're not very good at it. Hence, a new one, just like this one." He smiled. "Sorry. But if you want it to heal properly, that's what we have to do."

I said "damn him" to myself. I could've whacked him with it.

With my new cast, seemingly heavier than the last one, I saw Win in the waiting area.

She looked at my cast, raised her eyes to mine and lifted one eyebrow. "Chic."

"That's what I was going to say about yours. Bright blue? Really?"

"I asked for black," she said with a crooked smile. "I had my choice of Kelly green, neon pink or this. At least it doesn't weigh a ton." She rose, stuck the crutches under her arms. "Do we have to go back to the station? Or can we go home?"

"I'm ready for home with a fire in the fireplace and you by my side. Let's try to relax and not think about anything."

"Yeah, right."

* * *

I woke up to water gurgling in the downspout and dripping from the trees outside. I figured our February thaw had arrived at last. I slipped out of bed and stood for several silent minutes just looking at Win. Her face was so relaxed and reminded me of the kid I'd met in first grade. How long ago that seemed, yet the memory was still so sharp. Even though she'd tried, she'd remained on high alert last night. Her lovemaking hadn't been the thorough sensual enjoyment she normally showed.

I put on a robe and new shearling clogs and after the coffee started brewing, turned on TV. Instead of coming down from Canada, the weather was moving from the southwest and warm temperatures were slated for the next week. Damn. That meant flooding which would keep my deputies fully occupied as the winter's snow melted. We were stretched thin enough with regular patrols. Search and rescue missions, a certainty with flooding, would pull deputies away from their patrols and away from the station. I turned off the TV.

I built a fire, just to have some brightness in the gray dawn. As I sat on the couch, my hands wrapped around the mug, I couldn't decide what I was most worried about, the coming assault or Win. Time had taken such a big chunk of our lives before we got together, I couldn't stand the thought of...no, I couldn't go there.

Win was to be our lead sniper, stationed on the highest building on the square, the old Masonic Lodge. Leslie would be her backup on the roof. I'd thought about stationing two deputies by the stairs, but we just didn't have enough people. My main concern was how Win was going to work her way up all those flights of stairs.

I heard Win in the hall, the thumps mostly squeaks as she maneuvered into the bathroom. I got up, poured her a mug and myself a refill, all the while waiting for the clatter of crutches on the floor. Worry much, Sarah?

I heard her coming down the hall and met her at the couch. "I thought you might sleep in today."

"I awoke wifeless, though the bed was still warm on your side. Did I wake you? Was I dreaming?"

"Yes and yes. All night. What are the dreams about?"

"Don't remember. How can I change the dream if I don't realize I'm dreaming?" Win blew on her coffee and took a sip. "We finally got a Skype account set up with CELI. I won't have to go into campus until I'm off crutches. Got an email yesterday. Forgot to tell you."

"Wow. I didn't even know you were working on it."

She watched me with a question in her eyes. "Yes, you did. I told you when I first thought of it."

"Are you sure?"

"Yes. You've got too much on your mind to retain trivia." Win sat back, let out a long breath. "I wish to hell they'd speed up their schedule."

"CELI?"

"The Rangers, or whatever the nitwits are calling themselves. It's the waiting that's the hard part, always the waiting."

I nodded. Normally, waiting meant judges issuing warrants or for forensics to finish. I didn't think I'd ever get used to waiting for battle. "The snow's melting and I'm worried."

"About flooding?"

"Temps in the fifties and low sixties for the next seven days."

She took a deep breath. "How thin will that stretch your force?"

"Depends on how many idiots try and stay put at home too long."

Win leaned her head back and cradled her mug. "We need to do a sweep for explosive devices that morning. I'd use a diversion before I sent the force in."

"Enough! Can't we just take this time together and be together?"

Win turned to look at me. "I thought we did that last night."

"Your mind was working on countermeasures or some other stuff the whole time."

Win got up and put another log on the fire. "This is the time in an op when I do nothing but review the plan. Look for weaknesses. Make contingency plans. I'm not used to taking a break."

"Can you let it go for now?"

She leaned against the mantel, looking bruised and bushed. "I can try. I can't promise the result you want, Sarah." She pushed off the mantel and reached for her crutches. "You know what I was thinking about last night? When we were making love? What your chances of survival were if you were hit in the particular part of your body I was touching." She took a step forward. "I know you thought I was distracted. It's just...I love you so much."

CHAPTER FIFTY

Win and Sarah

Win

After Sarah called in to the station, we went back to bed. "Can we just touch?" I asked. "No goals. Just be here with one another?"

"You're asking a lot," she said. "You're supposed to be concentrating on me, remember? On my body and my desires and—"

"I want you in my arms, Sarah. Just here. Real." I touched her shoulder, ran my hand down her arm. "You've changed my life. I want to hold on to that change, just for a while when I can see where I've been, where I am now—before the next cycle of change that's inevitable."

Sarah moved to lay her head on my shoulder. I inhaled her scent and wrapped my arms around her. "It's not that I don't want you. I do. But right now, I need to know you're safe."

"When the attack goes down, we'll be separated," Sarah said after a long silence. "Can you handle that?"

"I'll have to." I ran my hand through her hair, kissed the spot below her ear. "I'll be on the com line. I'll have an idea of what's happening."

"You'll hear shots and shouts."

"Don't Sarah. Please. If you want me to awaken my desire, just shut up. I need to feel you in my arms so I can let go of the fear. Because that's all I feel most of the time since this started. I'm terrified this could be the last time we make love. Ever."

Sarah

Win spoke the words that took my breath away and stopped my heart. It was the thought I'd pushed away so many times. Especially since I saw her covered in blood and so still in the wreck.

"We can't think like that," I said. "We can't live like that."

"How can we not?" She tightened her embrace. "I'm okay with you going to work. It isn't you being a cop. This is so different, Sarah. This is a military raid orchestrated by fanatics."

I could hear her heart thumping, steady but way fast. "We've had advance notice and we've planned."

"Take it from a planner, anything can go wrong. Everything. Too many variables, too much unknown."

"My people will execute. They'll do what they have to do."

"It's not your deputies that give me nightmares."

I didn't want to push, but maybe Win remembered more than she thought. "Is that what the nightmares are about? Things going wrong?"

"I really don't remember them. I'm just assuming. The same thing happened every time I planned an op, nightmares. Then in the morning, something I'd overlooked popped into my mind."

"Anything pop now?"

"No."

I started to move my left hand to her face and ended up whacking her head with my cast.

"Get that weapon out of here," she said. "Roll over and we can spoon."

Win

Sarah shifted to her side and I held her close to me. Skin on skin. What could be more truthful? Real? Loving.

Had anything popped up from my subconscious? Diversion by explosives. Des and I could walk the square right before dawn, then the camera operators could pick up surveillance.

"You want to keep Des with you that day?" I asked.

"I thought we're supposed to be in a timeout. You're confusing me."

"Sorry. It just slipped out." I felt her ribs as she sighed.

"What did Em tell you to do? To let go of all the planning? Of what's coming?"

"Think about our photos."

Sarah turned to me. "When did she see them?"

"She went in to get a pillow for my head." I felt her tighten up. "Look at them, Sarah. They're beautiful."

"If I wanted everyone in the county to know what I looked like without clothes, I'd put my badge on my boob and go to work."

I kissed her neck. Whispered in her ear, "That'd be a unique way of collaring felons."

She pulled me into a deep embrace. "I'm tired of dealing with felons. I'd much rather collar you."

"I surrendered to you a long time ago. Remember?" I kissed her. Felt her breathing become more rapid. I willed thoughts of war and carnage out of my mind, thought about the woman in my arms. For the next hour, Sarah was going to be the only reality I knew.

CHAPTER FIFTY-ONE

Win

"I think I was right," Sarah said with a smile. She took another bite of her lamb sandwich. "We needed a timeout. I haven't felt so…rested in ages. Not since this started."

"That's because you fell asleep immediately after, Sarah." I picked up the sandwich, then put it down. "Do you realize all the food memories I have from growing up are from your mother? I don't think I'd ever had lamb before your house."

"I remember she fixed you a lamb sandwich one noontime and when she realized she'd fixed it without asking what you'd liked, she was flummoxed."

"She asked what I wanted on it. I didn't have a clue. You said to try it that way first. I did. Still eating it the same way."

"Didn't your mother ever cook?"

I put the sandwich down. "Cook? No. We had TV dinners. Oh, and hot dogs."

"Did you eat together?"

I shook my head. "We never knew when Dad would be home from work. So when we got hungry, we'd heat something up and eat it wherever we wanted. Mom didn't care."

She looked down.

I knew what she was thinking—cold house to grow up in. No walking in the back door and smelling the luscious scents of something good in the oven. Just Pine-Sol. Older brothers who were ready to pounce on me as soon as I walked in. No wonder I spent so much time at Sarah's house. No wonder I'd relished my life in military intelligence. Avoiding direct confrontation with the enemy or my brothers was one whole cloth.

"This is the home I never had. Warmth, good food, shared chores. So much that I missed growing up."

"How about a warm bed?"

I laughed. "I wasn't thinking about that when I was little. You are at the heart of my life, Sarah, then and now. Kind of a miracle, isn't it?"

"Fate, maybe." She reached across the table and took my hand in hers. "Whatever the cause, I'm eternally grateful. I've watched friends walk in here and their eyes light up because they feel the warmth and the love."

I felt pride in the physical structure I'd built. But I also was proud of what Sarah and I had built together, would continue building—if nothing happened to Sarah.

She must've noticed the dark cloud that passed over my face, squeezed my hand. "We'll be here together until we're old women, sitting in our rocking chairs on the porch in good weather."

"Emily taught me to examine what I was feeling. But sometimes, she said, I just needed to stop thinking. This is one of those times, Sarah. You were right."

"Then eat up and we can go back to bed." She waggled her eyebrows and laughed.

I shook my head. "I promise I will shove away every negative thought that comes through my mind. Tonight. In the morning, I get back to planning, making adjustments, trying to anticipate their actions. I really hope Nolan gets hold of me soon. I need his input."

"Tomorrow, Win."

* * *

Sarah was in the shower, Des outside. All was right in my world, especially after last night. I checked my phone while the coffee brewed. Three texts from Nolan. The last indicated he wanted a meeting. After such a short respite, back to worrying, to fear.

I texted back. *When? Where?* It wasn't more than a few seconds later when he texted back. *Dog's @ 9:00 a.m. Park in back. Use back door.*

Dog's? Did Micah set this up? I called Micah and asked.

"Just gave the boy some names of folk he could trust an' told him to use my name," Micah said. "Don't know what he did after that. Haven't seen him since."

"I've got a meet with Nolan there at nine. If you don't hear from me after, call the sheriff."

As I hung up, I thought Micah knew the ground better than I did. Still, it didn't hurt to be careful. Very careful.

As Sarah ate breakfast, I briefed her. "I'll call you after I leave. You have time to meet for lunch?"

"Come on by," she said. "We can always order in." She looked up at me. "So we're back to worrying about everything, aren't we?"

"Remember West Baden when it gets to be too much. Hot springs, soaking, massages. Promise."

I approached the Dog Pound with a circuitous route. Parked, tried the back door and found it was open. I stepped inside and saw an older man who might've been the father of the Dog I remembered.

"You Win Kirkland?"

I nodded. I'd changed too.

"My office—hall in back of you."

"Thanks." I turned around, found a door marked Office across from the bathrooms. I opened the door. Nolan sat with his feet resting on a heater by the desk.

"Hey." He put his feet down and handed me a phone. "Everything's there. All correspondence with Bill, background intel and as much of their plan that's set. I'll let you know about half an hour before they launch."

"How?"

"Text message. Win, these guys are gung-ho idiots. I've talked them out of grenades or other explosives, but it was a job. Had to blabber on about how insurgents I fought were fucking cowards and stooped to explosive vests because they couldn't win in a fair fight." He held up his hand. "I know, not the war either you or me fought. But these guys suck up war talk."

"The most dangerous kind of minds—haven't been there but saw it on TV."

"Yeah. Got photos of all of 'em on the phone with names and addresses. No com lines, we're running silent. All the weapons are semiautomatic except one guy's got a machine pistol."

"Shit. He could just spray the place and come away with multiple hits."

"I know. I'll try to divert him, but it's not going to be easy. Anyway, five go in the back entrance, five in the front—"

"That's the solution—have him lead the group to the back. We have a couple of surprises ready for them there."

"Wrapped in the new BearCat G3?"

Bill had gotten the sheriff's department a real deal on an armored vehicle to go with SWAT. Sarah had hesitated. I'd pushed. "Yeah. Nice wheels."

Nolan nodded. "I'll put him in the back assault group." He sighed. "Hope you have a few surprises for the front group too."

"Not so much. There's not a lot we can do with that open space. Bill lent us some dummies from the Fun House we'll use in the bullpen. SWAT will be there but hidden. I'll be on sniper duty."

"Don't let those bastards get away, Win." He smacked the desk. "I sure as hell didn't risk my neck abroad so I could come home to lunatics running the country."

"Me neither."

"How are you holding up? And Sarah?"

"Hanging in, but I sure hope this happens soon. It gets harder every day."

"Unless things get changed, it's going down tomorrow at noon."

The news took my breath away. I nodded. "Are you wearing ski masks? Something to disguise your faces?"

"Bandanas, fucking bandanas like we're in a western movie. Fucking stupid."

"Let me get your picture," I said. "I don't want someone shooting you. Do a full face and then one with something covering the bottom. Look mean, Nolan." I snapped a couple with my phone and then one three-quarter shot. "Take care of yourself, man."

He nodded. "Just make sure none of them make it out of there. If they get snickered and know it was a setup, the other ones are much more likely to crawl back under their rock."

Other ones. "Thanks, Nolan. Thanks so much."

He got up and I got a long bear hug. "I ran out on you once. This is just payback, only what I owe you."

I held him at arm's length. "You did what you were supposed to do. Get those guys to a medical facility ASAP. What I did was ignore orders."

"You ever sorry you retired?"

"No, not one moment."

He examined my face, then nodded. "Well, Colonel, this is my last mission before I retire. So you keep my butt safe, Sir."

I gave him a hug, saluted. Left without turning back.

CHAPTER FIFTY-TWO

Sarah

Win came into my office full of information. We went over everything on the phone Nolan gave us including detailed plans where possible, guesses about the personnel and their reactions to various scenarios.

"Whew," I said. "He's been really thorough and this is a goldmine."

"Nolan's a pro." Win took out her own phone.

"What's wrong?"

"We've got to make sure he's not accidentally shot. He won't be wearing a vest. Here, I took some shots of him. SWAT and the detectives and whoever else is involved inside need to know his face."

"We'll distribute copies."

"Not until tomorrow when everybody's here." Win shifted in her chair. "We don't know for sure that someone here wouldn't talk. Not necessarily on purpose, don't get me wrong. 'Loose lips sink ships.' Still goes."

I studied Win. She was a coiled snake ready to strike. It was absurd that image entered my mind, but it did. "Dad called and wants in on the party. I don't want him in the line of fire. Would you be comfortable with him at your back? Downstairs? If anyone tries to go up, he can nab them."

"I trust Micah to have my six as much as I trust you," she said, rolling her head.

"Need a back rub?"

"Tonight. I'd like a briefing with SWAT and one with the detectives and uniforms."

"Sure. Right now?"

"Tomorrow morning. Eight o'clock?"

"I'll set it up and I won't tell anyone we think it's tomorrow."

"Thanks. I know I'm sounding like a paranoid general. Sorry, I can't help it. I have to keep all of you safe and I promise I'll do my very best."

I sat back in my chair. "It's killing you, isn't it? Not being in the middle of this?"

Win expelled a long breath and nodded. "But I'd be a liability with this leg. I know I'm best where I'll be. It's just hard, Sarah."

We didn't leave the station until the early twilight had descended on the melting landscape. We traveled in that moment of blue when any light in a window cast an orange glow. Rivers and streams ran high and swift, their voices singing an unholy harmony. Bare trees rose in their stark blackness along the road, a whisper of warning from their limbs. I realized I'd been holding my breath when we pulled into the clearing where our home stood.

Safe, at least for the night.

As we fixed dinner, Win was silent and I thought she was going over the plan again, step by step. She ate the same way, in silence and preoccupied. After we finished the dinner dishes, she lit the fire and sat on the couch. She patted the spot next to her.

"Me or Des?" I asked.

"Whoever gets here first," she said with a grin.

I sat next to her and she put an arm around me. I nestled close to her and put my hand on her stomach. "I wish tomorrow would never come."

"Shhh," she said. "I'm trying my best to turn those thoughts off. Let's be here and now, enjoy the fire. Except for one question. Do you want Des with you tomorrow? Nolan said they weren't using explosives."

"No. I'd be too worried about her."

"I'll take her with me. I've got so much protection at my back, I won't be able to breathe. Now let's watch the dance."

"Dance?"

"Fire dance." She put both arms around me and kissed my forehead. I sighed and tried my best to watch the fire, but thoughts of tomorrow kept pushing into my mind. I was terrified for my people and for me. Could we really overpower a bunch of fanatics? We damn well better, but by all that's right we shouldn't have to.

"Let it go, Sarah. Wait for morning before you think about it again."

"That's usually my spiel. I'm scared."

"It's going to be okay." She turned my face toward her. "I'm not just saying that. I feel it in my bones. We're prepared. Your people know what to do. Have the skills to execute. We'll get the fuckers and we'll get them good."

* * *

After the briefings in the morning, I felt better. Win had done a full run-through with those who'd be involved, firing questions at them and none had hesitated. They knew where they were supposed to be and what they were supposed to do.

"Got a note from Nathan this morning," Win said as people filed out. "He's uploaded all your data and links to the Cloud. You have any old computers and monitors stashed away?"

"Yeah, a bunch in the basement we've never gotten around to scrubbing."

"Why don't you switch them out with what you use now? No use in damaging good equipment."

"Good idea." I took her hand. "Are you going up now?"

"Yeah." She pulled me to her. "You take care of yourself, stick to the plan even if they throw you surprises."

I leaned against her. "Don't say 'surprises,' please."

She kissed me and then she and Des were gone.

We switched out the computers, propped up the dummies and checked weapons. At eleven thirty people drifted to their assigned places.

I checked with Dory to see how she was doing. "Fine," she said. "Can't wait for the vermin to come." She opened the drawer beside her and I saw a Colt .45 revolver.

"Do you have a carry permit?"

"No. You gonna arrest me, Sarah?"

At three minutes to noon, Win alerted us that a black van had entered the parking lot in back. A few seconds later, one guy walked in the front door. He looked around, then leaned against the wall and texted. I held my breath. Would he notice the dummies? The old equipment? The new glass barriers? Had he texted *no* or *go?*

"Five men coming toward the front entrance. Get ready."

I saw the men through my window on the bullpen. They passed the outside window. "It's a go. Ready. They're through the door. Weapons drawn. *Go.*"

The next few moments were a blur of firing and return fire. My window shattered, glass spewed across the office. I crouched as I crossed it, weapon drawn. Over the constant gunfire, I heard heavy footsteps coming toward the door and moved back against the wall by the door. A big bald head led a fat body through the door. My rage exploded. I used my cast as I backhanded him mid-face with all my strength. He fell backward into the hall. I stood over him, my weapon at the ready. He was out cold, blood spurting from his nose.

Caleb rushed up. "You okay?"

"Fine." I became aware that the firing had ended. "Our guys?"

"A couple wounded I think, nothing life-threatening."

"Cuff him, would you."

Caleb holstered his weapon, turned the man over and dealt with him. We left him lying in the hall. When I stepped into the bullpen, a pall from the gunpowder hung over the wreckage.

"What a damn mess." One of the front windows had shattered, computer guts spilled out and monitors smoked. I glanced around the room and saw my deputies cuffing four men, two of whom seemed to be bleeding. "Everybody okay?" I shouted.

"Yo," Willy said with a big grin. "A couple of scratches, nothing more. But we will need a bus for a couple of them."

The front door opened and all weapons pointed to the door.

"Don't shoot," John said. "It's us with our prisoners." The guys who'd been in back pushed in five cuffed prisoners. "Mission accomplished without a shot. Where's Win?"

"I gather the raid is over?" Win said over my com line. "Your dad's got two more to add to the party. Heading down."

"See you soon."

We started getting organized to book them all, those unwounded first up. Two ambulances showed up and the EMTs took care of our guys first. I watched the organized chaos and then I saw Win on her crutches crossing the square with Des beside her. Dad was behind her with two guys cuffed together and poked by dad's Winchester. I smiled. We'd made it through and we were okay.

I heard a shot and saw Win fall backward. Two more shots. What the hell? I rushed through the front door, my weapon drawn and scanning the square for a shooter. God dammit, how the fuck could this happen?

CHAPTER FIFTY-THREE

Win

"You get him, Leslie?"

"Roger that, Win. You okay?"

"Basically. Good work."

Micah took my arm and helped me up. I saw Sarah running from the station. When she put on the brakes in front of me, I was afraid she'd hug me.

"Sniper on the roof of the drugstore," I said quickly. "My flak jacket caught the bullet, but I may be a bit sore tonight." I looked up. "Think it's our thirty-aught-six shooter. Can you get a couple of deputies up there?"

Sarah nodded, though she appeared stunned.

Micah shoved his two prisoners ahead. "I'll take care of it, Daughter. You help Win."

"You could've been killed. Why the hell did you pull a stunt like this? Set yourself up as a target?" she squeaked.

"I don't like assassinating someone now that I'm home."

"Let's get you to the hospital—"

"No." I glanced at the ambulances pulled up in front, lights still flashing. People were beginning to form groups by the other buildings on the square. "Let's go inside and assess the op."

"I just want to assess your injury," she said as she hurried beside me.

"You can do that tonight at your leisure."

She reached for the door.

"What the hell happened to your cast?"

Sarah raised it to see. "Oh. I used it as a weapon. I didn't want to risk giving him a verbal warning."

"You're the one who needs to go to the hospital, Sarah."

"Only if you come with me and get checked out."

I nodded. "Let's get the after-action started." I walked in and looked at the mess. "Okay, folks, damn good job. Somebody needs to photograph the scene, check on the surveillance cameras and see what they caught. Anybody get away?"

"No," Caleb said. "Better haul than we expected."

"Any cop need treatment?"

"We got it, Win. How about you getting Sarah to the hospital? She's got blood all over her cast," Caleb said.

Sarah looked down at it. "That's his, not mine."

Leslie walked in. "I'll be glad to take you, Sarah. You really should have that looked at right away. You may have done more damage."

"I did damage all right," Sarah said. "The guy's still out. First, we have to take photos of the scene to document intent."

We stayed out of the way as Vincente and Leslie moved around the scene, one taking video, the other stills. The place was a mess, glass shards all over the floor.

A couple of state cops walked in and started taking cop statements. Their presence was a detail I'd forgotten, evidently Sarah hadn't. As soon as Leslie was finished, we hightailed it to the hospital.

Sarah disappeared into one of the ER cubicles and I was ushered into another. When they peeled my sweater off, I had a bruise forming on my shoulder. They did an unnecessary X-ray. I could've told them nothing was broken. He was too far away with that caliber rifle.

When they finished with me, I walked over to the other cubicle. Found it empty. I began to panic, then felt foolish. She was probably having a new cast put on. Bet this time, they'd make it a really heavy one. Leslie was sitting in the waiting room. I sank down in an uncomfortable chair next to her. "They take Sarah for a new cast?"

"Yeah." She glanced over at me. "The doctor was really pissed at her and said she could've done damage that would never heal."

"Could've—not *did*?"

Leslie shrugged. "I'm not sure, Win. He just whisked her away while he was yelling."

I could feel my shoulder tightening up and put the ice pack on it. "They bring the sniper in?"

"Took him right up to surgery," she said. "He may not make it."

I heard the tone of regret in her voice. "How are you?"

She was silent for a minute. "A bit shaken. I've never shot anybody before."

"Be sure you see Emily—Dr. Peterson. She's good at helping you sort through all the feelings. But for what it's worth, you did what you had to. I have a feeling he's the man who left the Brownes to bleed to death. Wounded two deputies and tried to kill Sarah and me. You did a good deed for every person in uniform in this county."

* * *

When we got back to the station Sarah orchestrated the chaos. Documentation of the attack up the wazoo, identification of all the aggressors, statements from the few who talked. Regret after the fact is stupidity. Conference with the DA. Cleaning up the place without destroying evidence.

I looked for Nolan. Found him in a holding cell with three other guys. He had his sullen face on and I walked by. Neither of us showed any recognition. So how the hell was I going to get him out? He couldn't stay undercover. As the newest member of this band of not-so-merry men, he'd be the chief suspect for a leak. They had to know we'd been ready for the assault with a counterattack plan of our own.

I waited until Sarah had a lull, asked her.

"You think we really need to pull him out now?"

"Absolutely."

She thought for a minute. "We can question him last and then he can disappear before he gets to the jail. Sound okay?"

Was I letting my concern about Nolan get the best of my operational sense? Maybe. But he'd said this was his last op. Could he be traced back to Bill and his organization? Maybe. "Let me call Bill."

"Go ahead and have Sarah spring him," Bill said. "He's retiring and they'll never be able to connect him to MCIA. We've covered his tracks completely."

"Okay, but please be absolutely certain. And thanks for everything."

I nodded at Sarah. When he came in a half-hour later, he held up his handcuffs. "Is this the thanks I get?"

"You're sounding awfully cocky," I said. "For a felon, that is."

"Worked, didn't it? And I didn't get a scratch. Good job, all around."

Sarah unlocked his cuffs and gave him her thanks.

"So, what are you going to do now?" I asked. "Bill said you're retiring. Anything on the horizon?"

"Just a clear sky. Why?"

"I haven't talked this over with the sheriff yet—but how about spending your golden years in local law enforcement for McCrumb County?"

Sarah turned to me. Her eyebrows just about hit her hairline.

"Think about it, Sarah. Bill doesn't want these yahoos to know MCIA is involved. If Nolan signs on with us, he looks like a local cop. Besides, you'd get another member for SWAT. And a really great guy, to boot."

"Do I get a say in this?" Nolan asked. He grinned. "Actually, I was thinking about settling down somewhere I've never lived. I like the country around here because there are no big mountains, but it's not flat either. Close to Paducah."

I turned to Sarah. "Well?"

"The grant money would cover the hire for a couple of years. But I think you should meet Willy, our team leader. For right now, can you just disappear?"

"I'll go up to Indianapolis," he said. "Give you a call when I get settled." He gave me a big hug. "You've got a good set of officers, Sheriff. Much better than I thought I'd find in rural Indiana. If there's room, I'd like to join them."

* * *

We got home around eleven, which made it a fucking long day. Sarah was still wired. A clean op with the result she wanted—sweeping up all the trash. Except I didn't think all the garbage was in the local jail. Leatherby, our sniper, was in critical condition in the hospital, McNab and Salie were in the county jail. Hall, described as "office" when he, McNab and Leatherby had met at Dog's, was still at large. He seemed to be the local commander, the one who was getting orders from above. We still needed to know who that "above" included. If this were a national conspiracy, as Nathan and Bill thought, how would they take an absolute defeat? Retaliation? Or back to the drawing board? As I lit the fire, I couldn't help shake the feeling this wasn't over.

"How's your wrist," I asked as I settled on the couch next to Sarah.

"Throbbing."

"Whatever prompted you to hit that guy with your cast? Wasn't a loaded weapon good enough?"

She snuggled closer. "If I'd identified myself with my weapon drawn and he didn't surrender, I would've had to shoot him. I didn't want to do that."

"Shit." I put my arm around her. Felt the fabric under my fingertips, sensed the warm skin beneath her uniform.

She let out a long sigh, put her hand on my thigh. "I feel so relieved, like the weight of the world's off my back. I think I'm beginning to feel human again." She lifted her head to look into my eyes. "I can't thank you enough for being there, by my side in all the planning and execution—but if you ever set yourself up as bait again, I'll divorce you."

"Easier said than done. Ditto with the back rub you've offered."

"Would you really like one? I can do it one-handed."

I got up, told her to scoot over. Lay down on the couch with my head on her lap and my stockinged feet on the other arm.

She began tentatively, working in small areas. "I can't feel your muscles through this sweater."

"Easy remedy." I pushed myself up to a kneeling position and took it off. Groaned because my shoulder had stiffened up. "Is this really a back rub or should I take my bra off too?"

Sarah looked at the growing bruise. "That's got to hurt."

"It's okay. No permanent damage. Now answer my question."

"Yes and yes." She unclasped my bra with one hand, kept her arm around me. "I've been so scared, so constantly. If you hadn't been here by my side, I would've been carted off to the looney bin." Sarah stroked my back. "I'll never know how you did it all those years."

"Did what?"

"Lived with all that pressure, the planning and then the execution."

I sighed, couldn't help it. "You get into a rhythm, tunnel your thoughts about what you have to take into consideration. What you have to do. You go over the checklist until you're satisfied." I lay back down. "Just rub my back. Concentrate on the muscles—you should be able to feel the knots without a problem now."

She leaned over, kissed my back. Then started kneading the muscles around my neck.

Today had scared the shit out of both of us. I vowed I'd never let them get that close again.

CHAPTER FIFTY-FOUR

Waterstone picked up the call and glanced at his watch. Two thirty. It should be Al checking in from the op. "Waterstone."

"Disaster, man. Absolute disaster. All of 'em are in jail or the hospital. Should the rest of us spring 'em?"

"No. Although go ahead and spread the rumor. I have a plan B and I'll send you everything you'll need with my operative. Code name Walker, code word boom. In the meantime, have them go ahead with the diversion we talked about."

"But shouldn't we—"

"Follow orders. We'll take care of the others. Don't go home, go to Evansville Regional Airport, get a room at the Motel Six. We'll contact you there. Do it now."

He snapped his phone shut. "Fucking idiots." He turned and stared at two photographs on the wall he'd cut from the *Greenglen Sentinel*. "They're not finished with you yet, ladies. Soon, I promise you, soon."

CHAPTER FIFTY-FIVE

Sarah

"I don't have much I can release to you," I said to Zoe over the phone. I'd come in early to go over the statements and see if our inmates had given up any information at all.

"Was there an attack on the station?"

"Yes, an organized assault, but I don't know by whom and nor their motivation. To tell the truth, I'm hoping whoever is responsible will take credit, though since it was such a total failure, they probably won't."

"McCrumb County Rangers?"

"Possible, but I have no verification."

"Let me check our wall," Zoe said. "Maybe they posted something there or on Twitter. When you get a statement ready, please send it over. Indy media's sniffing around and Lloyd's having an anxiety attack about getting scooped on his own turf. It's already hit social media. I heard the state police were in on the bust."

"Dispatch called them and they were close."

"You're not going to be able to keep a lid on this."

"I don't want to, but until I have some concrete information, I'd be irresponsible to release speculation. Hang in, Zoe. Let me know if you pick up on something. Right now, every bit helps."

"Do you think this has something to do with your relationship with Win?"

"No, maybe, but I really don't know. One of the men we arrested has a record of violence against gays in the Bloomington area, but there's no evidence that was their motivation." I opened a file. "I can't release their names yet, but they lawyered up with one Gordon Quinlan. I don't know him and he doesn't live in the county."

"Interesting. I'll work on it. Glad no one from your department was seriously injured."

"You can't imagine how grateful I am." We hung up and a second later it rang again—the hospital with the news on the shooter. He'd make it. "How's the other guy? The one I concussed?"

"Let's just say you got him good. He's conscious, but his nose is shattered and there's some damage to the orbital rim. He'll go into surgery when the swelling goes down."

I thanked her, and rather than return to the statements, went upstairs. The front area and bullpen areas were dark because the window had been boarded up. The glazier was supposed to be here in the afternoon, but we'd lost the sign painted on the window in 1939. I hoped someone had saved the shards because it felt to me as if we'd lost a part of our tradition.

I walked into the forensics lab and saw Leslie concentrating on a monitor. "News," I said as I settled on a stool next to her. "Your shooter's still in critical condition, but he's going to make it."

She took a deep breath. "Good. I'm glad to hear it."

"How are you feeling?"

"Lousy. I know it was a righteous shoot, but it still seems so…"

"Brutal?"

"Yeah, that among other things. I wanted to be a cop to protect people, not shoot them."

I took her chin, made her look at me. "I've killed in the past because if I hadn't, my dad and Win would've been killed. Leslie, if you hadn't taken that shot, the man who shot Win could've gotten another shot off and killed her. Or any other cop who walked onto the square." I let my hand drop. "This might not help much, but what you did allows us to bring this man to justice. He'll have to stand trial for the murder of Linda and Barry Browne."

"And the other shootings."

I patted her shoulder. "You need to make an appointment with Dr. Peterson ASAP. That's an order since she's the department shrink. Now, you have the ballistics for the rifle we got from the roof?"

"I didn't touch any of it since I was in the action. Vincente did it all. He worked all night on all the ballistics. He'll be back this afternoon."

"Good—good chain-of-evidence procedure and good Vincente will be in later." I stood. "What does Deborah say about this?"

Leslie turned to the monitor. "I...I haven't talked to her since the incident."

"Call her now. She's probably heard the rumors and must be so worried. That's another order. Then finish this up and go visit her. You don't have to tell her what happened, just what you're feeling. You can't keep the shit from your partner or you'll shut her out of your life. Believe me."

* * *

By the time I got home, I was insurrectioned out. Caleb and I'd gone over all the statements with the proverbial comb for any clue to the organization that had launched the assault and found zilch. Nathan ran the names through all the databases he had and found a communication tree that led to the McCrumb County Rangers and back to 1776 Corps. They wouldn't be arraigned until court resumed after the weekend on Monday, so we had time. Vincente's forensics report nailed our shooter for not only his attempted murder of Win but other sniper attacks. He'd done a yeoman's job.

I also called Bill, but all he said was that he'd get back to me. Well, hell. Why would he cut me out now?

The deputy dropped me off in front of our home and I stood a moment, staring at the sky and the full moon. The temperature had dropped again, so the moonlight made the trees look like glittering spun-sugar. I let my breath out in a frosted billow.

Win opened the door, let Des out and me in. I embraced her and held her close. "I'm so lucky to come home to you."

"Your peg leg bride?"

"You getting cabin fever?" I asked as I let her go.

"So is Des. We'll work it out."

I hung up my coat and duty belt. "Only one more day until my days off. Where do you want to go?"

"Go? Snowshoeing, skiing. Before the snow gets too sloppy to do anything but watch it melt." She maneuvered into the kitchen. "I know. I'm turning into a fat, cranky woman. Where do I want to go? To the hospital where they'll take off this fucking cast."

"All in time, Win. I'd like to get rid of this too," I said as I held up my arm.

"Did you do any lasting damage?" Win asked.

"Not to my wrist, but his face is another matter. He's going to have to have extensive plastic surgery."

"So he'll be beautiful again?"

"He was pug-ugly to begin with, at least as much as I remember of his face, Win."

"Too bad you didn't have a baseball bat or a rifle butt."

"Are you going to stay cranky?"

Win took a deep breath, exhaled noisily. "I'll try to chipper up. No promises. Soup and sandwiches okay with you?"

We fixed dinner together and by the time we had everything on the table, Win had relaxed a bit. I thought she was more frustrated with having to use the crutches to get around than with the cast, but it was a toss-up.

"I had a talk with Leslie today and it was like you were sitting on my shoulder, telling me what to say."

"Yeah, I bet. Tactical talk?"

"No, she was upset about her shoot. I made her promise to call Em and set up an appointment. I also reamed her out for not calling Deborah."

"They still going strong?"

"Yeah. I told her while she didn't have to talk about the incident, she needed to share her feelings about it with Deborah. I sounded exactly like you."

Win looked up, searching my face. "You really said that?"

I nodded.

"Did you mean it?"

"Yes. I'll try, Win. No promises."

CHAPTER FIFTY-SIX

Win

Sarah wanted me to go to the station—but for what purpose? I'd done enough sitting around, so she left early. I began the housework. Dishes weren't a problem, getting the laundry to the washer was more of a problem. Dusting was impossible—find a place to rest crutches where they wouldn't fall, dust, hop to do more in the area, pick up crutches. Repeat. I woke up from a nap with sniffles and I sure as hell didn't need this shit.

Besides, I realized I was waiting for the next move of the planners of the debacle at the station. Even if it had been intended as a trial run, I didn't believe they'd retreat to their den to lick their wounds. I wouldn't. I'd come back with a strike that would let my opponent know I was still out there. Waiting. Ready to take them on again, waiting to crush them.

Was I warped? Or just well-trained?

I put away the cleaning supplies, settled down at the computer, went through all Nathan's notes again. I still couldn't figure out why they'd picked McCrumb County. A random dart to a US map? Or did they target the county for a specific reason like revenge for the Shamsi takedown in Greenglen and the weapons he'd stored here? Or did they have their eyes on some other local target?

I called Bill. "Two questions. Is there still chatter?"

"Yes. Two?"

"Any idea what they're planning?"

"No. We've got tons of data to go through, Win. I'll let you know if we get a solid lead."

"They're not going to let go. Any idea why they hit here?"

"That's three." He hung up.

"Fuck you."

I couldn't let it go. Why not pick a soft target if they only wanted to create panic? Fear? Why had they attacked a hard target, even if it was a county sheriff's department? Any unit of law enforcement was a hard target. Were they preparing to tackle the state police post? Why would they?

I thought of other hard targets in the area. Camp Atterbury. Crane Naval Warfare Center. Crane had a number of contractors in the area around it. One with a particular attraction to a paramilitary group? I almost called Bill, but knew I'd had all the answers I was going to get today.

I pulled up a list of businesses in the county, looked at more detail for some of them. Nothing. No armament manufacturers, none that handled expended radioactive materials.

These homegrown terrorists operated on their own wavelength.

I kept circling back to one question: what did they want?

I called Nolan. He picked up on the third ring. "Hey, Win. What's up?"

"You settled in?"

"Yeah. I'm getting fat on room service, compliments of MCIA."

I grinned. He'd never get fat. "You have any ideas on why they picked on the sheriff's station? It just doesn't make sense to me."

"Down to business right away. You haven't changed." He laughed. "Nope. The planning was in motion when I joined their effort. All I can say with certainty is that the order came from above, wherever that is." He exhaled a long breath. "For whatever good it does, making that kind of assault as your first statement is stupid."

My turn to sigh. "You think it was a statement? If so, what the hell does it mean? Nobody's published a manifesto. Our local newspaper looked at all the stuff on their timeline and Twitter. Nothing." I smacked the desk. "They swoop in. If they'd succeeded, what was the plan?"

"Swoop out. Disappear."

"Ah, fuck. This whole op is so fucking senseless." I doodled on my legal pad. "There's some indication this was practice for a bigger op. You get that sense?"

"I was the newbie, Win. If there were more plans, I never heard about them. You want me to go back in? As the fugitive? Thanks to the story Sarah put out, I escaped and am now on the lam."

"Too damn dangerous. They have to know there was a leak. Don't they?"

"Probably." He was quiet a minute. "There's one guy, McNab. He strikes me as the weak link."

"He's lawyered up. But I'll pass on the word about McNab. If you think of anything else, call."

"Right. Stay safe, Win."

I called Nathan. He picked up right away too. "You're going to ask me if there's anything new and the only answer I can give you is I'm not sure."

"You care to clarify that?" I waited. "It's driving me crazy. There's no reason behind the assault. It's a stupid move. If they were out to get Sarah, there was a fifty-fifty chance she wouldn't be there. From what Nolan says, the day and time was in the planning from the beginning. Why would they risk this? Why not blow a couple of bombs on Courthouse Square?"

"I don't know, Win," he said on a long exhalation.

"Look at the attack, Nathan. They could've used a couple of IEDs, done a drive-by and sprayed the front of the station. Public proof of power. They wouldn't even have had to kill anybody. The point would've been made."

"If it helps any, they're getting reamed out from the guys who issued the order. Well, the ones left."

"How many are left?"

"Twenty-some-odd. They don't seem leaderless either. I gather more recruits may be coming into the state."

"How soon?"

"Plan's still in the works."

"So they're not giving up."

"Doesn't look that way."

"Keep me in the loop. Please. Look for a reason why they picked McCrumb County for this exercise. Why *here*?"

"Lower your frustration level, Win."

"I can't. Not when I know this isn't over."

* * *

I broke for lunch. I tried to take a real break, but my mind kept turning over the same facts. The same questions with the same results. Nada. To a tactical officer, this made no sense at all.

So could I pretend to be somebody else? Maybe a county sheriff? No, not possible. I knew I couldn't approximate Sarah's mind when it came to this county. Its people, the land, the history. I tried to understand. Most times I failed.

I didn't know any of the sheriffs in surrounding counties. Besides, it'd look weird if I called them. Then a thought struck. I finished the sandwich with enthusiasm, rinsed my dishes, and picked up the phone.

"Hey Zoe. You up to your neck in work?"

"What work?" she asked. "About the little scrape the sheriff's department had with a gang of thugs? If Sarah doesn't release more information, I got nothin' to do."

"Can't do anything about Sarah. I had an idea though. What if you called sheriffs in the surrounding counties? Ask what their standard procedure would be in like circumstances?"

"What's this about, Win?"

I cleared my throat. "I can't figure out why they picked their target. The response of the other sheriffs might throw some light on it. Is there set procedure? Or did they never imagine anything like this could happen? What would they have done? Should give you a good sidebar."

"What's my deadline on this?"

I laughed. "Just get back to me when you get some answers."

"You think it's over?"

"No."

"I'll get right on it."

Des sat by the front door, her eyes bright with cabin fever, tail wagging. I got my parka, my phone and a travel pack of tissues. If I fell, I didn't want to wait until Sarah came home.

As soon as I opened the door, Des took off down her usual trail. I started around the yard. It was slippery. The constant temperature fluctuation the past few days had created layers of ice. As soon as I thought I was through to the ground, I'd break through another layer. Des had made her path just as slick. I turned to the other trail down to the creek. Pristine. Maybe it'd be easier.

I started carefully, placing and testing the crutches before I put my weight on them. I kept my eyes on the terrain. I was concentrating so hard, I wasn't aware of the two men until they were on me. One from each side. They knocked my crutches away. As I stood balancing on my good leg, one of them stuffed a hood over my head. I tried to strike out, but each took an arm and put some kind of tie on them.

I tried to shove one of the men. One of them cussed. I heard thundering paws and then a shot. A whine. I struck out blindly. Felt a hand at my throat. A thumb on my neck. Pressure on my neck.

CHAPTER FIFTY-SEVEN

Win and Sarah

Win

I regained consciousness in the back of a van. Though it was moving slowly, it skittered in icy ruts. The hood was still over my head, so the first task was maneuvering so I could see. The idiots had tied my hands in front. Unadulterated half-wits. I inched my hands up to the hood. Lifted it. Much better. I unzipped my pocket. Slowly, without sound. Then pulled my phone out, hit 7#, the emergency call Nathan had installed as part of my system that enabled the GPS. Pulled out the tissues and stuck the phone behind them. Put it all back in my pocket, re-zipped it and let the hood fall back over my face.

"Watch it, Don," the passenger said. "We don't need to end up in a fucking ditch with our cargo."

"Fuck you," the driver replied. "Fucking van's garbage and the road's nothing but ice."

The passenger grumbled but shut up.

I closed my eyes and went down Nathan's list of militia members. I couldn't remember a Don. Was he one of the guys from Idaho? I couldn't remember.

"Fucking stupid mission," Passenger said.

"Not for you to say. She awake yet?"

I could hear the front seat squeak. "Naw. You sure you didn't kill her?"

No answer.

"Why do they want her?"

"Shut your fucking mouth. We got orders, we carry them out. Period."

Sarah

Deputy Branch pulled into the area in front of our house and put the unit in park. "You want me to wait until you check everything?"

I started to say no, but the house was quiet and Win hadn't turned on any lights. Not that she needed to since it wasn't dark, but she usually did. A welcoming beacon, she'd said.

When I got out, I noticed the prints from her crutches heading away from the clearing, down the trail to the creek. Surely she hadn't tried that trail.

"Wait for a little bit, would you?" I asked. "Win took a trail and if she's down, I might need help getting her vertical."

"Yes ma'am."

I started down the trail and wondered where the hell Des was. By now, she should've been swarming me with her happy dance. Then I saw her, lying on her side, whining softly.

"Dave!" I waved at the patrol unit. "Branch! Come on!"

I went to Des, heart in my throat. I rubbed her neck. "What's the matter, baby? What happened?"

She looked into my eyes, tried to get up but couldn't.

The deputy came and knelt down, running his hand over her coat. "She's wounded, but it must be the other side. Should I take her to the squad car?"

"Yeah, but be careful. If she could, she'd be up and running." As he lifted her up, I saw the snow under Des was red.

My heart was beating fast. Des was down and there was no Win. I got up and followed my one-legged woman's tracks. A few steps further on, I saw her crutches—and the prints of two big-footed humans. It appeared that they had accosted her, then dragged her down the trail. I couldn't catch my breath.

I picked up the crutches and raced back to the car just as Dave placed Des gently on the backseat. He took off his parka and laid it on top of her. I slid in next to her so that her head was on my lap. "Call dispatch. Win's been abducted. Get a BOLO out—but I have no idea what kind of a vehicle she's in."

While he did that, I called Dr. Huff, Des's vet. "We'll be there in fifteen minutes."

"How do her gums look?" Huff asked.

"Not pink, but not gray yet," I replied. "Maybe the snow helped stop the bleeding a little."

"We'll be ready for her."

I gave her as much of a hug as I could, cuddled her to keep her warm and to keep my worst fears at bay.

Dave put on the lights and we made it to Doc Huff's in ten minutes. Huff had a gurney waiting outside, we transferred Des to it and Doc pushed it quickly inside. I followed weak-kneed and panicked. Dave helped me in, responding to his radio as he deposited me in a chair in the waiting room.

"How did they go? Where does the trail go?" he asked me.

"Down to the creek. From there, it's just a spit and a throw to the road."

My hands were shaking so much I could barely answer the phone when it rang. Nathan? Before I could say hello, he said, "Win's in trouble. I'm tracking her GPS. I can send the locations directly to units in the area."

"I'm out of the office so along with other units, send them directly to Unit Nine and I'll let dispatch know." So many questions raced through my mind, the uppermost being how he knew. Questions I could ask later when Win was safe.

"Stay on the line, Sarah. I'll keep you up to date."

"Nathan's sending you GPS coordinates for Win," I said to Dave. "Go after her, but please be careful. Backup's on its way. We've no idea who's got her."

He nodded and took off, again with lights and siren.

"I need to talk to Caleb," I said into the phone. "I'll call you back as soon as I'm finished."

"Stay cool, Sarah. We'll get her back safe."

I couldn't respond, just disconnected and called Caleb. I gave him a brief rundown of what had happened.

"We'll get the CSI van out to your place—can they tell where it went down?"

"It's on the trail to the left as they pull in the clearing. But you may want to send them down to where the creek meets the road. Maybe they can find tire tracks."

"They're on their way. What else?"

238 S. M. Harding

"We need SWAT in the area. Willy's got command. Des is at the vet's and Dave took the unit. I'm stranded."

"Which vet?"

"Doc Huff."

"No sweat, Sarah. I'll swing by and pick you up."

That's what I was afraid of. I started pacing.

Win

The van slowed down, took a turn. Bumpier here. Driveway? I had a rough idea where we were—out in the middle of nowhere. House? Barn? Other farm building? I just hoped to hell the GPS was working. That Nathan had been at home to pick up my emergency call. That all wasn't lost. I kept kicking myself for being such easy prey. I hadn't even bloodied a nose. It wasn't over yet.

The van stopped, both doors slammed shut, then the side door rolled open. I felt the cold air sweep in.

"She still out?"

"Yeah."

I felt myself dragged over the metal floor. Lifted out of the van and slung over the guy's shoulder. The hood fell off with a little help. He was breathing hard by the time I heard a door creak open on rusty hinges. Some sort of out building. As we entered, I took a quick peek. Barn.

He deposited me on the ground with an umph.

"How long is she gonna be out?" I thought it was Passenger.

"'Til she wakes up. Maybe I tapped her a little harder than I thought."

"Maybe? What if she dies?"

No answer.

"Just find the damn heater and get it going. Fucking cold in here."

I heard some banging around. Then the roar of a small engine. I began to feel the heat. The van had been chilly and my muscles were beginning to tighten up.

"Please tell me why we're doin' this," Passenger said.

"Need to know."

"I need to know. Come on, Don."

"We're gonna trade her for our men. Not the locals, just us."

"Jesus," said Passenger. "You think they'll go for that?"

"They better, or they'll get one dead bitch back, after we play with her a bit. We might even send a finger of hers if they don't cave at first."

"Ah, Jesus. I don't mind shooting the enemy, but torturing women…"

"Shut up, Phil. Just shut the fucking up."

I heard something being dragged across the dirt. Something to sit on? Not for me. I wondered if I should "wake up" now. Or begin to scare the shit out of Passenger and remain comatose? Then a thought occurred to me. If I woke up only speaking Tajik, they'd think I was crazy from lack of oxygen to my brain, maybe get them to lower their defenses. But how the hell was I going to do anything offensive with no crutches and one leg to stand on?

The biggest part of tae kwon do is mind. Mr. Kim said that was my missing education, so that's what we'd been working on. Now might be a good time to practice. Draw the chi within, find the moves I was capable of. Practice them in my mind until it was time.

Sarah

Nathan guided the chase while I paced at the vet's. Caleb arrived within fifteen minutes, the longest fifteen minutes in my life. As I fastened my seat belt, I asked, "Any word from Branch?"

"Nathan says he's pretty close behind," Caleb said. "But no sighting yet."

"Has he cut the siren and lights? I'd rather a visual than provoke a car chase, especially since the roads are in such crappy shape."

He relayed the order and settled in to cover ground without landing us in a ditch.

Win's face, asleep this morning, popped into my mind. She's so beautiful and while she acknowledges it, says offhandedly it was the one good thing she got from her mom. Asleep, all the tension she carried was gone and her frown replaced by a peaceful rest. I swallowed.

Dave's voice came on the radio. "Got them in sight." He gave the license plate and description of a white Chevy van. "They're turning into a lane that leads to a barn. I'm continuing on. Will stop when I'm out of their sight."

"Roger that, Unit Nine. How many suspects?"

"Only saw two men in the van, but I've no idea how many could be in the barn."

"Stay close Dave. Get yourself a perch."

"Ten-four."

"Where's SWAT?"

"Close to that location." Caleb watched the car's computer monitor.

"Have them meet us here." I pointed to the next road on the screen. "We can go through Major's Woods and come out in back of the barn. I think Ronnie Major still uses it, though his acreage is about a mile away."

"You're beginning to sound like Micah," Caleb said with a grin. "Knowing every structure and every owner in the county."

"Guess that's one of the things I got from him."

"There's the barn," I said. "Keep on to the next road and take a left."

"Yes, ma'am."

"Sorry. I'm damn scared."

He took a hand off the steering wheel and patted mine. I felt like crying.

About ten minutes after Caleb parked on a logging road, SWAT arrived. We'd have easy access to the back of the barn. Willy took the lead with his three team members behind him. I followed them while Caleb stayed at the car to coordinate other units in the area.

When we got to the edge of the woods, Willy signaled a short trek through the woods until we were positioned behind the barn. He examined the building with binoculars. "Is this barn used regularly?"

"It's an overflow barn for hay," I said. "If you're asking if Ronnie keeps it in good shape, the answer is yes."

He nodded. "Looks to me like one of the loft doors is open a tad." He handed me the binoculars. "If we could get up there, we'd have the upper hand. Think the pulley will hold?"

I took a good, close look. "Should. It's shiny, so it's been used recently."

Pointing to his crew he said, "You two—target the loft. For God's sake, be quiet. You take the small back door."

"And me?" I asked. "Or do I have to stay here and be terrified?"

"You can follow me to the front, but stay behind me. You haven't trained with us, Sarah."

Despite feeling sidelined in my county, I reined in my temper. He was right. He was in charge. I nodded.

"Anybody see any eyes on us?" Willy asked.

Three people answered in unison "Negative."

"Let's go."

Win

Every time Passenger tried to ask a question, Don shut him up. I thought I could use the tension between them. Careful Win. I also thought my time-out was almost at its end. Otherwise, I'd have to play dead.

Strange how your other senses perk up when your eyes are closed. I thought I heard a squeaky brush against the back wall, like a running shoe on clean linoleum. A different sound from what I'd been hearing. Another one, farther up on the wall. Then a third, almost to the hay loft. Sarah and the cavalry? I could only hope. Another scrape lower down. Another person? Or no entry from above? Or was I just going crazy? Hearing things that weren't there?

Take it like any other op, Win. Work to gain advantage.

I moaned. Whimpered. Opened my eyes. Kept them unfocused. I said "cold" in Tajik. Blinked. Pantomimed "cold."

They both looked at me. Passenger stood.

"Tough shit," Don said.

"Let me sit her on a bale," Passenger said. "Won't do any harm."

"Fuck you, bleeding heart."

Passenger walked over, took two bales off the stack. Took me under the arms and pulled me up. I wobbled. He guided me as I hopped over to the closest bale.

"Thank you," I whispered as he helped me sit.

He went back to his own bale. "How much longer?"

"He'll call when he calls," Don said. "Now for the last time, shut up."

I kept blinking. Slumped. Started muttering in Tajik. If there was an op or not, these two guys were going to meet the Madwoman of Afghanistan. I listened intently. I felt a cold draft, carefully glanced up. Two figures. *Yes!* Thank the stars my captives had seated themselves with their backs toward the loft.

I began speaking Tajik. Did a translation of Rumi in my head. I got louder. More agitated. Strange to hear such beautiful words said with fear, anger. Craziness. I began to shout.

Sarah

"She's got to be aware we're here," said a whispered voice over the com line. "She's going ballistic, making a lot of noise."

"Either that or she's got her own plan," I whispered to Willy.

He nodded. "How many perpetrators?"

"Two."

"Thea, give us the go."

I could hear Win's voice, rising in hysteria. She was speaking a foreign language and trying to do what? Make them think she was in another place at another time? Was her PTSD taking over? Win, please, *please* don't do anything that will cost you! We're here!

"Four, three, two, one—go!"

Win

I'd gotten to Don. Agitated, he told me to shut up. Stood and walked toward me. Leaning over me, menace painted every feature on his face. "I told you to shut your fucking mouth. Do it or I'll do it for you."

I pushed off with my good leg, head-butted the oaf and swung my interlaced hands into his neck with as much force as I could muster.

He toppled over.

Sarah

Willy pushed through the small door with me hot on his heels. "Hands up! Sheriff! Now, now, now," Willy yelled. The cry was yelled by every officer.

One of the kidnappers toppled over. I'd heard no shots. Heart attack? Or had he just fainted? The other looked at us and threw his hands up.

"Kneel down. Hands at the back of your head," Thea yelled from the loft.

He did so without hesitation. The other guy was still down.

While the others went to cuff our prisoners, I holstered my weapon and went to Win.

She wore a wide grin. "You like my performance?"

"You're okay?"

Win nodded and held up her hands with a plastic tie on them. I cut it off. Win opened her arms to me.

I walked into them. "Damn, I was so scared."

She hugged me close. "How's Des? Did they—"

"We got her to the vet right away and she's in surgery. Doc Huff's taking care of her."

"Can you let your people clean up? Can we go to Des?"

I nodded, unable to trust my voice. I took off the com set and asked Willy if he could take it from here. He nodded with a big smile. Happy that I'd relinquished control? "Good job, Willy. We have a wounded dog to tend." I called Branch and asked him to bring his unit to the barn. "The crutches still in the back?"

"Yes, ma'am. Shall I bring them in?"

"Yes, if you will."

CHAPTER FIFTY-EIGHT

Sarah

Once Win got the crutches in place, she steamed along on her own power. In the backseat of the unit I took Win's hand in mine. Now that she was safe, I could worry about Des. I wondered what would happen to Win if Des didn't make it. Would it throw her back into the killing fields? I checked my phone for messages. Nothing from Doc Huff, but three from dispatch. I didn't want to answer, but I thought I'd better. "Operation's over and Win's okay."

"Thank the Lord," Dory said. "I called 'cause we've had two calls from a man who says you should talk to him."

"About what?"

"He wouldn't say, Sarah. But he sounded creepy. After the first call, I asked Nathan to trace the call. Virginia. Now who'd be callin' from Virginia?"

"If he calls again, patch him through, Dory."

"You give Win a big hug for me, you hear?"

"Promise."

I took Win's hand again. "What was your performance about?"

"Masking any noise you might make getting in place," she said, leaning her head back. "Or if they thought I was hallucinating, get my own op going. Take down Don. See if the other guy wouldn't cooperate."

"You got the big guy down?"

"Yeah. Bigger they are, harder they fall," Win said. "He was the one in charge. Drove, gave orders. I think they planned to trade me for Leatherby and McNab."

"Trade?" I told Win about the calls. "Maybe that's what the caller from Virginia wanted to set up."

"If he doesn't know I'm free, we could set a trap. You need to get hold of Don's phone, check if he's received any calls from the number."

We pulled into Doc Huff's parking lot. I helped Win get out and followed her into the office. As she eased herself into a chair, her face looked drawn and tired. The receptionist told me Doc was still in surgery, but it shouldn't be long. I sat down beside Win.

"She was conscious when we brought her in," I said. "And Doc thought she hadn't lost too much blood because the snow made it clot faster."

Win took my hand. "I know you did everything you could. She wasn't even close. Down at the other end of the trail, terrorizing small critters. I remember thinking I was glad she wasn't there. I…"

I squeezed her hand. I didn't know what to say. Des and I had a bond, but Win and Des? They'd merged soul-deep. All they did was look at one another and they'd know what was up. No words needed and certainly no commands. If Des didn't make it, Win's grief would be soul-deep.

Doc appeared at the door to the back of the clinic, still in his bloody scrubs. "Sorry to take so long," he said, walking toward us.

"Is she—"

"Shh," Win said.

"After a period of recuperation, she'll be fine," he said, sitting down next to Win. "Maybe not a hundred percent right away. The bullet missed any important organs, but tore up some muscle and connective tissue. She'll be taking it slow for a while."

Win shut her eyes tight, but tears still leaked through. I put her hand between mine.

"She had a lot of scarring from her previous surgery and I took the opportunity to clean some of that up. Took longer, but I think the long-term benefits outweighed the risk. She's one strong dog."

Win nodded, still unable to talk.

"Can we wait until she wakes up? I think she needs to see Win's okay."

Doc looked at Win, who still struggled to regain her composure. "Sure, no problem. I'll call you as soon as she's awake."

As he walked away, Win broke down. I held her in my arms, told her everything was going to be all right.

With Des, yes. With the rest of McCrumb County? Who the hell knew?

* * *

We got home late and I could tell Win was exhausted. She flopped on the couch, leaned her head back and closed her eyes.

I lit the fire and sat beside her. "I can't do this anymore."

She looked up at me. "You want a divorce?"

"Divorce? No. What are you thinking?"

"You said...I just thought...Shit, Sarah. I'm so tired I don't know what end's up."

"I know, I know." I put my arm around her. "We've both had quite a day. Quite a day in a long line of quite-a-days. I'm going to resign."

"Resign? From what?"

"Sheriff's office."

Win examined my face. "Not tonight, you're not. Not tomorrow, either."

"What? I thought you'd be happy." Who was this woman?

She pulled me close. "Part of you is the sheriff's department. I love you, even the sheriff part. I've worked hard to accept that part. You wouldn't be the same woman without it. I think it's vacation time. You need time away."

"I have to be here to oversee all the charges, trial prep and then the trial."

Win shook her head. "Tomorrow, which is your day off, you can get everything rolling. The trial isn't going to be next week. As a matter of fact, I think you should transfer these last two guys to Bill. I'm surprised you haven't heard from him yet."

I was quiet for a minute and looked into the fire. "Bill can sweat them for intel in a way I never could."

"There is that."

"Win, I'm sworn to uphold the law. I can't turn them over for a trip to Gitmo or wherever they take prisoners like this. They broke county and state laws. I caught them, therefore they stay in county jail."

Win shrugged. "That's fine. You still need to get away from the stress. We could go to the Bahamas, Costa Rica, someplace with a nice beach and nothing to do but lie around. Make love all day."

"On the beach?"

"We can go wherever you want to go. You just need time away."

"What about Des?"

She grimaced. "Yeah. But promise me, no resignation until you've had time away. We'll go down to West Baden for a couple of days. Doc isn't going to release Des right away. Even if we just go for a day. Please Sarah."

"You win this round." I snuggled into her. "Des sure was glad to see you. I thought her tail was going to tear her stitches."

Win was quiet and leaned her head against me. I watched the fire and thought about the day. If they'd wanted to terrorize me, they'd succeeded. I wanted to hunt down all the bastards and put them on a spit with a slow fire.

Win must've felt my muscles tightening. She leaned over and kissed me. "Let's just go to bed."

"Make wild and passionate love?"

"Uh, not until this damn cast is off."

CHAPTER FIFTY-NINE

Win

The next day, I'd packed up all the burn phones I'd bought over the last couple of years. Made Sarah's driver stop at a convenience store. When we got to the station, I asked Sarah if there was a quiet place I could work.

"Caleb's office good enough?"

"Sure. Won't he be in today?"

"He's in court all morning, maybe this afternoon. The DA didn't want to postpone his testimony."

As soon as I settled in the chair, I began to unpack. The first thing I did was call Nathan on the land line. "Hey, Nathan. So what do we know today that we didn't know yesterday?"

He laughed. "Morning, Win. Very glad to hear your voice." His desk chair creaked. "The guy in Virginia used a burn phone. Got a call from this area code just about the time your kidnappers made it back to town. Seems like he had eyes on the sheriff's building."

"Shit. Sure wish we'd been able to reel him in." I took a deep breath. "I want to know what the hell is going on. Is this a national conspiracy? Most of all, I want to know why they picked McCrumb County."

"Good questions Win. Wish I had answers for you." His chair squawked. "What do you need me to look for?"

"A high-profile target worth the risk. Is there any business or installation in the county that needs a full-force attack? For a prize worth it?"

"Shoot. Nothing I can think of right off the bat. But I'll look. What kind of prize are we looking for?"

"No idea. I was thinking along the lines of material to make a dirty bomb. I couldn't find anything. But some kind of WMD. Something that can't be obtained easily anywhere else." I sighed.

"I'll think and I'll look. Anything else?"

"Yeah. I've got four phones here I need a new identity for. Can you do it?"

"Easy. You have new cards for them?"

"Yeah."

"Turn them on one at a time. Wait 'til I switch it, then load the card. I'll turn it off. You'll be in business."

"Thanks, Nathan. I seem to thank you a lot. If I can ever return the favors, just holler."

"Just be good to Sarah."

We went through the process with each phone. I numbered them, then opened my laptop. While I was talking to Nathan, a thought had occurred to me. I typed in "chemical weapon storage." The pages came up for Pueblo Colorado, Umatilla Oregon and Tooele Utah. Nothing in Indiana or even the surrounding states. I thought I remembered one in Indiana. And maybe one in Kentucky. Had they been closed?

A shadow fell on the desk. Micah. I smiled and motioned him in.

"You takin' up the job of Chief Deputy?"

"No, never. Just borrowed the desk until Caleb gets out of court."

"Mind if I set a while?"

"Please do. Let me ask you something. Wasn't there a chemical depot in Indiana?"

"Sure was. Down at Ridley Forge. Made VX gas 'til—well, reckon I don't know when. Tore down the facility what made the gas in aught-six or so. Army turned over the depot to locals in twenty-ten. Had this big plan to reuse the facility, but that kinda fizzled. It's just settin' there."

"All the VX was destroyed?"

"Yep. Well that's what they said."

"But?"

Micah stretched out his long legs. "Don't know nothin' for sure. Just heard rumors, an' you know what rumors are like in the county. I would venture to say your friend Bill might know more."

"Did they build an incinerator there?"

"Yep. Folk was upset. Wanted the gas gone, but didn't want it destroyed there either. Dilemma."

"Have you been down there since the army moved out?"

"Reckon not. Wanna go?"

I nodded. "This afternoon?"

"Fine with me—if you an' Sarah will accompany me to lunch at the establishment of your choice."

"Can't speak for Sarah, but I'd love to. You'll have to charm her yourself."

* * *

"So where did you and Dad go this afternoon?" Sarah asked as we ate dinner.

"Driving. He thought I should refamiliarize myself with the county." I kept my gaze on my food. Took a quick bite of the sausage and tomato casserole.

"Truth, Win."

I finished chewing. "I wanted to take a look at what used to be the Ridley Forge Chemical Depot, supposed to be shut down in 2010."

"Why?"

"Why what?"

"Dammit, Win. Talk to me."

"Woman can't even eat dinner in peace around here." I started to take another bite, thought better of it. "It could be what the Rangers were practicing for."

Sarah took a bite. Thinking, turning it over. "What did you see?"

"The railroad tracks were shiny on the spur into the facility."

"What does that mean? You think they didn't really shut it down?"

I shrugged. "It's a spur line that only goes to the incinerator. The county had this big reuse plan. Nothing happened. Just a thought, Sarah. Something to keep on the back burner."

"Oh, hell and damnation." She threw her fork down. "You still don't want me to resign from this insanity? Because how the hell am I supposed to think about VX gas without wanting to run away?"

I examined her face. Could see how overwhelmed she felt. Which is why I didn't want to tell her about our trip. "No, I don't want you to quit. We'll face this together."

"Win, you could've been killed when they kidnapped you. What if the girls had been here? To come all the way from Afghanistan to be safe—and then go through this kind of trauma with their new family here?" Her voice rose with every word.

"They weren't here. I'm not saying you have to be sheriff forever. I'm just saying you shouldn't resign right now. Give it some distance. Besides, Ridley Forge could be a figment of my imagination."

She glared at me.

"Any chance we can get away before Des comes home?"

Sarah shook her head. "There's so much paperwork to finish. Plus, figuring out the right charges that the DA can prosecute and all the different jurisdictions involved. But I promise I'll take the weekend off."

"Swell."

CHAPTER SIXTY

Sarah

The week slid by in a blizzard of conferences and paperwork. The high point was leaving work early on Friday to pick up Win for a trip to Doc Huff's. Des limped out slowly, but she had regained the light in her eyes. Win insisted on lifting Des into the backseat, afraid that my cast would cause damage. What a crew we were, the Three Wounded Musketeers. I wondered if having Des home, as a reminder of the trauma, would cause Win to change her mind and want me to get out of a war where I didn't even know whom I was fighting.

Des slowly made her way to the fireplace and then turned around as if to say, "Where's the fire? Get cracking."

I got a blanket she could settle on and then lit the fire. I was aware Win still stood at the entry, watching me tend Des. There was a definite conspiracy between them. After all, both my legs were functioning. "You want me to put you to bed too?"

Win grinned. "I'll settle for the couch. How about we order something in tonight? I don't feel like cooking." She took off her jacket and thumped to the couch. When she had her leg on the pillow, she looked up at me. "Pizza? Calzones? Both?"

I ordered, fetched a couple of beers from the fridge and sat next to her and leaned my head back. What a fucking week. At least all of the felons were still behind bars. The judge thought they provided a serious enough threat to the community that he'd refused bail. Our two kidnappers were up for bail next. Caleb would be at the hearing, handling the evidence for the DA.

The Indy and Louisville media had covered both the arraignment and bail hearing and had buzzed around for a few days. Then they'd hared off after the latest sensational story. They made me appreciate the calm coverage Lloyd and Zoe offered, though Zoe wasn't satisfied with my answers. "What groups are behind these guys?" became her mantra, though she changed the wording. "What was the purpose of the attack?" her other favorite question. I shrugged and said we just didn't have enough information yet. I shouldn't have said "yet."

I looked over at Win. She was asleep. She hadn't said another word about me resigning. I thought she'd support me no matter what I decided. Why the hell did she feel I should stay? She was the one who worried about my safety every day. If I was no longer sheriff, what the hell could I do? We needed the income with two kids coming. Our ISP district commander had talked to me about teaching at the state academy, but those were six-month-long periods outside of Indianapolis. Come home on the weekends while Win was away teaching in Bloomington? It sounded like Dad would be raising the girls. The basic fact was that if I resigned as sheriff, I didn't want to join any other law enforcement agency. What the hell could I do to earn money?

What the hell did I want to do? Was it too late to change course?

The fire popped at the same time the alarm pinged. I got up and checked the monitor, went to the door and paid the driver. The scent of pizza should wake Win up. It certainly had Des's attention.

We ate quickly, without much conversation. After I closed the box, I leaned back. "We now have four days together. Anything special you want to do?"

Win leaned back and put her arm around me. "We are confined to the house and environs until Gimpy does more healing."

"Which Gimpy?"

"Dogs heal fast. We don't," Win said. "When does your cast come off?"

"The doctor's vague. He said I did more damage when I used the cast as an offensive weapon. How about you?"

"Next week. If he hadn't said that, I would've taken a saw to the damn thing myself." She pulled me to her. "We've had a couple of close calls, Sarah. But we're still here. All of us. Healing."

We sat that way for a while. Des was asleep. I hated to disturb the peace, but the fire was dying. When I sat back down, Win asked what I was fretting about.

"What I want to do when I grow up," I said.

"Really?" She twisted around to look into my eyes.

"I don't know what else I can do, other than law enforcement."

"You've always liked literature. Couldn't you teach?"

"After I spent four or five years in graduate school and then found a job close by." I sighed. "Win, I'm not equipped to do anything else but be sheriff."

"Sarah, you've been preparing yourself for the office since we were kids. No wonder you don't know what else you could do." She ran her hand up my arm. "We just have to figure out some way to lessen the stress for now."

"I can post signs at the county borders: No felons allowed."

"Let's talk to Emily. Both of us. Together. So we can check on one another. Keep stress levels low. Like tonight. Fire, dog, two women relaxing together."

"You make it sound so easy, Win."

"It's not and I should know." She took a deep breath. "Whatever you do, I'll stand with you. But—"

"I knew there'd be a but."

"But you're the finest law enforcement officer I've ever known." She gave me a long look and ran her hand through my hair. "I love you so much. Still can't believe that you love me back. If you want to walk away from the job you love, do it. I'll love you even if it's the wrong decision. I won't say a word if you turn in your resignation. But I'll be sad."

* * *

We went to Em on Monday and she gave us several suggestions as well as a ritual. When we got home from the day's work, we were to write down the stressors of the day, talk about them and then burn them. When Win was in Bloomington, we'd save our papers and burn them when she got home. I thought the deep breathing exercises would be more beneficial. Win surprised me by wanting to begin the practice that night.

"Look Sarah, I know you don't like this idea," Win said at dinner. "But some of the weird stuff Emily does has really helped me. Helped us. Even if you still blush when we talk about sex."

I could feel the blood rising to my face. "What if we keep writing down the same stuff, day after day? What good is that going to do?"

"That tells us we're not making progress, not finding better ways of dealing with it."

I knew Win wanted to say more, so I shut up and waited.

"I need to understand the attack. I'm going to keep probing. Does that bother you?" Win asked.

"Of course." I choked back an angry retort. "I don't want you hurt again. I worry about you when you're investigating. But what worries me more is that you think they're still out there."

"They are, Sarah. Somebody's paying for that fancy legal team for the guys who staged the assault. Zoe, with all her contacts, got nowhere. Nathan's working on that part. But I have a feeling he's working more for Bill than with us. There are still a lot of unanswered questions. I won't feel safe until I have the answers."

"We may never know the answers, Win."

"Gotta try." She watched the fire, then turned back to me. "It depends on how well we do with the exercises Emily gave us." She rubbed my arm and it was like an electric current. "Want to do the list now?"

I didn't, but it seemed to help Win, which in turn, helped me. Des watched us as we burned the slips of paper. I thought she looked as skeptical as I felt. It seemed to relax Win. I knew I kept pushing the worries to the bottom of my mind because I wanted to concentrate on the sense of peace our home exuded and Win, cast or no cast.

I thought about what Win had said, that she was amazed I loved her back. How could I not? She was always there, at my side or covering my back. She protected me, soothed me and gave me a new life. How could I not return her love and try my best to protect her, soothe her and give her a new life too?

I nuzzled her neck and pulled her into a long kiss.

"Damn this cast," she said. "Doesn't let me do what I want to do with you."

I smiled. "Don't tell me the intelligence wizard can't figure out how to work around one simple obstacle."

CHAPTER SIXTY-ONE

Win

When Sarah was occupied elsewhere I talked to Nathan. I had a feeling he knew more than he was telling. Fuck it! Did he think I was going to jeopardize a national op just to protect Sarah? Would I? I wanted her safe. By my side rearing two little girls who'd already seen too much violence. Why the hell couldn't I tell Sarah to walk away from the danger? Walk away from the job?

I couldn't. It would change the woman I loved. Maybe in ways I couldn't even imagine. Would she blame me? Especially for bringing two children into the mix? If she walked away from her job, would she resent the choice? Feel that she was forced to make it? My gut told me yes.

"You get a name on Don's pal yet?"

Sarah looked up from her book. "Pal? Really?"

"I got the feeling the other guy regretted getting involved with this. So maybe he's not a pal. You have a real name?"

"Everett T. Gorman."

"Background?"

"Use my computer and tap into our records. Everything should be there."

Sarah knew the background. She wasn't going to help me directly. She didn't want to think about that stuff on her day off. I left her to her reading and logged on. I scanned the background check they'd done. Then the deep background Nathan had run. Interesting. The man was single. Never married. Parents dead. Rest of family scattered across the country. I took notes and signed off.

"I'd like to meet him," I said as I sat next to Sarah. "I have a feeling he'll talk to me. Can we go into the station this afternoon?"

Sarah sighed. "Can't you do that tomorrow?"

"I teach tomorrow."

Sarah slipped her bookmark into her place and closed the book. "Let me change clothes."

"Civies," I said. "Don't give your people any ideas."

We worked out a strategy on the way into town. I had a small amount of time with Everett. I waited until Sarah and the lawyer entered the other interrogation room. I opened the other door. Everett sat at the table with his head in his hands.

"What do your friends call you?" I asked as I sat across from him.

He looked up. "Tom. You really are Colonel Kirkland, aren't you?"

I nodded. "Retired…Gunny? Shit! I didn't recognize you with the beard and those extra pounds you're carrying. What the hell are you doing here? In cahoots with these men?"

He shook his head. "Hell if I know. When I got out, I couldn't find a job. This guy told me about a security company that was training men. Didn't realize he meant mercenaries."

"What company?"

"Rattler."

Shit, one of Nathan's snake companies. "Was this in a camp in Idaho?"

"Yeah. That's where I started hearing all this stuff about how the government was planning on taking away our rights. Didn't make a lot of sense to me. But it was a paycheck and I was good at training men. I thought this little trip was a training mission for the Rangers. Didn't turn out that way."

"The man who first approached you—who was he?"

"Ed Rokita. Owns the Cross-Hairs Gun Club."

"Which hate groups are behind this? Do you know?"

He sighed. "Just about all the crazies in the area. Real religious strain, but I don't know who's in charge. Some skinheads along for the ride. But there's a core of command and I got no idea who's running them."

"We don't have much time because your lawyer's going to be coming in with the sheriff. By the way, follow your lawyer's instructions." I slid a phone across the table to him. "My number's programmed in. When you're alone, text the names of all the men involved you can. Then what you remember of the plans."

"Won't they confiscate this at the jail?"

"No, per the sheriff's instructions. Keep it hidden from other inmates. Use it only when you're alone."

"Colonel, I've heard talk about a jailbreak."

"From inmates?"

"Should've said 'overheard.' No, I think the Rangers are going to break us out."

"Shit." Fanatics never give up. I should've remembered that. "We'll see if we can't get you into witness protection. No promises. I'll do what I can."

He nodded. I slipped out.

CHAPTER SIXTY-TWO

Sarah

Win had been moody since her visit with "Tom," the reluctant terrorist. He'd agreed to testify against his pal. She told me about the jailbreak and given me her list of countermeasures, all of which I'd put into effect. Nolan was back in the county and training to become a deputy. He'd attend the academy with the next intake. I'd protected Bill's op, but at what cost to Nolan?

Win's cast came off on schedule to be replaced by a walking boot that looked like something out of the Transformers. I'd accompanied Win to her appointment but the doctor wouldn't talk to me. "You want to have a wrist that bends and fingers that work? Then come back when I've scheduled your next appointment," was his only comment.

Win celebrated her freedom that night, so much so that we overslept that morning. I was two hours late for my shift.

The weather continued to be weird, the temperature moving from the mid-twenties to the mid-fifties. The rivers rose, our Search and Rescue was called out again and again. The folks we saved weren't stupid, just stubborn. They were trying to hold on to the lives they'd built. I understood that, but it did nothing to alleviate my sense of frustration. We only had so many resources and they were spread so thin right now, if we added any more water, we'd split up the seam.

Win kept probing for intel about the Rangers and those who stood behind them. I returned to everyday duty, petty crimes and felonies. The one advantage of the flooding was that criminal activity was kept to a minimum. They were as hamstrung as we.

Win began going into Bloomington again for her classes. She asked if I wanted Des to stay with me. What she didn't say was "in case I needed added protection." I refused. Des had healed fast and was almost back to her usual self. I thought I saw some hesitancy when she took off to chase some critter. "She remembers the last time she took off after someone," Win said. "That she's still chasing is a good sign."

"So how's life?" Em asked when I ran into her at Rhomer's.

I glared at her. "Here?"

She laughed. "Make an appointment soon."

I ran late for it because of a domestic call. When I entered the waiting room, Em's office door was open and she yelled, "Come on in, Sarah."

"You install a security system?" I asked as I sank into the chair opposite her.

She nodded. "A little barn door action—shutting it after the horse, the pig and the goat are long gone. I hope. What's up?"

"The stress stuff isn't working, Em. At least not for me." I crossed my legs. "I want to resign as sheriff and Win doesn't want me to. She'll support whatever choice I make, but she said it'd make her sad."

Em nodded. "Would it make you sad?"

"I don't know. I just feel I need the relief."

She stared at me until I began to squirm. "I'm not a butterfly to add to your collection, so stop staring at me like you're pinning me down."

"Fanciful image, but that wasn't what I was doing." She slammed her notebook shut. "The one complaint you've seen me for is stress. Stress from the relationship with Win, stress from the job. But you've never wanted to figure it out—you just want a quick remedy.

"If Win had had that same attitude, she'd still be having screaming nightmares and ducking at every unexpected sound. She worked at it, dove deep into her psyche. She keeps working. She's never asked for a quick and easy remedy."

"Thanks, Em."

We sat in silence for several minutes.

"If you don't stop avoiding the introspection, you'll never resolve this. I can give you a referral to a therapist who might do you some good."

"No." The thought was terrifying. "I don't want to bare my soul to some stranger."

"Is that what it means to you? Baring your soul?"

"Yes." I recrossed my legs. "I've never been introspective."

"Just leaped into the latest breach? Saw what had to be done and did it?"

"Pretty much. Except maybe when Hugh died. There was nothing I could do."

"Hugh was your husband?"

"He was a state trooper and was murdered before you moved here. I could never even talk about his death until I met Win again. We'd talked about him the first time Win kissed me."

Em was quiet again.

"It's not that I don't think about why I do stuff like shooting to kill. I am clear about that. It's just…"

"You don't like thinking about things that are murky and don't have clear answers," Em said. "Your attraction to Win—you didn't think about that?"

"Of course I did, at least a little. Okay, not a lot. I kind of rushed ahead blindly. I fell for Win and wanted to find out what it was like."

"It?"

"Loving a woman," I said, running my fingers down the crease of my pants. Em didn't say anything. "Okay, making love with a woman."

"You thought more about the physical act than about an intimate, emotional response. Interesting. Are you seeing a pattern here?"

"I chase criminals and I chased Win."

"Bullshit." Em stood. "I can't take you on as a client. I can see you with Win, or for a specific incident involving the sheriff's office. But that's all." She went to her desk, rummaged around and came back to hand me a card. "This is the therapist I mentioned. Call her. But Sarah, you're not going to get relief until you face your underlying feelings."

I felt like crying, but I'd be damned before I'd give Em the satisfaction. I took the card, put it in my pocket and left.

CHAPTER SIXTY-THREE

Win

I'd kept digging into the snake companies and had a thick binder I'd printed out. Nathan had been right to target them, even though they weren't the usual culprit fields of inquiry we looked for. I called him for any updates on them. "Um, nothing really new," he said. Bullshit. Definitely closed out of the loop and I couldn't figure out why. Maybe because this was a threat to national security? One small cog in a mesh of agencies? I didn't think Bill trusted any other agency at this point.

I didn't talk to Bill, except to tell him to give Sarah a heads-up if something popped up about the county. I also told him about a jailbreak. "We need to bring these men to trial ASAP. There's been enough blood shed and bones broken."

Sarah had been a giant pain in the ass since she'd seen Emily. My guess was that she'd had her butt kicked. It was only a guess because Sarah refused to talk about it. After a few attempts to snuggle, even Des had given up. Then I'd found the therapist's card in her shirt pocket. Had Emily kicked her out? Tried to refer her? If Sarah wasn't talking to me, I doubted she'd talk to a "stranger." Shit.

At least she'd finally had her damn cast off yesterday. I was tired of getting clunked on various body parts when Sarah forgot she was wearing it. She was as rebellious about wearing the support splint as talking about what was going on with her. Or doing rehab. I tried to encourage her but failed miserably. I shut up about it and took shelter with Des.

Des walked over and put her muzzle on my leg. "You wanna go play with Sarah?" I asked. She whined, looked away. I got down on my knees next to her, wrapped my arms around her. Rubbed my face on her fur. "Humans are weird creatures, Des. We try so hard to protect ourselves. Be invulnerable. And that's the very thing that brings us down." I kissed her between her eyes. "Sarah will be okay. Eventually."

"Are you guys hiding from me?" Sarah asked as she leaned over the back of the couch.

Des lay down, flattened her ears. "Yes, we are," I said. "You're in a really pissy mood. You're scaring both of us."

She walked into the kitchen. It was time to take this bullshit by the horns. I followed her. "So what did Emily ream you out about?"

"What did she tell you?"

"Nothing. Haven't talked to her. But you've been in a shitty mood since you saw her."

"What do you want for dinner?"

"Cut the crap, Sarah. Talk to me."

"All I wanted were some techniques to lessen the stress and she says she can't take me as a client. Well screw her. The firing range is a great way to—"

"She can't take you because I'm still her client. That's the way it works. My question is, why did she think you need therapy?"

"Or do you want to order in?"

I put my hands on her shoulders, turned her around. "If you don't want me to take Des and move into Bloomington until the end of the semester, talk to me now."

"You don't mean that. You wouldn't do that."

"Yes. I do. I would. You're stewing about something. If you don't trust me enough to talk about it, then find a therapist. I saved the card before I put your shirt in the laundry. You want it?"

She shook her head. "Give me a little more time—"

"No! Spill the beans or I start packing."

"You're bullying me, Win."

"No. I'm just tired of tiptoeing around you. We haven't made love in more than a week. That's another milestone and not a good one. What the hell have you got to lose?"

She leaned into me. Put her arms around my waist. "Don't take away the one thing I'm sure of. Please."

"The one thing?"

"Your love. Your presence in my life, in our bed, even if we don't make love. You're at the center of my life, Win. *Please*."

"Is that it? Is it that the sheriff's department used to be the center?"

"You're not going to let this go, are you?"

"No." I took her hand and led her to the couch. "I understand the impulse to handle it yourself. When you're in a command position, that's what you do. But not with what's eating you up on the inside. Or don't you really trust me?"

"I trust you with my heart," she said, her eyes wide. She fidgeted. "This is something I've wrestled with a long time, even before we got together. I worked hard, pushed myself to be the best cop ever. Dumb, huh?"

"No. Idealistic. Dedicated."

"Well, that was me. When it became evident how Mac was damaging the sheriff's office, a group of other dedicated officers got together. We had to run someone against Mac and I got the short straw. It was fine with me because I could take the crap and know it was crap. And I didn't think I had a chance in hell to win."

"You cleaned up the department from what I've heard," I said.

Sarah nodded. "A lot of housecleaning, which is a good detail job for a woman. About two years in, the weight of the badge started to hit. We had a couple of horrendous cases where good people did appalling things. Those cases rested on my shoulders, not just to solve, but somehow rectify. I know what you're going to say—I have a whole department to share the load. But that's not how it feels."

"But you ran again."

"Only because Dad backed me into the wall. I signed the forms because he got me so mad." She took a deep breath. "It's a huge responsibility to have people's lives in my hands, both the victim and the perpetrator."

"Like the girl who committed suicide because she was gang raped?"

She nodded. "But it's all the weight. Duty decisions, budget, the stupid crimes that destroy lives, how thin we're stretched. Had I known what I was signing up for the first time, I don't think I would've."

"Wow. I had no idea. You ran because you thought you'd lose?"

Sarah nodded, tucked her head onto my chest. Whispered, "My secret. I didn't think I was ready."

"But you pour your whole being into the job…"

"I can't fail the people who elected me." She burrowed deeper. "It's more a love-hate relationship. I love putting the bad guys away. I love justice. Most people in the county are good. If we don't stand between them and the criminals, then who does? I'm good at what I do. In a lot of ways, I love my job. I just hate the responsibility of making it all work."

I put my arm around her and kissed the top of her head. We sat a long time, breathing together. I took the shrink's card from my pocket and handed it to Sarah. "You need someone to help you sort. This is beyond my skillset. Will you do it? For us? For the kids? But most of all, for you?"

She looked at the card like it was laced with anthrax. "I'll go once. If I don't like her, I'm not going back."

"Once is better than never." I kissed her. With this attitude, I doubted if she'd ever go back to a shrink she was determined to dislike.

* * *

"They're bugging out," Bill said. "We've been keeping the farm under surveillance, eyes on the ground and in the sky. All of 'em should be gone by tomorrow late. This time, we have the advantage. We can tail the bastards and listen in to their fucking chatter."

"That's a load off. I kept waiting for something to happen. A jailbreak. Or an RPG through the front window of the sheriff's station. Some kind of revenge."

"Well, that's the other part of the news. Their 'strategic re-deployment' will end with 'the last word,' or so they say."

"What does that mean?" My stomach did a flip.

"Don't know. They're leaving four guys behind to deliver their surprise, and then they'll catch up to the main detachment. It may be nothing, Win."

"Yeah, right. What kind of firepower do they have?"

"Nolan didn't see any trace of advanced weapons. Not even RPGs."

That was good. No dirty bombs. No Sidewinder missiles. Still... "Four guys." I thought how much havoc four trained fighters could wreak. "You better dig on this, Bill. Talk to Tom—he's going to testify against the other kidnapper."

"We'll do everything we can. You know that. I'm sending backup."

"You better send a fucking battalion." I tried to calm the knot my stomach had become. "Tell Sarah. I'm not delivering this news."

I hung up with sheer dread surrounding me like a fishnet. I was trapped in horrendous scenarios that raced through my mind, each worse than the next. Why the hell hadn't I told Sarah to quit? Run for the hills? Except for Bill's limited intel, we were riding blind this time. Why the fuck couldn't they let us alone?

I called Micah. "Hell's bells," he said. He was silent for a full minute. "Got eyes on that old depot, down at Ridley Forge. Trains comin' in regular an' deliverin' somethin'. Rumor goin' 'round, sayin' the army's started it back up, usin' it to finish up the depot down in Kentucky. Possible, Win?"

"At this point, I have no idea. Bill's holding his intel close." I started pacing. "But, yeah. I guess it's possible. Thought the one in Kentucky had been closed too. Hope to hell they're not shipping nerve gas across the country."

He was silent again. "If those punks are leavin', mebbe they gone an' give up on the depot and McCrumb County."

"Maybe." I stopped pacing, stared out the window. "Sarah's going to implode."

He was quiet again. "Can't do nothin' but be there for her, Win. Give whatever aid she'll accept."

I knew he heard the frustration in my voice when I said, "Sometimes your daughter isn't very comfortable accepting help." I leaned my head against the windowpane. "Keep up your surveillance on the depot, if you would. And keep your fingers crossed."

I called Nathan. "You get any intel on the county, you shoot it to Sarah," I said without a preamble. "Bill's playing this too close to the vest. Sarah could get hurt. Or worse."

"That's what I've been thinking too," he said. "Consider it done."

CHAPTER SIXTY-FOUR

Sarah

"What the hell's going on, Win?" were my first words when I got home from work.

She looked up from her veggie prep. "What happened to 'Honey, I'm home'?"

"Win look at me. Tell me what's going on."

She kept her head down. "Bill called, I told him to call you with his intel. Then I called Nathan. Told him to shoot you any chatter he's picking up. Bill's not sharing much. Nathan agreed. That's all I know."

Win still didn't look at me. I'd hurled all the day's frustration and anger at her. I hung my jacket and duty belt on pegs by the door and I took several deep breaths before I walked into the kitchen and slipped my arms around her waist. "I'm sorry. What an awful thing to say first thing home." I turned her around and saw the scar on her forehead was bright red. I touched it softly.

She didn't say anything and I felt her muscles tighten. "What are you making?"

"No idea." She started on a carrot. "I needed to do something. I cut veggies. You can put them in a casserole or eat them raw. I don't care."

I released her, walked to the bathroom and took a long shower. She was really pissed at me and probably with good reason. I was so tired of all of this, and tired of being tired. I hadn't been sleeping well, though for the life of me, I couldn't remember any dreams.

I got out, toweled off and put on my sweats and socks. When I walked back into the kitchen, she was still chopping. I took a deep breath. "Vegetable soup?"

"Told you, I don't care."

"And I told you I was sorry." I pulled out our stockpot, put some butter on the bottom and turned on the burner. I started collecting the veggies strewn over the top of the island into a colander. Win hadn't started on the onions yet, so I diced one and a couple of chilies. I threw them in the pot and turned to her. "I am sorry. I had no reason to yell at you."

Win stopped chopping. "No you didn't. I did exactly what you've asked me to do, stepped away and told Bill and Nathan to talk to you directly. They evidently think there's a continuing threat. More pressure just when you felt it was all over. I understand, Sarah. But don't ever use me as your whipping boy." She bent back to her task.

"Don't shut me out. Please."

"Shut *you* out? What the hell do you think you do to me?" She slammed her chopper onto the counter. "It's like digging to China to get you to talk to me, Sarah. Endless. Impossible."

"I don't have to answer your questions."

"You don't have to live here either." Win looked away, crossed her arms and shook her head. "We're sniping at one another. I'm sorry. I'm trying to do what you want me to do, but it's hard to figure out what you want. Do you know?"

I took a shaky breath. "No. All I feel is a deep desire for this damn pressure to be over."

Win walked over to the pot, stirred it and then turned to me. "Let's get this soup cooking. Sit down and talk. Can we do that?"

I nodded. We made short work of adding all the ingredients and broth, then sat on the couch with a cushion between us. Win's words still stung.

"Do you really want me to move out?" I asked, afraid of hearing Win's answer, but afraid not to.

"Of course not. That was just a response to 'I don't have to answer your questions.' I regretted the words as soon as I said them. I'm sorry." Win turned to me and put her arm on the back of the couch. "I really don't know where you are. You've become so quiet. I don't know where you want me to be. Covering your back? At your side? At home being safe?"

"All of the above," I said, touching her hand on the back of the couch. "I want you safe, always. At the same time, I need your strength and skill. Why the hell are they doing this? I don't even know what 'this' is, Win. I've never dealt with this kind of crap before."

"Don't fight me, please. Do you want my analysis on this latest intel? Or shall I join you with our heads in the sand?"

"That's not fair. If my head was in the sand, we'd all be dead from their last attack." I leaned my head back. "Give me your analysis."

"If I put myself in the insurgents' place and I were running an op against local authority, I'd wait a while. If this was the Middle East, then I'd attack with a suicide bomber or two. I don't think these guys are willing to do that. How about a fertilizer bomb like Oklahoma City?"

I felt like she'd hit me over the head with a dread stick. "Oh, hell. We can't close the square or put Jersey barriers up all over town."

"Why not? Announce that the city planners are thinking about making the square a pedestrian-only space," Win said.

"The business owners would roast us," I said. "Including Tillie. They depend on the on-the-street parking. Especially if nothing happens, they'd be furious."

Win shook her head. "They'll be more upset if the sheriff's station blows up and takes that whole side of the square with it. Plus…"

"Plus what?"

"These guys like to use secondary explosions that injure first responders."

I closed my eyes, but it was too late because tears were flowing freely. "This is too much, way too much. How can I protect the public and our people from something like that?"

CHAPTER SIXTY-FIVE

Win and Sarah

Win

I left the Bloomington campus right after class on Thursday. CELI was having a full day of meetings tomorrow. For full-time faculty. While I wondered what was going on, I was glad I didn't have to go. I had another agenda on my mind—Sarah's welfare.

After I made it through the door at home, assured Des of my love, I looked at Sarah at the stove. She looked exhausted—shoulders slumped, movements slow. I walked behind her and put my arms around her. Kissed the back of her neck.

"I'm glad you're home," she said. "Safe."

"Anything new?"

"Check your email. Nathan said he was sending you some stuff."

"Nathan? Why didn't he send it to you?" I felt her stiffen.

"Because I'm too tired to make any sense of it," she said. "I've had a couple of sleepless nights."

"You missed me?"

"So much, Win. So much. I kept having nightmares that those skinheads in Bloomington would beat you until you're nothing but a pulpy mass of blood and bones."

I tightened my embrace. "Haven't heard from them lately, students haven't either." I turned her around. "Why don't you go shower then get into bed. I'll bring dinner in."

"Dinner in bed? I don't know if I can stay awake that long."

"That's what the shower's for. Now go." I watched her go down the hall, not sure if she'd make it. Swell. Sarah needed to be on top of her game and she wasn't. She was barely vertical.

I put two mini-loaves of French bread in the oven, sniffed the soup and added a few spices. Got out two bowls that I'd found in Brown County last fall. I'd bought them because they had lids. For times like this.

I heard the shower going and figured I had a few minutes. I resisted looking at Nathan's email. I'd wait until the first thing in the morning. When the oven dinged, the water stopped in the bathroom. Perfect timing.

We'd eat. Make love. Sleep.

Sarah

Last night had been soul-deep wonderful and I'd slept like a log. I woke up to find Win at her desk, going over the emails Nathan had sent. "Find anything?" I asked, yawning.

"Coffee's ready," Win said. "Nothing that makes sense. What time do we have to go in?"

"We?"

"I'm coming with you. I can't access the databases here." She grinned. "That sounds like a country-and-western song, doesn't it? 'Been searchin' fer my true love an' I ain't got no databases left.'"

I poured a mug of coffee. "You're giving country music a bad name."

I walked to the desk and stared at the screen. "I repeat—find anything?"

"Not finished yet." She pulled me close. "So far, Nathan identified three of the four men who've stayed behind. I went ahead and sent the pics to the station for a BOLO—eyes only. Okay?"

I nodded. "If you were in Afghanistan, what would you do with those men?"

She took a deep breath. "Pick them up for interrogation. If we couldn't pick them up, kill them. But Sarah, they'd be firing back at us."

I felt chilled. She'd said it so matter-of-factly. I sipped my coffee.

Win turned to me. "That's in-country. I wouldn't do that here. Even though the stakes are the same. Collateral damage. Bombs take out people who don't have diddly to do with any cause. Think of Boston."

"All the violence is just bewildering. I don't understand how people can think about wiping out the maximum of human lives."

"I'm still working on understanding taking one life," Win said, taking my hand. "Yet, I've done it. Multiple times. Never an assassination, always under combat conditions."

I put the coffee down, leaned down to kiss her. "Think they'd go away if I resigned?"

"No." She scrolled down the intel. "Any way to track the fertilizer purchases in the county?"

"You've got to be kidding. This is primarily a farming county and I can track thefts, but not purchases."

She nodded. "Then we've got nothing." She turned to look up at me. "Rumor has it that Bill's got eyes on these guys. We'll see."

Win

Friday morning had been quiet. We'd stationed deputies atop buildings where streets entered the square, but when a domestic call turned wicked, Sarah released them for normal duty. I wished she hadn't, but what the hell were they supposed to be looking for? A Ryder truck? Guys with big backpacks?

I leaned against the wall by the newly reinstalled window in Sarah's office. Watched the square, looked for disaster to appear and hoped it was clearly visible ahead of time. I glanced at Sarah. Still working her way through paperwork. May the blizzard of paper be her worst concern.

A UPS truck stopped, then backed up over the curb at the back of the courthouse. "Is that usual?" I asked.

Sarah looked up, got up to stand beside me. "The UPS truck? No, they usually block the street."

We watched the driver step down from his seat with a clipboard and several packages. He began to trot around to the front. His cap was down low and he wore sunglasses.

"Is the courthouse back door locked?"

"No, it's always opened when the courthouse is open. Maybe it's a new driver and he doesn't know."

"I don't like this, Sarah." I started out the office door to the bullpen when I saw a flash and the ground shook. The truck disappeared in a dense cloud. I stumbled, caught Sarah as she pitched into a desk.

Two deputies ran out the front door with Caleb on their heels. "No!" I yelled. The word had barely left my throat when the first deputy fell. Then the second. Then Caleb. We heard the shots.

"Oh my God," Sarah whispered as she stood at my shoulder.

"Snipers, Sarah! Get the rifles and John Morgan. Get to the roof and shoot those fuckers." I turned to her. "You're sure you can shoot with that damn wrist?"

She nodded, her gaze still on the street outside.

I shook her shoulder. "Sarah! *Now*."

"But Caleb and—"

"I'll get them. Where's the key to the BearCat?"

"On the board, but—"

"Go, Sarah. Please. Put the plan into action now." I heard more rifle shots.

John appeared on the steps, two Mark 12s in his hands. "Ready?"

I pushed her toward the stairs and grabbed the key for the BearCat. Stopped at dispatch. "Call the ambulance services, the hospital and fire department. No personnel in the square, no vehicles. Shut it down. Have them stop at the corners until we give them the all clear."

As I approached the back door I had my weapon drawn. No snipers on the building behind the station were visible, so I made a mad zigzag dash for the armored vehicle. Dove in. The thing handled like a fucking tank, but nothing under a .50 mm round could penetrate it.

I manhandled it to the street, then took a wide turn toward the wounded men. Shots peppered the windshield. Pulling the BearCat in front to protect the wounded, I crawled out the back and saw Caleb smile up at me. He rolled over so he was well behind the open doors. "Got my vest on. Sore ribs, but I'm okay."

"Help me get these guys in, if you can."

He pushed himself up with a groan. We got both of the men in.

I heard two quick shots. Then two more almost in unison. Heavy weaponry like a Mark 12.

Caleb closed his door and I picked up the mic. "Closest ambulance?"

"Back up to the corner behind you. They should be there," dispatch said.

The firing had stopped. I turned the corner and saw a couple of ambulances, their lights flashing, parked at the side of the street. "How are the deputies?" I asked as I locked down.

"Not good," Caleb said. "Safe to open the doors?"

"Yeah. Just don't go dancing in the square."

Sarah

When the ground shook, my first thought was an earthquake. Then I saw the cloud from the explosion. An explosion? I couldn't believe what I saw. Win was saying something. She pushed me toward the stairs where John gave me a Mark 12. I took it and he turned and pelted up the stairs. I followed him.

On the way to the roof, I tried to unscramble my brain and remember our plan. Snipers would be on rooftops and we were to snipe the snipers.

"The parapet's only three feet tall, so stay down. I think one of them is on top of Korhner's, one on top of Tillie's. The third one could be on top of the old Masonic Lodge. I'll take closest guy, you take farthest, then we'll meet at the one at the diner."

He nodded and stoop-walked to the front of the building as I did the same to the rear. I peeked over and saw a guy on the roof below, dressed in full battle gear. I looked at John. With his weapon ready at a crenellation, I caught his eye. "Go!"

I popped up, rested the rifle on wall and found the shooter's head in my scope. I fired. John fired. Then I moved the weapon to the middle of the block. That shooter was aiming at John. I fired again. Not a kill shot, but John finished the job.

My hands began to shake. Fight it, Sarah, fight it. Your duty isn't finished yet. John came up to me and held out a hand to help me up. "Good shooting, John."

He nodded. "This time."

We headed back downstairs. "There are wounded on the front steps of the courthouse—civilians," dispatch said.

"Let's make sure all the snipers are down before we send anybody out," I said.

I heard a loud diesel engine and saw another armored vehicle head toward the front of the courthouse. Was this the next thing they were going to throw at us?

"Marines have landed," dispatch said. "You want to talk to them?"

I nodded and took the headset. "Sheriff here."

"All of you okay?" It was Bill's voice.

"Three officers down, don't know how seriously wounded. Three snipers down."

"Good work, Sarah. We'll get the wounded at the courthouse secured and then you can send in the ambulances."

"Thanks." I handed the set back to dispatch. "Stay on the line. Bill will tell you when it's safe to send in medical personnel. How many of our units are close?"

"One at each corner of the square."

I nodded. "Get additional units back here. There'll be wounded snipers on top of the old Masonic Lodge, Korhner's and Tillie's diner. We need to collect them."

Dispatch nodded. I was still gun-shy, so I went out the back door. When I got to the street, I saw our BearCat at the corner. Our wounded men weren't on the street and I hoped they were getting medical attention. Had Win succeeded in moving them out of the line of fire?

I hurried down the street and saw Win talking to Caleb.

CHAPTER SIXTY-SIX

Win

The two ambulances took off with sirens shrieking. The medic left to deal with other injuries but said she thought Caleb had cracked ribs.

"I'll stop by the hospital after we know what happened," he protested.

"Go now," I said. "Otherwise, you'll be useless. A hindrance to any mop-up."

"Shit, Win. You sure know how to make a guy feel good."

I grinned at him then caught sight of Sarah. She still looked dazed. Wait until she saw the back of the courthouse, or what had been the back of the building. She walked up.

"You get the snipers?" I asked before she had time to turn around and look at the mess.

She nodded. "First time I've ever aimed at a man's head. They were in full battle gear, Win. There was no other way to stop them."

I put my hand on her shoulder. "I hope you didn't hesitate."

"I didn't have a choice. With all the body armor, there were heads or legs left. Legs wouldn't have stopped them from firing."

I pulled her to me in a brief embrace. "I heard the marines arrived."

Sarah nodded. "A little after the fact, but they secured the wounded in the front of the courthouse."

"Let's check it out," I said. "But first, would you order your chief deputy to go to the hospital and get his ribs taped up?"

Sarah turned to him. "Taped?"

"My vest caught the bullet but I'm a little bruised," Caleb said.

"Go," Sarah said. "There'll be plenty to do when you get back."

Sighing, he saluted.

Sarah turned around and got a full view of the damage. "Oh my god!"

I examined the gaping, blackened hole that had been the back of the building. "Without that solid stone facade, it would've been a lot worse."

Sarah started jogging toward the front of the building. I'd heard shots after the three cops had been hit. Four ambulances were pulled up on the square, Marines still watched the perimeter. I saw Bill on the lawn. It was a long time since I'd seen him in full battle gear.

Sarah charged up to him. She leaned into him, said in a low voice, "I thought you were supposed to have eyes on these bastards."

"Not here," he said. "I'll give you a debriefing tomorrow."

"What the hell do you mean—"

I grabbed her arm, tugged her back. "We're needed at HQ, double-time Sarah."

She looked furious. I tugged again. She finally turned on her heel and followed me back to the station.

I could see her rage, ready to strike out at anyone who came within range. I felt the same and recognized the pain below it. Figured the safest place for Sarah was in her own bailiwick. But, like Sarah, I wondered, how he'd lost the shooters.

* * *

We didn't get home until midnight. I'd made a run around dinnertime to let Des out and feed her. The rest of the time had been chaos. At times, controlled chaos. But shit, I didn't envy Sarah her job.

When Sarah just stood in our entry hall, I collected her jacket and duty belt. I got two beers from the fridge, walked to the couch and handed one to Sarah. I thought I saw a slight tremor in her hand. "You want me to light a fire?"

She nodded. Sat with the beer in both hands, stared into space.

I got the fire started, returned to the couch, put an arm around her. Felt her trembling. I pulled her to me, held her tightly. She started sobbing. The storm lasted a long time. I don't think she felt my arms around her, nor heard the comforting sounds I made. Finally, it abated.

"What are you feeling, Sarah? Right now?"

"Everything, all at once. Terror. I couldn't even believe what I was seeing. Rage. I could've killed Bill. I did kill the snipers. Numb. Just fucking numb."

I kissed her forehead. Took the beer from her hands and set it on the side table. "All the feelings all mixed up? Sweeping over you like waves?"

She nodded.

"You'll probably find more and they won't let you alone for a while. You need to talk to Emily."

She kept her face buried, but shook her head.

That was a battle for another day. I rubbed her back with both my hands. I felt her quiet down. The fire popped and she started.

"What the hell did they prove, Win?" She sat up, ran her hands through her hair. "Three civilians dead and one of my officers. So many civilians wounded and some critical. For *what?*"

I started rubbing her back again. "Fanatics pave their way to heaven with dead bodies. For them, there is no collateral damage."

What I didn't say was that "heaven" meant sheer power to some. And they never quit.

CHAPTER SIXTY-SEVEN

Sarah

Saturday morning, I handed the investigative lead to the FBI, assisted by ATF. Homeland Security had put pressure on me to do their bidding. I told the special agent in charge our suspicion that this wasn't just a local plot and gently steered him toward the information we'd gathered. I omitted everything Bill had found, figuring it was his job to disclose his findings and share intel. Explaining the decision to let the FBI lead to the media, who were buzzing around like flies to a corpse, was trickier. It was especially hard with Lloyd and Zoe, who had more questions than I had easy answers for. Between the bombing and the previous assault on the station, we were national news and the *Greenglen Sentinel* wasn't good at printing guesses.

I wore my full-dress uniform and campaign hat for the funeral of Billy Weber, my deputy who'd died in the street in front of the station. The mix of emotions I felt during the proceedings was almost overwhelming, but it was my duty to execute the complicated funeral of a law enforcement officer. We had representatives from all over Indiana and Kentucky, plus a good sprinkling from the rest of the states. I only lost it once—when the riderless horse passed by. Tears crept down my face regardless.

Win was my rock over the following weeks, beside me when I needed her and not pressing me about seeing the new shrink. Finally, though, she got tired of my nightmares and maybe my shot of bourbon before I could sleep.

"I get it, Sarah," she said. "You were ticked at Emily for saying you needed therapy. Get over it. You do."

I'd told Em I wasn't going to do therapy for the long run. "This is our standard after-incident clearance, nothing more."

"I won't do it, Sarah," she said. "You need to unpack what you're feeling and a couple of sessions just aren't going to do it. I gave you the name of a therapist. Use it."

I stomped out of her office but when I told Win, she sided with Em. "Look at the major cases you've had lately. Not the usual run of domestic homicides and drug busts most county sheriffs come up against." She'd started enumerating, holding a finger up for each. When all five fingers on one hand were open, I'd stopped her. "I'll think about it, Win. Right now, I need to concentrate on the bombing until all the federal charges are filed."

I had thought about it and all the feelings I was dragging behind me, rather like the warrior brother who'd drug rusted armor up a jungle trail in *The Mission*. It kept dragging him back down the mountain. I didn't want to find myself up to my neck in mud, unable to move forward. But right now, I needed to hang on and not fly apart in the face of horror.

Win didn't hassle me, but kept her distance. Most nights, after my bourbon, I fell into bed and into immediate sleep. I hadn't had a day off since the bombing, almost three weeks now, and we hadn't made love since the explosion and its aftermath. Win stayed beside me during the day, when she could, and yet disappeared beneath covers at night. The only comment she'd offered was that she didn't like bourbon and had a particularly bad memory associated with its taste. She wouldn't tell me what.

The Feds were trying to tie in our prisoners from the station attack to the bombing. I reluctantly gave them what we had on our attackers and even if the Feds didn't come up with extra charges, we had enough to put all the felons behind bars for the rest of their lives. The judge was tired of the defense team's delaying tactics and had set the station attack trial for early May.

Then their glitzy defense team had abandoned the cause and left their clients to local lawyers.

Spring began to stick her toe tentatively in the stream of changing seasons. The first flush of buds on trees, the early breaking of soil by the heartiest of sprouts. But I knew spring was a tease and didn't trust the warmer weather. I felt I didn't trust much at all.

One Friday I came home, exhausted by the continuing questions from federal agents. Win was already home and I detected something in her demeanor that said her days of "hands off" my exhaustion were over. We ate dinner with minimal talk and I was thinking about going to bed when Win brought her laptop to the couch.

"I want you to look at this," she said, opening to a commercial page.

"French Lick?"

"I have an ultimatum. Either you go into therapy now or we go to French Lick next weekend. I've made a reservation at a place that has cabins and a spa package for the resort. We leave next Saturday morning, come back Tuesday night." She turned to me. "I realize the strain you're under to present the perfect case to the Feds. But I can't take your silence anymore. You need to seek treatment. If you won't do that, at least try a temporary fix."

"French Lick is a temporary fix?"

"A completely new environment, no hauntings."

"Win, I don't have time—"

"Make it."

"Or?"

Win took my hand, rubbed her thumb over the back of it, fingered my wedding band. "I want us to walk the long road together. But I'm tired of this distance between us. Tired of your denial of the trauma you experienced. We have to do something to get out of this rut."

* * *

We arrived at the Springs Cabins early this morning. When Win gave me her ultimatum, I'd caved and I'd never asked her the "or what" question again. I couldn't imagine my life without her.

"What are we going to do besides spa stuff?" I asked as we unpacked. "I mean, other than mind-blowing sex?"

Win laughed. "Relax, Sarah. It's warm enough to go hiking and cool enough at night for a fire. We can visit a winery. Get a tour of the restoration of the grand hotel. I suppose we could go gambling."

"I gamble every day when I strap on my weapon," I said.

"I know," Win said quietly. She hung a pair of slacks in the closet. "Anyway, we're due for our first soak in the medicinal waters in half an hour. Pick up some brochures at the hotel. We'll go over them tonight."

I was imagining an erotic exchange in a pool with the hot spring waters lapping the edge. What I got was my own tub. Tub? Damn. But I had to admit, I did manage to relax a bit into the experience, letting my head rest against the pile of towels on the lip. When time was up, I was whisked into a thick terrycloth robe and led to the massage rooms. Again, not what I'd imagined for a "couples massage." Two tables, with Win close enough to hear my masseuse's running commentary on my tight muscles and general state of tension. I heard her laugh at a couple of the remarks.

We had lunch at a vegetarian place and Win actually drank one of their special juices, though I'm not sure she enjoyed it.

"I packed for a sexy vacation," I said as we walked to the hotel for a second round of soaking and massage. "Is it going to happen?"

She took my hand. "You need to relax, Sarah. You're wound so tight, you'd come if I looked at you naked. I want all the pleasure of a slow dance."

"I just want to dance."

We'd done our second massage round and I did find myself easing off the treadmill the bombing case had become. I welcomed the work that had begun to reconstruct the destroyed back of the courthouse. One reminder going away, so many more to go.

Win treated me to a scrumptious dinner at the West Baden Springs Hotel, where I gawked at the Atrium like an out-of-towner with neck cramps in New York City. To think this extravagance had existed among corn and soybean fields for a hundred and twenty-five years boggled my mind. "This is some place, Win. Thanks for bringing me here. It must be costing you a bundle."

"Naw," she said with a grin. "Military discount."

* * *

Win bent over the kindling in the fireplace and coaxed a flame into existence. She was good at that, building all kind of fires. She walked back to the couch, took my hands and pulled me to my feet. "Feel like some slow dancing?"

"I'm so stuffed, I'm not sure I can do more than lean against you."

"That's just fine," Win said, bending over to push play on the boom box she'd brought. The music started and she pulled me close. I felt her body so close to mine, in movement, swaying together to the same melody. I slipped my hands under her sweater. When I tried to undo her bra, she pulled away. "Slow down, speedy. Just enjoy the moment."

"I was."

She let go of me and stepped back. "Sarah, I've got something to say. I really want you to listen."

I nodded and sank down on the couch with a feeling in the pit of my stomach that felt like a cannon ball. "What?"

"You need therapy," she said, sitting beside me. "The nightmares haven't stopped. If anything, I think they're getting worse."

"How do you know? I can't even remember having one."

"That's part of it. You shove everything down so deep, no wonder you don't know what's there." She stroked my hair. "But you're the one who has to realize you need help. You have to ask for it. I know it isn't easy. I *know*. But going to therapy was the best decision I ever made. What Emily gave me was the ability to be with you. Fully and completely with you."

"I just need to get—"

Win held up her hand. "I'm not giving you a deadline. I'm just asking you to seriously consider it. When it's right for you, promise me you'll go."

"Why can't I just talk to you?"

Win grimaced. "You think that much of Emily's rubbed off on me?"

"Yes."

"You need someone who's objective. Who won't be seduced when you look at her the way you're looking at me now." She leaned over and kissed me. "I can't tell you how important this is to me. To us."

"You think I have PTSD?"

"I think it'd be amazing if you didn't. Plus a good part of your department. Your people all have been through two major traumas."

"If I don't, would you leave me?"

Win ducked her head. "I couldn't stay and watch you self-destruct like Laura."

"She had such severe physical trauma—"

"That's not what drove her. The horror in her head broke her." Win leaned toward me. "Therapy isn't a death sentence. It's a chance to heal. Think about unburdening yourself, freeing yourself for more love. Getting ready to help two little girls bloom in McCrumb County soil. Just getting to know yourself better. You'll like the woman you've become. Deal?"

I nodded and found it difficult to say anything. I felt pathetic, but I realized what Win asked of me would require more strength than I had. "Deal."

Win stood. "May I have this dance, Sarah?"

"I love you Win Kirkland." I stood and entered into the circle of her arms and felt safe and protected—for the moment.

And I wondered what the Rangers were planning tonight. Push it down, Sarah, push it down and dance, dance while we can.

Bella Books, Inc.

Women. Books. Even Better Together.

P.O. Box 10543
Tallahassee, FL 32302

Phone: 800-729-4992
www.bellabooks.com